BRIGHT
SWORD
OF
JUSTICE

GUARDIANS OF THE NORTH

By Honor Bound
Heart of Valor
Bright Sword of Justice

9705

ALAN MORRIS

GUARDIANS OF THE NORTH

BRIGHT SWORD OF JUSTICE

BETHANY HOUSE PUBLISHERS
MINNEAPOLIS, MINNESOTA 55438

Bright Sword of Justice
Copyright © 1997
Alan Morris

Cover illustration by Joe Nordstrom

Published by Bethany House Publishers
A Ministry of Bethany Fellowship, Inc.
11300 Hampshire Avenue South
Minneapolis, Minnesota 55438

Printed in the United States of America.

Library of Congress Cataloging-in-Publication Data

Morris, Alan B., 1959–
    Bright sword of justice / by Alan B. Morris.
      p.   cm. — (Guardians of the north ; 3)
    ISBN 1–55661–694–5 (pbk.)
    I. Title. II. Series: Morris, Alan B., 1959–   Guardians of the
north ; 3.
PS3563.O87395B75   1997
813'.54—dc21   97–21021
                                             CIP

To my sister Lynn

For all those times I needed
a friend, a mentor, an ear,
a pat on the back, a hearth,
and, most of all, a big sister
who loved me without condition.

ALAN MORRIS is a full-time writer who has also coauthored a series of books with his father, best-selling author Gilbert Morris. Learning the craft of writing from his father, Alan has launched his first solo series, GUARDIANS OF THE NORTH. He makes his home in Texas.

CONTENTS

Part Four: The Noble Heart

THE RULE OF MEN'S MINDS

Omnia enim plerumque quae absunt vehementius hominum mentes perturbant.

As a rule men's minds are more deeply disturbed by what they do not see.

C. Julius Caesar
Commentarii de bello Gallico

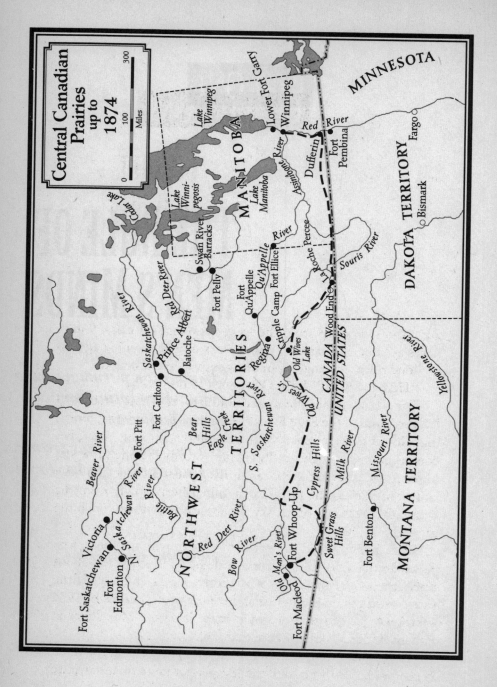

Central Canadian Prairies up to 1874

MINNESOTA

DAKOTA TERRITORY

Fargo

Bismark

MONTANA TERRITORY

Fort Benton

NORTHWEST TERRITORIES

MANITOBA

Winnipeg

Lower Fort Garry

Fort Pembina

Dufferin

Lake Winnipeg

Cedar Lake

Lake Winnipegosis

Lake Manitoba

Swan River Barracks

Fort Pelly

Fort Qu'Appelle

Qu'Appelle River

Cripple Camp

Fort Ellice

Regina

La Roche Percee

Wood End

Old Wives Lake

Old Wives C.

Cypress Hills

Fort Whoop-Up

Old Man's River

Fort Madeod

Sweet Grass Hills

Milk River

Souris River

Red River

Assinboine River

Missouri River

Yellowstone River

Bow River

Red Deer River

S. Saskatchewan River

Eagle Creek

Bear Hills

Fort Carlton

Fort Pitt

Battle River

Prince Albert

Batoche

Saskatchewan River

Red Deer River

Victoria

Fort Saskatchewan

Fort Edmonton

N. Saskatchewan River

Beaver River

CANADA

UNITED STATES

Miles
0   100   300

CHAPTER ONE

Curtain of White

A wind sprang up from the west, crisp and odorless. Snow-flakes as large as quarters began to descend at an angle against the lone rider, no longer spiraling gently in silent beauty.

"Here it comes," Liam O'Donnell told himself.

The wind had been brisk and cold but refreshing when he'd left the banks of the Sage River in Montana Territory that morning. Now it gathered speed with an ominous keening moan, becoming an increasingly deadly enemy. Already the fine snow was blowing so hard that it appeared to be sheeting past him on a course parallel to the plains, as if falling horizontally from the west rather than out of the sky, and destined never to touch the ground.

Liam had watched the gathering storm with apprehension. As he'd ridden north, the storm had appeared to his left about midafternoon in the form of a ghostly cloud clinging to the earth. With the prairie so vast and seemingly never ending, he'd mistakenly judged that he could make it to the Milk River in Canada in time to camp there that night.

Twenty years old, Liam was of medium height and rode well in the saddle. As if he were the last perfect piece in an intricate

11

family puzzle, Liam embodied an eerie combination of his two older sisters. He had Reena's bright, blazing blue eyes and Megan's golden brown hair. He possessed a well-proportioned and reliable frame that fit somewhere between Reena's slim build and Megan's well-rounded one. If he had a single characteristic to tilt his looks in one sister's favor, it would be his high, handsome cheekbones that were the duplicate of Reena's.

Liam's feet and the exposed flesh of his face began to register the increased bite of the weather. His horse, a roan he'd purchased in Fort Benton from a man named Hudson, began to labor in the snow that seemed to deepen by the minute. An hour before, his flanks had been sweating with effort; now, the perspiration was drying in clouds of vapor that the wind carried quickly away. Liam rubbed the horse's neck vigorously. "Come on, boy," he called over the bleak wind, "you can do it." His words sounded hollow, even to himself. Hudson had told him the name of the horse, but it had been some sort of French name that Liam quickly forgot.

"What's a Frenchman doing out here in the middle of nowhere, anyway?" he muttered through lips grown stiff with cold. "Must have been lost. *Real* lost."

Liam had talked to himself on and off for the last three days out of Fort Benton. Every time he spoke, the roan would pitch his ears back, as if what his master was saying was of utmost importance and couldn't be missed. It amused Liam, and he'd learned to like the roan. This time, however, the horse ignored him as he picked his way over the blinding-white prairie.

Hudson had looked at Liam strangely when he'd learned of Liam's destination. "You got a death wish or somethin', boy? Nobody travels alone over the plains to Canada. If the Sioux or Cheyenne don't get you, a Crow will. Then, if you get there with your scalp intact, you just might have the opportunity to offer it to a Blackfoot or a Cree."

"I'll take my chances," Liam had informed him. He avoided looking the man in the face because one of Hudson's eyes was so clouded with cataracts that it seemed to stare out at him like a robin's egg.

"You'll take your chances, all right—*big* chances. That's just the savage element I was talkin' about," Hudson went on. "Then you got your bad white men—there's plenty of those around, too—and Mother Nature. You can't leave her out. She can blow a blizzard over you quicker than a train runnin' full speed. Then there's cougars and wolves that ain't scared of *no* man, not to mention bears." His cataract-ridden eyes grew round as he said, "Don't let them legends fool you. Some bears don't *never* hibernate, and they're *hungry*. Seen one in January myself one time. He chased me and my horse for miles and would've caught me if'n he hadn't found a buffalo carcass to feed on."

Liam had smiled weakly at Hudson when he'd finished saddling the roan. "Thanks for the advice."

"You got kin?"

"Of course."

"You wanna leave me a letter to 'em just in case a bullwhacker comes across your corpse come spring?"

Liam mounted the horse without a word, but something in his belly twisted with nausea at the thought.

"I'm serious, son!"

"Thanks for the roan," Liam told him as he wheeled the horse and rode out of town. He'd traveled nearly two thousand miles from Virginia, first by train, then by steamboat from St. Louis to Fort Benton. To have come this far only to be scalped was unthinkable.

He'd seen no Indians or any of the other man-eating animals Hudson had cheerfully informed him about. Once he had spotted a small herd of deer and spurred the roan toward them, happy to find that the little horse could cover distance quickly, even in snow. That night, Liam had feasted on venison haunch until he found himself groaning with discomfort. He still carried what was left of the deer over the roan's rump.

The only consolation Liam could find in the intensifying

blizzard was that his eyes weren't quite so uncomfortable now from the reflection of the sun on the snow as they'd been for the past two and a half days. At times he had raised his bandanna all the way over his eyes to get relief from the brilliant, piercing light, but that had proven to be impractical. Now the sun was hidden behind the storm's fury and would be setting within two hours; however, his whole world was still bleached white with the snow covering the ground and dancing thickly all around him.

He raised the bandanna over his nose, seeking to put warmth in his face. With eyes watering heavily in the harsh wind, Liam had no idea in which direction he was heading. For all he knew, the roan could be heading south back to Fort Benton. He would have to make a decision soon on where to stop for the night. The chances of finding a farmhouse with a warm barn were practically zero. He suddenly remembered the venison, and his stomach growled.

The thought of shelter was heavy on his mind, but finding a copse of trees to camp under was impossible. Eventually, he came to what he thought and hoped was the beginning of the Milk River Canyon. The visibility was so poor, the roan almost fell right into it. Liam managed to divert him just in time.

Blackness moved across the sky toward him like an unrolling carpet. It was time to find a spot to camp, and soon.

Liam rode around the canyon edge until he found what he judged to be a passable trail down. The roan, thankfully, proved to be surefooted. The snow seemed to be falling even harder in the shallow canyon. He steered the horse close to the walls in the hope of finding a sandstone outcropping he could camp under. The flakes bit at his face in fiery stabs and the wind sucked his breath away, but after a few hundred feet he found a suitable overhang.

When he'd seen to the horse's needs, Liam found a small cottonwood tree perfect for firewood. With stiff hands he broke off what branches he could, dragging them back to the shelter. His fingers were so numb he had trouble striking a match, but soon he had a blaze going under the outcropping. In spite of the welcome heat, Liam couldn't seem to get warm. Shivering, he ate some of the venison and the last of the biscuits he'd brought.

After he ate, he picked up his canteen for a drink to wash down the food, only to find that the water was frozen. He put the canteen by the fire to melt, but fatigue struck him like a mailed fist. He struggled up, wrapped the roan in one blanket, himself in another, and threw himself down against the wall farthest from the blowing snow. But the blanket offered little protection. The wind and the sheer weight of the coldness seeped through the covering, first penetrating his legs, then his bones.

Shaking violently, he nevertheless fell asleep, despite the rioting racket of the wind moaning through the shelter.

———

Pain awoke him.

The wind had stopped, but when he opened his eyes to see if it was still snowing, he cried out and shut them quickly. He heard the roan stir nearby. Liam's blanket fell to his waist when he rose to a sitting position and put his hands to his eyes. Rubbing them only caused more intense discomfort. He tried opening them again, and it felt as if someone were sticking needles into them.

He had a desperate thought of what it would mean to be trapped in a blizzard with his eyes gone, and he hugged the blanket closer, shivering in the bitter cold. He had no idea what time it was, and finally he drifted back into a fitful sleep, which was broken by recurring frightful dreams.

He came awake with a start, all his fears rising again. This time he didn't bother trying to open his eyes—he knew it would be fruitless. The only way he could have described his pain was to liken it to hot coals being held against his eyes or a cattle iron branding them.

Rolling over and keeping his eyes tightly shut, he began to crawl toward the opening of the outcropping—but stopped when he felt snow under his hands. The wind had blown it in, almost to where he'd lain.

Hearing himself panting hoarsely, he scooped up two handfuls and pressed the snow against his eyes. The cold was shocking but didn't curb the pain one bit. Desperately, Liam sat down cross-legged and gathered all his willpower. He brought his hands to his face, and with two fingers he forced his eyes open.

He could see nothing.

"The night's too black," he told himself, closing his eyes again and gently massaging around the orbital bones. "It must be pitch black out here!"

Even as he spoke the words, he knew he was wrong, for the snow on the ground would provide an eerie illumination even without a moon.

He tested his eyes again, with the same result. Starting to panic, he rose quickly and banged his head on the roof of the outcropping. With pain shooting through his scalp, he managed to stumble out into the falling snow.

"Dear Lord!" he cried, his voice muffled against his hands. "Dear Lord. Please don't let this be happening! Tell me this isn't happening!"

Then he heard the last thing in the world he expected to hear: the hammer of a gun being cocked. Instinctively, he reached for his own gun, which he'd taken off in order to sleep. He heard men's laughter.

"Forget something, young fella?" a pleasant voice asked.

Liam hesitated, well aware that he was in a tough situation. He couldn't see, and a man in his circumstances was cannon fodder in the wastes of the prairies. From the sound of the laughter, there were at least five men nearby. If they discovered he was blind, he could very well be killed just for his horse.

Holding his eyes open by sheer will, Liam fixed his gaze on the area from which the voice had come. He tried to sound as casual as possible when he commented, "I sure didn't expect to see anyone else out here. What are you men doing traveling in the middle of the night?"

A horse sneezed, but there was no answer.

Inwardly, Liam cringed at his own stupidity. He had discovered on his way west that many of the men who crossed the plains weren't quite normal. They were hard men and private. The majority of them kept their business to themselves. Liam held his breath while waiting for someone to answer, even though holding his eyes open and fixing them on the same spot was proving to be torturous.

Finally the same pleasant voice spoke. "Why, we were just passing by on that mesa over there and saw you jumping around. Thought you might need some help."

Liam took another chance. "Then why are you pointing that pistol at me?" Again his question was met with silence, only this time he heard a strange noise from one of the men. It sounded like a surprised chuckle, but he couldn't be sure.

After what seemed like an eternity, Liam heard a new voice that wasn't as pleasant as the first. It grated on his ears and brought visions of chaos. "That pup's blind, Fitz."

"No, I'm not!" Liam called immediately.

"Then how many fingers am I holding up?"

Liam paused, then said, "Three."

Laughter broke out, and Liam knew that he'd blundered—there were more than ten men in the group.

"What's your name, boy?" the gruff voice demanded.

"What's yours?" Liam returned, then he heard a low, gravelly chuckle.

"You may be blind, but you got spunk. My name's James Coffin."

He hated being blind. The whole world was a groping, backward blur. The men knew he was blind. He'd been foolish to think he could hide the fact in the first place. To curb the agony in his eyes, he shut them and kept them shut.

"We're waiting," Coffin growled.

"Liam O'Donnell. And I'm just snow-blind, not permanently blind." He turned in the direction of the kindly voice. "And what's your name?"

"Fitz Meecham, at your service."

"Where are you headed, Mr. Meecham?"

17

"North to Canada. And you?"

"Me too."

Coffin said, "We need to move, Fitz."

"I know, I know."

Liam heard the creak of leather and the hammer of the gun being uncocked.

"O'Donnell, it's Coffin who was holding down on you," Meecham said. "And we saw you because it was nearly dawn. Now it's full dawn, and that's why your eyes are really starting to hurt. Newby, put a blindfold on the boy."

"I'd appreciate it if I could come along with you, Mr. Meecham. I don't want to stay here until my vision returns."

Coffin remarked, "You may not like where we're going, boy."

"It's north, Mr. Coffin. That's good enough for me." Liam heard the man he supposed was named Newby walk behind him. His bandanna was untied from around his neck and retied around his eyes. With a sickening feeling, Liam suddenly thought of himself as being in front of a firing squad. "You're not going to shoot me, are you, Mr. Coffin?"

More laughter. "You're blind, O'Donnell. If we were going to shoot you we wouldn't have to blindfold you. Fitz, this boy may be too dumb to ride with us."

"He sounds educated. Where are you from, O'Donnell?"

"Chicago, sir."

"Long way from home."

"It's not my home anymore."

"Fitz, he's just another mouth to feed. Besides, he can't take care of himself. We'd have to wet-nurse him all the way," Coffin complained.

"You just help me saddle my horse and put me on it," Liam declared defiantly, "and I won't be any trouble. I have my own food; you don't have to feed me." Panic gripped him—he did *not* want to be left alone while blind. "Please, Mr. Meecham."

A heavy sigh. "All right. You just remember that you wanted to come along, no matter what. If you prove to be a good hand once you get your sight back, I'll even hire you on. Newby, while you're down there, saddle that roan for him."

"Yes, sir."

Liam was startled and looked up when Newby spoke. His voice came from high above; the man had to be six and a half feet tall. Relief washed over Liam as he realized that he was going to be all right. "I thank you, Mr. Meecham. You won't regret it."

Coffin chuckled in his deep, rasping way. "We probably won't regret it, kid. *You* might."

Liam didn't like the sound of that, but he soon forgot it.

———

Newby held the roan's reins and led Liam all day. Several times Liam had tried to start a conversation with the man, but he was met with absolute silence. Finally, a young-sounding voice spoke up from Liam's left.

"Newby don't talk much." Liam felt his hand being taken and pumped vigorously for a long moment. "My name's Pod. Well, that ain't actually my name—it's Podolnaya—but nobody ever remembers that, so they call me Pod. Hey, what you doin' out here alone, anyways?"

"I just wanted to see a foreign country."

"And now you're blind. Ain't that a kicker?"

"Yes, it's a kicker all right."

"How old are you?"

"Twenty."

"I think I'm about twenty, too. Feels like it, anyways."

Liam detected no remorse from the young man over the fact that he didn't know how old he was. From what he'd heard, there were a lot of men like that in the West.

They rode along in silence for a while. Liam's pain became acute despite wearing the bandanna. There was no way to keep all the sunlight from seeping through, and his eyes felt as if they were filled with grating sand. He tried holding his hand over his eyes, and it seemed to help somewhat, though it was awkward.

"Pretty painful, huh?" Pod asked. "Hey, Newby, you ever been snow-blind? Me neither. And from the looks of this feller, I never wanna be. I think ol' Rodriguez might have a cure in mind. He's a doctor of sorts from Mexico. We come across him on the Milk River a few months ago. He was eatin' a muskrat. 'Bout starved to death. You ever eat a muskrat, Liam?"

"No, I haven't."

"What kinda name is Liam, anyways?"

"You say 'anyways' a lot."

"So? Somethin' wrong with that?" Pod suddenly had an edge to his voice.

"Not at all. I was just—"

"Well, keep your observin' to yourself. Now, how about that name?"

Liam was growing tired of Pod's banter and useless information. Unfortunately, there was no way to get away from him. "It's Irish."

"You Irish?"

"Yes." Liam began to realize that Pod was something of a simpleton.

"Now, what was we talkin' about? Oh, yeah, didja ever eat a muskrat?"

"No."

"Too bad. Kinda tough, but it'll do." Pod paused, then commented, "Ol' Rodriguez will probably fix you up tonight."

On and on Pod talked for over an hour. Soon he stopped asking questions and seemed to become content to just let Liam listen to him. Liam doubted that Pod had ever had a captive audience, and he was deeply annoyed that it had turned out to be him.

At one point during the afternoon, someone spotted a herd of pronghorn, and Meecham sent Pod and another man to shoot two of them. Liam enjoyed the break from Pod's endless chatter.

That night, Rodriguez did indeed have an idea for Liam's condition. "We'll put your head over a boiling pot of tea. It'll take some of the pain away."

"You don't have an accent," Liam observed. "Pod said you were from Mexico."

"That Pod is an idiot, or haven't you figured that out yet? I'm from Missouri, born and bred."

When the tea was ready, Rodriguez sat Liam down on a stump and placed a blanket over his head. "Keep your eyes open and let the steam go into them."

"Thanks, Rodriguez." The tea smelled good—tangy and strong. However, for all the good it did his eyes, he might as well have been drinking it. When Rodriguez came back for him, his eyes still felt like red-hot rivets.

Liam's sleep that night was filled with pain and nightmares. In the morning, the only improvement was a yellow haze, through which he could dimly make out the shapes of men. The sun still sent lightning bolts of pain through him, and he again donned the bandanna.

At midafternoon of the second day, they stopped the horses but didn't dismount. Liam heard Coffin and Meecham talking in muffled tones. "What's happening?" Liam asked the ever present Pod.

"Got a job to do. Mr. Meecham's decidin' how to do it."

"What kind of job?"

Amazingly, Pod didn't say anything. Liam sensed a charge in the air that he didn't like. Something was about to happen, something dangerous, maybe even illegal. He started to question Pod again, but Coffin spoke first.

"Gossett, you stay with the blind kid. The rest of you come with me."

Liam hadn't heard Pod mention Gossett before, though he'd talked about many of the men. The men rode away, and Liam felt alone and exposed. "Is someone there? Gossett?"

"Yeah, I'm here," Gossett said, sounding disappointed. He seemed to be speaking around a large wad of tobacco. "I'm right here, missin' all the fun."

"What fun? What's going on?" In the distance, Liam heard shouting and a woman's scream. Then two gunshots. "Gossett, what's happening?" Liam fairly shouted.

Gossett grunted. "What's happening is that Mr. Meecham's feeling a bit bloody today."

"What do you mean?" All at once, Liam felt a debilitating nausea in the pit of his stomach.

"I mean, he just shot a farmer for no reason at all."

CHAPTER TWO

Reena's Partner

Reena O'Donnell stood in the snow, wrapped in a buffalo robe, watching some of the men in the Blackfoot tribe play snow-snake. It was a simple game. A long rut was dug into the snow, creating an alley. The braves broke into two teams at each end and took turns throwing a dart as far as they could along the ice. The dart was three feet long, capped on one end with a piece of buffalo rib and feathered on the other. One point was scored in each round for the team with the longest throw. Some of the men could heave the dart an impressively long distance.

Beside Reena, a boy named One Spot watched the men in admiration and jealousy. "We started that game," he glowered, looking at the other boys gathered around him, then back at Reena. "They run us off."

"Ran," Reena corrected, "they ran you off."

"Ran *and* runned."

Reena covered a smile. The children were awkward with the English language, and some of the gems that came from their mouths were amusing.

She'd been with the Blackfoot tribe for almost a year. Having successfully started her mission work with an Assiniboine tribe in the Cypress Hills three years before, she'd come to the Blackfoot thinking it would be just as easy to convert them to Christianity. She'd been wrong. The language was more difficult, and the tribe had proven cautious and hesitant to receive her. Reena had persevered, however, and now the Indians accepted her as part of the scenery, though only a few had converted to Christ.

One Spot hadn't finished his grumbling. "We dig that hole all morning. Now we don't even get to play in it."

"They'll be finished soon. Then you can play." Reena reached down and ruffled his fine ebony hair. Standing at five foot eight, she towered over most of the Blackfoot—even the men. Her hair was every bit as dark as theirs, and if it wasn't for her light blue eyes, she could have been mistaken for an Indian. She dressed mostly in wool dresses, but occasionally, as on this day, she wore a warm deerskin dress that had been made for her by her Assiniboine friend, Gray Dawn.

Reena heard a wagon approaching and turned to find Del Dekko and her sister Megan rolling into the camp. She waved and made her way over to them.

"Mornin', Miss Reena!" Del called as he stopped the team of horses. He was an older man, short in stature, with a bushy gray beard and one strange eye that seemed to wander. "We brought you some flour and salt. Miss Megan thought she was gonna bring 'em herself, but I put a stop to that pronto."

"Thank you, Del," Reena said gratefully. She was almost out of both staples and had been planning a trip to Fort Macleod any day.

Megan brushed honey-colored hair back from her face. She was beautiful, with a well-rounded figure and a frank, direct gaze. "Del's been around Hunter and Vic too much. He's grown almost as stubborn as they."

"That's saying a lot," Reena agreed.

Del shook his head sadly. "That's the thanks I get for hauling you all over the countryside, Miss Megan? You compare me to those two characters?"

"You're my hero, Del, and you know it." Megan looked at

Reena and winked. "I proposed to him on the way out here, and he turned me down. Can you believe that?"

Del blushed and tried to hide it by climbing down from the wagon. He began untying the sacks in the bed. "Tempting as the offer was, I'm a confirmed bachelor, and you know it. There ain't no way around that. 'Sides, I'm old enough to be your daddy."

"You're just a heartbreaker, Del." Megan climbed down and gave Reena a small hug. She only came to her sister's chin. "How are you?"

"You didn't have to come out here, Megan. Del could have brought it by himself."

"I know. But it's Saturday and there's no school, so I was bored." Megan, along with their friend Jenny Sweet, had started a school for the settlers' children in the area around Fort Macleod. At first there'd been only ten, but the presence of the Mounties had encouraged more people to travel west. Now there were nineteen children at the school.

"Why didn't Vic bring you?" Sub-Inspector Jaye Eliot Vickersham, "Vic" to his friends, had been spending more and more time with Megan, and it was no secret that they were attracted to each other. However, Megan's husband, Louis, had been killed only six months before, and she was still a bit guarded around men. Louis had turned out to be a rogue who sold whiskey to the Indians and had started abusing Megan just prior to his death at the hands of another whiskey trader. Megan was by no means in mourning, but the events had scarred her.

In response to Reena's question, Megan said, "Oh, you haven't heard. There's a ruthless gang terrorizing the countryside east of us. When I left the fort, Vic and Hunter had an appointment with Colonel Macleod."

"What do you mean by terrorizing? And how ruthless?"

"Very. They've been attacking the settlers and stealing livestock. I think there have been some deaths."

Reena sighed heavily. The beautiful morning seemed to have turned darker with Megan's news. Reena was in love with Sub-

Inspector Hunter Stone, and he with her, but because Hunter did not share her deep faith, Reena wouldn't allow their relationship to go beyond friendship. Reena had made it plain to Hunter that she wouldn't marry a non-believer, and he respected her for standing firm in her belief. Besides, he didn't want to convert to Christ just to win her. He knew it would be a mockery to do so.

Reena knew Hunter's job was dangerous. Before the North-West Mounted Police had arrived on the plains, lawlessness was notorious. Despite the Mounties' presence, there still existed a good number of bad men in the area. It seemed that it was always Hunter and Vic who were chosen to lead the patrols sent out to track down the villains. Of course, Hunter was known for having made more arrests and for having risen in rank faster than anyone in the Mounted. Colonel Macleod, the man for whom the fort was named, trusted Hunter implicitly and knew that when he assigned Hunter a job it would be carried out proficiently.

But Hunter's bravery and competence didn't help Reena cope with the danger she knew he often faced. Though she was proud of him, she worried about him almost constantly.

"So," Megan continued, as if reading Reena's mind, "since they're going out on patrol, I suppose it's time for you to start worrying. Or do you never stop?"

Del came around the wagon carrying a five-pound sack of salt. "You don't have to worry about those boys, ladies. They can take care of themselves."

"Aren't you going with them to scout, Del?" Reena asked.

"Yep, I gotta get back pretty soon. Prob'ly headin' out in the mornin'. Where you want this stuff, Miss Reena?"

Reena pointed to her tepee, and while Del unloaded the supplies, she heard the arrival of another wagon. A lone man in a black suit and caped overcoat guided two mules toward them. The braves stopped playing snow-snake and met the stranger at the edge of the village. The boys who'd dug the trench were delighted and immediately took over the darts.

The man stopped the wagon at a respectful distance and let

the braves come to him, showing them he was unarmed.

"Who's that?" Megan asked Reena.

"I have no idea." Reena saw that the man communicated in some sort of Indian dialect, but not Blackfoot, because he also used sign language. At one point the whole group turned around and looked at Reena, with one brave pointing to her.

Megan looked at her. "You're popular today."

The braves let the wagon through, and the man steered the rig toward Reena and Megan.

"He sure is handsome," Megan remarked.

As he came nearer, Reena saw that her sister was right. His light red hair was of medium length, and his oval face contained pleasant features. He smiled at them, revealing strong white teeth and twin dimples. His good looks were edged with a tiredness that showed around his eyes.

"Good morning, ladies," he greeted, touching the brim of his felt Stetson.

"Good morning," Reena returned, and Megan nodded.

"My name is Reverend Jack Sheffield. I'd heard there was a missionary in the area?"

"That's me," Reena replied.

"And you are. . . ?"

Reena introduced herself and Megan. Del strode up to retrieve the last sack of flour, and Reena introduced him also.

"Howdy," Del said shortly, barely glancing at the man as he walked away with the last bag.

"Mr. Dekko, it's a pleasure—" Sheffield stopped when he found he was speaking to Del's receding back and gave the women a questioning glance.

Megan explained. "Del's not much of a conversationalist unless he knows you pretty well."

"Obviously." Sheffield climbed down and dusted himself off, though there was no sign of dirt on him. His suit was well cared for and neatly tailored. He stood only an inch or two taller than Reena.

The Blackfoot braves were standing nearby watching them.

Few of them had bothered learning English from Reena, and she was certain they were curious about what was being said. She smiled at them reassuringly.

"What brings you out here, Reverend?" Megan asked in her direct, no-nonsense way.

"I've been working with a Sarcee tribe to the east. In a roundabout way I heard of Miss O'Donnell's work, and I thought I'd come meet her."

"Would you like some lunch?" Reena asked him. He was well mannered and seemed kind, but Reena wondered what his real intentions were. She'd heard of other missionaries in the area, but she'd never been inclined to go meet them. Could that be his only reason for being here?

"Lunch sounds wonderful."

Del returned, wiping his hands on his bibbed tan shirt. "Somebody mention food?"

Reena, with help from her Blackfoot friend Raindrop, prepared fried corn cakes and venison bacon in her tepee. Reena's home was spacious, with a writing table and chair, and an ever-burning fire in the center. The tepee was ingenious in that the smoke drew directly up through a small hole at the top where the support poles met.

Megan told Reena about the schoolchildren while they cooked, then asked, "Do you remember Lydia?"

"Of course."

Lydia Meecham was a quiet, introverted five-year-old whom Jenny Sweet met when she had arrived at Fort Macleod. Jenny's father, Armand, had been a ruthless outlaw and a whiskey runner, who had cruelly abused Jenny. Her lack of exposure to people other than her father's renegade friends had left Jenny socially scarred to the point of making her extremely shy and withdrawn. Constable Dirk Becker, a handsome young Mountie who'd saved Jenny from an outlaw named Sad Sid, had tried to introduce her to the outside world, only to be rebuffed over and over. Instead,

Jenny had found a kinship with Lydia, who showed signs of having family problems herself.

"Lydia and Jenny are nearly inseparable during school hours," Megan informed her sister. "After Jenny learned to read, there was no stopping her. She read everything I had, then read every book we ordered for the school. She's practically greedy about it!"

Reena turned one of the corn cakes in the skillet. "If she's read that much in so little time, she must learn fast." Megan had just taught Jenny to read in the summer past.

"She's a smart girl. She's just never had the chance to show it or to develop her talents. You should see her with the children, Reena. Not just with Lydia, but with all of them. They see her not only as a teacher but as one of their own. I don't know what I'm even doing there anymore."

"Now, don't say that, Megan. You've helped those children and Jenny so much. Just think of where they'd all be if the Lord hadn't sent you here."

"Well, I was going to tell you that Lydia's doing well, too. She's talking more, and that strange impairment she has with her reading is getting a little bit better."

"I'm glad." Reena glanced over at Del and Sheffield, who sat cross-legged around the fire in uncomfortable silence. She'd noticed that Sheffield had tried to start a conversation a few times, but Del would have none of it. Reena had been listening to Megan, but in the back of her mind she was still gnawing the question of why Reverend Sheffield was here.

As they ate lunch, Sheffield told them about his endeavors with the Sarcee tribe. "I've set up a Methodist mission and have begun to teach them English, general knowledge, and agriculture. They've come along very well."

Del, who was eating heartily, piped up and said around a mouthful of corn, "Them Sarcee are the gentlest of the Blackfoot Nation. You've had it easy, padre. You should try educatin' these difficult ones Reena's got to deal with day in and day out."

"Del!" Megan exclaimed. "They're just distrustful of white

people. And why shouldn't they be? For years they've known us as renegade whiskey traders and murderous land stealers."

Del shrugged indifferently. "Sarcees have seen the same thing. They're just more easygoing than those you got here is all I'm sayin'." He glanced over at Sheffield defiantly.

Silence ruled for a while as they ate. Sheffield eyed Del a few times with something close to resentment. Then he asked Reena, "What religious denomination do you represent, Miss O'Donnell?"

Reena was caught with a mouthful of food but was grateful, for it gave her time to think. Was this the reason for his visit? "I'm not under any specific denomination, Reverend. Why do you ask?"

Sheffield put his plate down in front of him and carefully wiped his lips with the knuckle of one finger. "So what, if I may ask, is your authority with these Blackfoot?" He stared steadily at her, trying to keep a casual smile fixed on his face, but Reena knew it was a challenge.

"Authority!" Del erupted. "What authority does she need to teach the Word of God? She has *God's* authority."

Reena and Megan were deeply surprised. Del wasn't a Christian, yet he was defending Reena's right to be there. The little man never ceased to amaze her, and she felt a new rush of affection for him.

"Mr. Dekko—"

"Del. Nobody calls me that."

"Del, then," Sheffield amended carefully, trying to control his impatience. "I appreciate your trying to help, but may I speak directly to Miss O'Donnell?"

"In other words, will I shut up while you pepper her with stupid questions? I'd say that's up to Miss Reena." He threw a look at Reena that was both questioning and amused.

"It's all right, Del. Reverend, I frankly couldn't have given you a better answer than my friend. I feel it's our Higher Authority who's sanctioned my being here. I tell you in all humbleness that many Assiniboine and a few Blackfoot have come to

Christ since I've been among them. In view of that, I don't see how it matters that I'm not under a certain religion's official cover."

Sheffield nodded slowly, still managing to keep the smile on his face.

"How long were you planning to stay, Reverend?"

Sheffield shifted on the dirt floor and cleared his throat. He seemed confused and unsure. "Actually, I left one of my assistants in charge with the Sarcee. He's very capable. I was going to offer my help to you if our religions didn't . . . um . . . clash."

Reena nodded and waited.

"I thought you may be Roman Catholic, and in that case our different doctrines would have caused a problem."

"What Del told you is at least partially correct. I've had trouble bonding with this tribe. No matter how much I teach the children, who are wonderful and trusting as are all children, the adults are still wary of me. I've been trying to find a way to gain their trust, and you've mentioned something that may work."

"What's that?"

"Agriculture. I'm not a farmer, and you could help me teach the Blackfoot how to grow their own crops so they would not be dependent on outside means."

"That's a good idea, Reena," Megan said.

"Yep," Del agreed, "she *is* smart." He looked over at Sheffield again, as if daring him to challenge Reena's intelligence.

Sheffield ignored him and pursed his lips as he thought. "Yes, it's obviously a good idea, but there are other . . . matters that have to be addressed before we reach an agreement."

"Like theology?" Reena asked.

"Yes, exactly."

Reena spread her hands and raised her eyebrows. "I have all day."

"You just watch that feller," Del warned Reena as he and Megan mounted the wagon. "I don't trust 'im."

"You don't trust anyone, Del," Reena grinned.

"Hunter ain't gonna like it."

"Why not? What does this have to do with him?"

Del eyed her knowingly. "You know."

"No, I don't."

"He just ain't gonna like it."

"Del, you're always the voice of doom!" Megan said. "If it bothers you so much, you don't have to tell him."

Del looked at her and shrank back slightly. "You mean hide something from my friends? I got few enough as it is, thank you very much, and I don't intend to lose one of 'em by stabbin' him in the back."

"Stab! What are you talking about?" Megan frowned.

Reena laughed and touched her sister's knee. "Don't try to make sense of Del's reasoning, Megan. You know better than that. Besides, how in the world are you going to stop Del from gossiping? It's his favorite pastime."

"Well, Hunter has no hold over you, anyway," Megan sniffed. She turned to Del pointedly. "As much as I like Hunter, he has no right to be jealous of a handsome man spending time with Reena."

"Practically *living* with her, you mean," Del mumbled.

"Del!"

"Miss Reena, if that padre gives you any more trouble about this religion business, you just give me a holler. I'll come back here and crack his pretty head. Or better yet, I'll bring Hunter and Vic—they could arrest him for something, keep him out of the way for a while so's he won't wanna come back here."

Megan rolled her eyes. "I can't believe I'm hearing this blatant talk of twisting the law to fit one person's desires. Del, this isn't the Spanish Inquisition!"

"The what?"

"Never mind, you two," Reena interrupted with a smile. "You've got time to argue all the way back to the fort. Del, I want you back in time to go out with Hunter. You're the best scout they've got."

"Oh, we'll be back in plenty of time," Del assured her, jamming his hat down on his head and grabbing the reins.

"All of you be careful . . . and thanks for the supplies."

"You're welcome, dear," Megan said. She glanced at Del with a mischievous glint in her dark brown eyes. "And keep Reverend Sheffield in line and happy."

"That does it," Del pronounced with a scowl. "I'm tellin' Hunter."

CHAPTER THREE

Patrol Orders

Hunter Stone sat on his bed, his back to the wall of the officers' quarters he shared with his friend, Jaye Eliot Vickersham. His booted feet were propped up on one corner of a chair that sat in front of him. Beside his feet sat his white helmet, upside down, slowly filling up with the cards he was lazily throwing into it.

Stone looked over at Vic, who sat on his bunk polishing his boots. "You know, you're going to scrub the shine right off those boots."

Vic looked up and grinned. His features reflected the British aristocratic blood that ran through his veins. The son of an earl, Vic was six feet tall, a bit thin, but carried a wiry strength. His nose, cheekbones, and jaw were sharp, but not unattractive, and his chocolate brown eyes usually reflected merriment, as if he were amused by the world in general. In his clipped, proper British accent he answered, "It never hurts to put on an extra coat of polish when going to see the man. You never know what he'll notice, the rascal."

Stone was still dressed in trousers, suspenders, and white cotton shirt. His scarlet jacket hung neatly on a rack beside his bed. "Something's really bothering me, Vic," he commented as he continued sailing cards into his hat.

"What's that?"

"Here we are, dressed exactly alike—blue trousers with yellow stripes down the sides, white cotton shirts, and suspenders. Yet you look neater than I do. Why is that?"

"I think it's because the strength of my character shows through in my dress. Since you're inferior, it's only natural that you appear slovenly."

Stone laughed long and hard, and Vic along with him. Throwing his last card, Stone picked up the helmet and emptied the contents on the bed beside him. A few cards were scattered on the floor, but not many; Stone didn't miss much. "You should have been Irish, Vic. You definitely have the gift of the blarney about you."

"The truth hurts, my friend. There's no blarney about it."

Stone began going through the deck of cards again. They sat in companionable silence, the swish and squeak of Vic's cloth and the flutter of playing cards the only sound between them.

Stone glanced occasionally over at his friend, smiling a secret smile. Vic was so intent on his job that his brow was furrowed and he chewed on his lower lip. If there was one thing in the world that Stone could count on, it was that Jaye Eliot Vickersham, no matter what calamity befell him, could be counted on to look like a professional soldier.

The thought of calamities brought the events of the past year to his mind. Vic had been wounded by one of Armand Sweet's men and had nearly died. Megan and Reena had taken care of him in Baker's Boardinghouse in the burg of Fort Macleod. Stone had eventually caught up with Sweet, and the confrontation had ended with exploding results.

Vic's wound had brought with it a life-changing decision. While he was under Reena's care, both he and Megan had become Christians—a conversion that hadn't happened to Stone when he had been in the same situation a few years before. Left for dead by a renegade Crow named Red Wolf, Stone was found by Reena, who nursed him back to health in the Assiniboine village. She had witnessed to him many times, but Stone's heart was consumed with revenge after Red Wolf had murdered his wife, Betsy.

Now it seemed that everyone around Stone was a Christian except him. It was a disturbing thought, and he often found himself wondering what it was he was missing that his friends enjoyed so much.

"Hunter?"

"What?"

"Didn't you hear me?"

"No."

Vic's eyes narrowed as he capped the polishing cream and began slipping on his boots. "Are you going deaf?"

"Crazy, maybe. Not deaf."

"You're too serious, Hunter."

"Believe it or not, I've been told that before," Stone remarked with a wry grin.

"I was saying that it's almost time to go. We certainly can't keep Macleod waiting."

"Right." Stone gathered the cards and slipped on the wool jacket. "Say, Vic, do you ever think about getting shot again?"

Vic looked surprised at the question. "Why, no, I don't. At least not very often. Do you?"

"I wasn't shot. I was stabbed."

"Ah, yes."

"Twice."

"I remember."

"Very painful. More painful than being shot, I'd imagine."

"Frightfully easy to make that assessment when you haven't taken a bullet to the chest. Would you like to be put in a position to compare them? I'll be glad to oblige."

Stone grinned and finished buttoning his coat all the way to his neck.

"I worry about you sometimes, old chap," Vic said, his face turning serious. "You can be sitting on your bunk, but you're not really there. It's very nearly like Jenny Sweet and her spells. How do you do that?"

Stone had slipped on his helmet and was adjusting the chin strap in the mirror over their washbasin when suddenly he stopped. Vic's comparison of Stone's deep musings to Jenny's catatonic seizures was disturbing. "I don't really know. It's like . . . it's as if I fall so deep into thought that I just erase everything around me."

Vic slapped him on the back lightheartedly. "I'll just have to keep my eye on you, I suppose. One of these days you're going to run into a tree while you're doing that."

"Maybe it'll knock some sense into my head."

At the door, Vickersham took hold of Stone's arm before he could open it. "Hold on there, Hunter, old boy. What's all this talk about getting shot?"

"Nothing really."

"Who do you think you're talking to? You don't ask questions lightly or without a reason. What's going on in that thick skull of yours?"

Stone reached out and picked a piece of lint from the front of Vickersham's uniform. "It's a dangerous line of work we're in. It just . . . crosses my mind sometimes. Doesn't it yours?"

"Occasionally." He thought a moment, then nodded. "Yes, I see what you mean."

"But it doesn't do any good to dwell on it."

"Quite right. Shall we go?"

———

Assistant Commissioner James Farquharson Macleod, who preferred just to be called Colonel, had the most erect posture of any person Stone or Vic had ever seen. Standing ramrod straight, Macleod formally greeted them in his office. "Sub-Inspector Vickersham, Sub-Inspector Stone."

The office was neat and tidy. Stone sat beside a small table on which sat a hand-carved ivory chess set. Vickersham sat under a mounted deer's head. Macleod went around behind his huge oak desk but didn't seat himself. In typical Macleod fashion, he got right down to business. "Are you gentlemen ready for an adventure?"

"Always, sir," Vic replied, and Stone nodded.

"Then I'm going to make you happy men today." He turned to a map of the North-West Territories behind him. Stone and Vic leaned forward in order to see better. A pointer appeared in Macleod's hand, and he tapped the map with it in three places. "Battle Creek, just east of Bad Water Lake, and, in our own backyard so to speak, Chin Coulée." He faced them and paused.

Stone, being sure that the hesitation was for dramatic effect, prompted him anyway. "What about them, Colonel?"

"Attacks on settlers. Burning of barns and houses, theft of livestock, and in two instances out-and-out murder." Suddenly he slapped the pointer down on the desk with a crack as sharp as a rifle report, splintering the thick piece of ash into four pieces. "In *our* territory!"

Stone and Vic regarded each other warily. They had witnessed Macleod's temper before—his face reddened, his eyes seemed to smolder like blacksmith's coals, and he invariably clasped his hands behind his back and tortured them by wringing them unmercifully. But never had they seen him show any sort of violent behavior.

Macleod's face was now red, his eyes were embers, and he did indeed clasp his hands behind his back, but he quickly brought them around in front of himself as he sat down heavily in the padded chair. His dark eyes went from one of them to the other as if waiting for a response.

Stone had no idea what to say at that moment; silence seemed to be the most prudent response. The fire behind him popped loudly. A clock over the fireplace mantel softly ticked off the passing seconds.

Macleod ran his hands through his thinning brown hair and sighed deeply. "We came here to protect those people, mainly from the Indian element, and now we have this."

"We know for a fact the attackers aren't Indians, sir?" Vic asked.

"Yes. There have been survivors—women and children mainly—who've told of masked riders. They say the men were white with no discernible accent, so they weren't Metis." The Metis were a race of mixed origin who still lived in the Eastern Territories, descendants from French trappers who settled in the area and took Indian wives.

"When was the first attack?" Stone asked.

"A week ago at Battle Creek, then Chin Coulée, then Bad Water Lake. There were a couple of days between each attack, so I believe they're going over the border to sell the livestock, then coming back."

Vickersham asked, "Why do they come to Canada to steal? Why don't they carry out their crimes close to the buyers in the United States?"

Macleod looked pained. "It's a slap in the face to the Mounted, Vickersham. Obviously they feel that the United States Cavalry in Montana Territory are more formidable than we are." He paused and observed both of them, smiling when he saw Stone. "I see that grates against you, Stone."

"Yes, sir, it does."

"Whenever you get that look, I know trouble's coming. Go find them for me and bring them back. You go with him, Vickersham."

"Both of us?" Vickersham asked. For the past few months, Stone and Vickersham hadn't been assigned together for a duty. Desertions in the ranks over the past summer had caused the need for new recruits, which meant training patrols. Stone and Vickersham had had to do most of the training.

"Yes, both of you," Macleod answered. "You two are the best, and I don't want this thing botched."

"How many men, Colonel?"

"That brings up the last piece of news I have for you, and it's not good. Witnesses say there are as many as a dozen men in the gang."

Vickersham whistled softly. "A dozen?"

"Right. Take the most seasoned men—no trainees. I should think about twenty will do, don't you, Stone?"

"Absolutely, sir."

Macleod stood and said, "Leave in the morning at first light. Head for Bad Water Lake and try to pick up a trail there."

Vickersham and Stone were heading out the door when Macleod spoke again.

"Oh, and, gentlemen? Take great care on this one. I don't like the feel of it."

———————

Stone and Vickersham found Dirk Becker near a storage shed loading supplies into a wagon. Despite the cold weather, he wore no coat. His suspenders hung loosely at his sides, and his dark blue cotton undershirt stretched tautly against his broad back when he tossed sacks into the bed. Stuck in his trousers at the small of his back was a large knife; Stone had never seen him without it.

"Constable Becker," Stone said accusingly, "you've been reading my mind."

Becker turned, surprised. "How's that, sir?"

"We were just looking for you to tell you to get a wagon loaded for patrol."

Becker grinned, revealing strong white teeth. "I'm way ahead of you, sir." He was extremely handsome, with light brown hair and a determined square chin. Unfortunately, a scar ran from just below his left eye to his jawline, marring his good looks. At six feet four inches and solidly muscled, Becker could take most any man in a fistfight. For the men who knew him, a knife fight with Becker was out of the question; his ability with knives was nearly magical.

Vickersham watched Becker throw a seventy-five pound sack of horse feed into the wagon with alarming ease. "What, may I be so bold as to ask, possessed you to begin loading a wagon, Becker?"

Becker looked at him as if he'd suddenly gone daft. "Patrol, sir."

"Becker, *we* didn't even know about a patrol until just now."

"You know how it is, sir. Word gets around a police post when there's murdering going on."

Stone and Vickersham exchanged glances. Stone asked, "Why didn't you tell us you knew something?"

"You mean you hadn't heard? I thought you knew."

"Do me a favor—next time you hear something, come tell us." To Vickersham he asked, "How is it we're the last to know these things, yet we're supposed to be in charge?"

Vickersham shrugged and grinned. "You know how the men are—they love to gossip."

"Yes, and Del is the worst one."

Becker asked, "When do we leave, sir?"

"Who said you were going?" Stone asked.

"But . . . you've *got* to let me go, sir!"

"Why's that?" Stone, like everyone else, loved baiting the boy. His enthusiasm and curiosity, combined with his size, prompted Del to nickname him "Bear Cub."

Becker looked confused, then saw Stone smile slightly. "You're having me on, aren't you, Sub-Inspector?"

Vickersham suddenly shouted, "You there, Stride! Come over here."

Sergeant Preston Stride, who'd just been about to step into the barracks, strode over to them on long legs. A professional British soldier before the Mounties were established, he'd come to Canada at the request of Macleod. Tough and wiry, he was an excellent disciplinarian. Both Stone and Vickersham trusted him with their lives.

Stopping at full attention in front of them, Stride said, "Yes, sir!"

"At ease, Sergeant," Vickersham told him. "We'll be heading out in the morning. Seems we have some bad men to catch."

"Very good, sir."

"I want you to handpick fifteen men. We want veterans who

can ride long and hard, and who can take the cold. Sub-Inspector Stone and I will brief you this evening after mess."

"As you wish, sir."

Stone watched him go and thought again about how glad he was that Stride was on their side. He took an immense load of work and responsibility off of Stone's shoulders.

Turning back to Becker he said, "Get someone else to load that wagon. I want you to help Sergeant Stride find the men he needs."

"All right." Becker began pulling on his scarlet jacket. It was a bit too small for him, but a reorder would arrive any day.

"Also, I want you to make sure that every man cleans his fire-arms tonight."

"Yes, sir."

"I mean it, Becker. I want you to stand over them while they're doing it. I don't want to run up against this gang we're after and have any misfires. It looks like we may need all the fire-power we can manage."

"Is it that bad, sir?"

"It could be," Stone said.

"All right," Becker conceded.

After Stone left, Vickersham looked at Becker. "What's the matter with you?"

Becker finished buttoning his tunic, his eyes on Stone as he walked away. "I've never seen him like that."

"Like what?"

"I think he's actually worried. I didn't know he *ever* worried."

"Oh, I don't think he is. He's just a bit grumpy because he didn't sleep very well last night." This wasn't true, but Vickersham could see that Becker was concerned. If the men sensed the officers were anxious, then they would be anxious also. That wouldn't do.

Vickersham himself had felt somewhat worried after hearing the size of the outlaw gang and their viciousness. He made a mental note to speak to Hunter about exuding confidence in front of the men instead of doubt. He also knew he would have to make himself shift into the same frame of behavior, though the only feeling he was really aware of regarding the coming patrol was a strange dread.

———

The North-West Mounted Police issued one Snider-Enfield single-shot carbine and one Adams .450 pistol to every new recruit. The Snider-Enfield was a stubby, ugly thing, but if sighted correctly, it was reliable. Though it was relatively easy to clean, the men still moaned when Becker informed them of Stone's order that all weapons be inspected and cleaned.

"Now what does he think he's going to prove with that order?" Gustav Boogaard whined. Boogaard had the unfortunate but predictable nickname of "Booger." He fell back on his bunk in the sub-constables' barracks and moaned.

"Sub-Inspector Stone doesn't have to prove anything, Booger," Becker told him. "You've got to be the laziest man I've ever seen."

"Thank you, Constable."

"You're welcome."

"It's some kind of power play of Stone's," Andy Doe announced quietly.

Becker walked over to him and stuck a thick finger in his young face. "I've warned you about calling the officers by their names without their rank in front of it. This is the last time I'm telling you."

"Okay, okay. What's the matter with you today, Constable?"

Due to Becker's bravery and his actions in Armand Sweet's cabin the previous year, Becker had been promoted to full constable. Being addressed as something other than Becker by men who were older than he had been difficult for him to get used to. "There's nothing the matter with me. We've just got a lot to do tonight."

"You know what I think?" Ken Garner asked, nudging Doe beside him.

"What?"

"I think the constable here hasn't seen the Sweet girl in a while, and he's taking it out on us."

Good-natured laughter went all around the room, and even Becker had to smile. "I saw her yesterday, Garner, so that blows a hole in your theory."

"Maybe he just misses the South," Boogaard mused. "I hear once Dixie's in your blood, you never really leave her, Constable. Does that make you feel better?"

"Booger, just when I start thinking you're not only the laziest man in the world, but the dumbest, too, you come up with a diamond like that. You're most certainly right. I miss Dixie a lot sometimes, but I've still got her up here." Becker tapped the side of his head. "Now, listen up everybody. Get started on your weapons. I'm staying right here to make sure it's done so Sub-Inspector Stone doesn't take your head off."

After a few more moans, the sound of lockers being opened and the clinking of iron filled the room.

"Hey," Garner asked, seeing Becker just standing and watching, "don't you have to clean yours, too?"

"Mind your own business, Garner."

"He cleans his every night," Doe informed Garner. "Didn't you know that?"

"What for?"

"I don't know—ask him."

Becker said, "Your rifle and pistol are your best friends."

"Why, that's the most ridiculous thing I ever heard," Garner mumbled. "Andy Doe's my best friend."

"What if he's dead and can't help you?"

"Now, wait a minute!" Doe argued. "What's this talk about me being dead?" He was twenty-two, with a baby face and large brown eyes. At the moment, his eyes were as large as they could be.

Becker shrugged. "It's a hypothetical situation."

"A what? Where'd you get that twenty dollar word?"

"What, situation?" Becker grinned.

45

"Of course not! That other one."

Becker rolled his eyes and looked heavenward. "Why, oh why, can't I find a man to converse with intelligently?"

"Well, I don't want to be dead," Doe announced stubbornly. "Have somebody else dying in your fancy situation."

Sub-Constable Gerard D'Artigue, a Frenchman with a thick accent, said to Becker, "I would think your best friends were your knives, Constable."

Becker smiled and sat down on a vacant bunk. "They can't be classified as just 'best friends.' They're on a whole level by themselves." He withdrew the knife tucked in the small of his back, gently slid it from its sheath, and held it up fondly. Its haft was hand carved from a deer antler, and the blade was six inches long with one razor-sharp edge. The lamplight gleamed along the honed blade ominously.

D'Artigue looked at the knife with appreciation, but Boogaard practically shuddered. "You're too spooky, Dirk. To have one of those things open up your face like that, and still you like them. There's something wrong with that."

Becker stopped smiling when his scar was mentioned. "It wasn't the knife that did this. It was the man holding it." When Becker had been a brash teenager, he'd accepted a bet from a drifter on what he thought would be an innocent knife fight. The man had cut Becker open, taken his money, and walked out of his life forever.

Garner said quietly, "I bet you'd like to meet up with that fellow again, eh?"

Becker balanced the knife point down on his palm and said nothing. Lightning quick, his hand was a blur as he twitched, then he was holding the knife by the handle. He performed the maneuver again, then again.

Noticing the men watching him in amazement and admiration, Becker pointed at their weapons with the point of the knife and said, "Get back to work."

CHAPTER FOUR

Among the Carnage

Snow was blowing at dawn the next morning when the nineteen Mounties pulled out of Fort Macleod. One of the men Stride had chosen was overcome with a high fever during the night, and instead of choosing another man and waiting for him to ready himself, Stone opted to go with what he had.

As the troop passed by Macleod's quarters, Stone saw the man watching them through ice-encrusted windows. Stone saluted, and Macleod returned it.

After Stone and Vickersham had briefed Stride, Stone had gone to the quartermaster and ordered nearly three times as much ammunition for the troop as was usual. The man had looked at him strangely, but he'd done his job. Stone could see that the two pack mules were loaded down with boxes of bullets. Weapons and ammunition were on Stone's mind for some reason—he had even dreamed about them.

Vickersham and Del appeared beside him in the swirling snow. Del wore a bearskin coat taken from a grizzly he'd killed himself. Stone thought he looked warmer than any of them. "How long do you think, Del?"

"Oh, we should be there tomorrow mornin' sometime.

Don't know why we're goin', really. Any tracks they left, the snow will have covered up by now."

"We're going because they're out there somewhere, so we need to be out there, too."

"Fine with me. Looks like we could be headin' into a bush-whackin', though."

"Why's that?" Vickersham asked.

Del turned and looked pointedly at the long line of men, the supply wagon, pack mules, and extra horses. "How long you think we're gonna be a secret? Everyone in the Territory is gonna know we're out here and why we're out here. Them fellers we're after might just wanna up and give us a surprise party."

"You are gloomy, Del, I must say," Vic replied.

Stone shook his head. "Nothing wrong with that kind of thinking. We can't be too cautious on this trip. Del, why don't you take Garner and two others and move ahead of us about a mile. And keep your eyes open."

"Right."

"Wait a minute," Vickersham said. "Hunter, don't you think he should take at least five men? Three wouldn't have a chance if they were attacked."

Stone thought a moment, then nodded. "Okay. Del, take five men."

"You got it."

When Del was out of hearing distance, Stone said, "I was thinking we should keep every man we could here with the supplies. What if we're attacked from the rear?"

Vickersham looked at him. "Why, you're angry at me for countermanding your orders, aren't you? I can see it in your face."

Stone realized he was being foolish and his features softened. "We've never talked about it, Vic, but who's ultimately in charge when we're on the same patrol? You were promoted before me, so I guess—"

"Come now, Hunter, I was *handed* my rank because my father is an earl. You've received two promotions because of your accomplishments, which were impressive. I think you should be—"

"Forget it, Vic. You've got seniority, and that's that."

"Is that an order?"

"Yes, sir. The last one I'm giving you, sir."

Vickersham laughed. "Don't 'sir' me."

They passed by Baker's Boardinghouse in the town, and Stone looked over at his friend slyly. "Care to stop the whole troop so you can say good-bye to Miss Megan?"

"No, I wouldn't, thank you very much."

"You want to and you know it. You just won't admit it."

Vickersham looked up at the two-story building. The snow was blowing in on the porch—a porch on which he'd sat many times with Megan while recovering from his wound. That was where he'd learned about her likes, her desires, her dreams. It had been a difficult time for her since her husband had come to the Territory under the guise of escorting Megan to visit her sister, Reena, after the death of their mother. But instead, Megan discovered that he'd only been looking for someone to deal the whiskey he shipped from Chicago.

"She's a wonderful woman," Stone commented, catching Vic's wistful look.

"Yes, she is."

They rode all day with only one minor incident: a wagon wheel got stuck in a crevice the driver hadn't seen because of the deep snow. The Mounties, including Stone and Vickersham, had had to dismount and push until it cleared the fissure. Most of the men had slipped and fallen into the snow during the action, and one man sprained a wrist. By dusk, everyone was more than ready to stop for the night, but Stone pushed them until almost dark. They camped in a copse of aspens and had a supper of beans, beef ribs, and hard bread.

The snow had stopped about midafternoon, which pleased Del. Sitting with Stone and Vickersham around a fire, he said, "This may be good news. It looks like it hasn't snowed around here for a few days, so maybe we'll find some tracks."

"We're still miles from the farm that was attacked," Stone reminded him.

"Don't discourage him, Hunter," Vic said with a smile. "That's one of the few positive things I've ever heard Del say."

"Don't you two start in on me," Del warned them. "I'll just go to bed if you do."

Stone sipped the last of his coffee, then threw the dregs into the fire. "Sounds like a good idea to me. I think we should all turn in early. Del, will you go tell the men?"

The enlisted men were gathered around a huge fire. Some of them were chatting and smoking cigars, while another group was gathered around an ammunition box playing cards. The night wasn't very cold, so they were comfortable. Stone watched them and wondered if any of them missed their families. Enlisted men weren't allowed to be married, but Stone knew that some of them had left sweethearts behind in the East.

"Are you still apprehensive, Hunter?" Vickersham asked him.

"No, why?"

"Because you look it."

"It's just hard to believe, looking at those boys, that some of them could get hurt or even killed on this patrol."

Vickersham grinned. "And that's not apprehensive?"

"Yeah, I guess you're right." He poked the fire with an aspen branch and watched the sparks rise. "I feel we're wasting time just sitting around."

"Can't track at night, old boy."

"I know. I just want this over with."

Vickersham watched him for a moment, then said softly, "If I didn't know better, I'd say you were frightened, Hunter."

Stone kept poking the fire but didn't answer.

"What *is* it? I've never seen you like this, and quite frankly, it's frightening *me*."

"I don't know, okay? I just don't know."

Vickersham pushed his beaver hat back and found an excuse to look at his feet. Taking a deep breath of the cool air, he let it slide out slowly as he revealed, "I'm different from what I was, Hunter . . . before becoming a Christian, I mean. I see the world in a new way, I think differently, and sometimes when I look in a mirror, I think I even look different. Isn't that strange?"

"Which part?"

"I'm serious, Hunter."

"So am I."

"I suppose what I'm trying to say . . ." Vic paused and couldn't meet Stone's gray eyes. "I'm trying to say that I'm not worried about dying anymore, because I know what's going to happen to me. I'm at peace about living or dying." He looked up and found Stone staring at him steadily. "You need peace, too, Hunter."

"Do all you Christians worry about what everyone else needs? Why don't you worry about yourselves?" Stone tried to keep the edge from his voice, but he heard it clearly, and he was sure his friend did also.

Vic's face fell, and he pursed his lips as if biting back a reply.

"I'm sorry, Vic. I think you already answered my question. You don't have to worry about yourselves because you know where you're going when you die. As for me . . ."

"I don't know what's in your heart, Hunter. No one knows another man's heart. But I do know that if you don't accept Jesus, it doesn't matter how good you are—and you are a good, decent man—it's still not going to bode well for you in eternity."

"I'm starting to realize that, I think. It's just . . . hard, you know?"

"I know how you feel. I don't mean to be a mother hen and all that rot, but I'm afraid for you—for your soul. And I'm afraid for those boys over there, all but one."

"Who's that?"

"Becker."

Stone nodded and looked at the young man who was supervising the men as they prepared for bedding down. Becker had an easy way about him, and the men liked and respected him. Stone didn't doubt that they also respected him, but liking him was another matter. As he watched, Andy Doe jabbed Becker playfully with a stick, pretending it was a sword. Becker grabbed the stick, then tweaked Doe's ear.

Stone smiled faintly. Under no circumstances would any of the men try that with him, and he found himself somewhat wistful at the thought.

"Anyway," Vickersham said lightly, standing and slapping Stone on the back, "enough death talk for tonight. Let's get some sleep."

The troop eventually piled into their two tents for the night. Stone listened to the restless movements of the men who couldn't fall asleep and the snoring of the ones who could. It seemed to him that he was the last to drift off.

Dirk Becker woke the next morning to the sounds of Del's coughing and to his own sore throat. Del's coughing wasn't unusual—it seemed to be a timely ritual for him—but Becker's sore throat was.

He drank some water as the camp stirred around him. He was amused to see Hunter Stone already dressed and saddling his horse, Buck, in the gray, iron-colored dawn. "The man never stops," Becker commented to himself and found that his voice was as harsh as a rasp.

"What was that, Dirk?"

Becker turned to find Vickersham also fully dressed and looking as spotless and confident as always. "Morning, sir. I was just wondering—does Sub-Inspector Stone ever sleep, or is he always on duty?"

"I've caught him sleeping a time or two. The only trouble is, even when he's sleeping he's still on duty, I believe."

"That doesn't surprise me."

"Having trouble with the voice this morning, Becker?"

"A little throat problem. It'll probably be better in an hour or two."

"You need to see Dr. Carson about that."

Becker finished the cup of water, which was cool and soothing on his fiery throat. "He's busy bandaging Michael's sprained wrist."

"That wasn't a request; it was an order," Vickersham returned pleasantly. "We need every man we've got in good health."

"Yes, sir." Becker watched him walk off, stopping and chatting with some of the men as they prepared a quick breakfast. It struck him that Vickersham and Stone complemented each other well in their leadership styles. Stone's quiet, no-nonsense approach that invoked loyalty and Vickersham's smooth, seemingly effortless ability to inspire confidence in himself were in complete opposition, yet the two fit well when combined.

He looked over at Stone again. When Becker had joined the Mounties, he'd practically worshiped the big blond man. At that time, Stone had been responsible for multiple arrests, had received several promotions, and everyone looked to him when trouble was brewing. Becker loved to go on patrol with Stone to see the manner in which he carefully considered every decision before making it, and to observe his openness to hearing suggestions from the newest recruit. True, Stone rarely took the advice given, but the Mountie was left with the impression that his opinion had been duly considered by one of the finest officers in the Mounted Police, and it gave him a feeling of importance.

One incident from Stone's legend that Becker wished he'd been there to see had taken place the same year that the North-West Mounted Police had come to the Territory. Whenever Becker heard the story told of Stone's insubordination and desertion in order to save Reena from the formidable Red Wolf, it was always spoken of in hushed tones and fascinated awe.

When Becker had first heard the tale, he'd been sure that Garner was having him on. Hunter Stone defy the great Macleod and desert? At first Becker had laughed, and then he'd seen the serious faces in front of him.

"You'd better believe it," Garner had whispered with a look over his shoulder, "because every word is true."

"I was there," D'Artigue assured Becker, "and it truly happened that way. Sub-Inspector Stone was a crazed man. Even Sub-Inspector Vickersham tried to go with him, but Stone wouldn't have it."

"Vickersham?" Becker had asked in amazement. "Now I *know* you're telling lies."

D'Artigue had raised a hand solemnly. "On my honor."

Becker found himself stroking the scar on his face as he often did while in deep thought. Stone had finished saddling his horse and was staring at Becker expectantly. Becker raised a hand and turned away quickly as if to eat some breakfast. He didn't want any of the hard biscuits or the sausage. His throat would rebel at rough food being forced down it. He felt Stone's eyes on his back and expected a tap on his shoulder at any instant, but when he cast a glance back, Stone was talking to Del, towering over the little scout.

Becker went over to Dr. Carson, who gave him some horrible-tasting elixir to take. Nearly choking, Becker gasped, "This is supposed to help?"

"It *will* help," replied the short, stocky man. His hair was ebony and full, and he sported an impressive goatee. "You'll feel better in no time."

Stone pushed them hard during the beautiful morning. The sun was bright and blinding, but at midmorning they saw the first brown grass they'd seen in a week. The fire in Becker's throat had indeed abated, but not to the point where it was totally healed. Just after he asked for and received another dose of medicine from Carson, the scouts topped a small rise and stopped abruptly at the horrific sight that stretched before them in a small valley below.

A stone chimney reached pitifully into the sky, while the blackened remains of a house lay to its side. What had probably been a barn had been burned down also. The only structure untouched was a divided corral around the flattened barn. Becker could see Del and the four men with him looking down at them expectantly.

Stone spurred Buck into a gallop, and the troop did likewise, except for D'Artigue, who was driving the wagon. When they reached the scouts, Becker positioned himself as close as possible in order to hear.

"Our luck nearly ran out, but not completely," Del reported grimly. "Look around. There's not a bit of snow to be found."

"No tracks, either?" Vickersham wanted to know.

"Yep, that's the one bit of luck we had left. There's some prints over that way." He pointed to the other side of the chimney.

"Did you see which direction they were heading?" Stone asked.

Del shifted in his saddle and looked uncomfortable, then he pointed and said, "Yonder. They're headed northwest."

Becker saw Stone and Vickersham exchange meaningful glances and wondered why this piece of news was so important.

"Maybe those tracks belong to someone else," Garner offered hopefully.

Del shook his head. "Nope. The tracks are a bit old, but it looks like those are the fellers we're after. There's about twelve or thirteen sets."

"No livestock tracks?" Becker asked.

"Nope."

Becker looked at Stone. "But . . . what does that mean?"

Stone didn't answer immediately. He was looking around at the burned-out shambles that had once been someone's home. His face was tight as he studied the remains with perfect gravity, then a shadow descended in his eyes. "It means they burned this place down just for the fun of it. They probably got nothing from these poor people except a little afternoon excitement."

The whole gathering of men were stunned by this grim observation and remained silent. Becker knew there were men in the world like that, but he never thought he would be chasing them.

Stone withdrew his Henry rifle from its sheath behind his left thigh and checked the magazine. It was a beautiful piece of work

55

with no stock—the gleaming barrel ran unhindered right up to the chamber. It held fifteen rounds, and it was said that Stone could hit objects with it that others couldn't even see. His voice was gravelly as he said, "Vic, one of us has to stay with the supplies. You or me?"

"I'll stay. You have more at stake in this than I do." He stopped and began pointing. "Becker, D'Artigue, Garner, Doe, Boogaard—go with the sub-inspector."

Stone replaced the Henry in its carrier. "Every man going with me get some extra ammunition. Not too much, because we're riding hard and fast, and we don't want to weigh down the horses. Take thirty rounds each."

All but Becker whirled their mounts and went to do what they'd been told. Stone looked at him and asked dryly, "Was there something else, Becker?"

"Ah, yes, I forgot," Vickersham said. "Becker's a bit sick." He turned to another man. "Cochran, you go with—"

"I'm fine, sir, really," Becker interrupted, pleading. He looked at Stone and didn't waver his gaze when he repeated, "Really."

"Then what are you waiting for?"

"I was just wondering, sir, where are we going? Where do those tracks lead?"

Stone's jaw twitched once, and his almost colorless eyes narrowed to cold beams. "Straight toward Reena's Blackfoot village."

CHAPTER FIVE

The Current of Touch

Plenty Trees gazed at Jack Sheffield with black eyes and level expectancy. The husband of Reena's friend, Raindrop, Plenty Trees had turned his life around with the help of God. The year before, he'd been a renegade, interested only in where his next drink of rotgut whiskey was coming from. Now he was a leader in the Blackfoot village, almost as respected as the chief, Powder Moon, and the medicine man, Wolf Carrier. Plenty Trees sat in his tepee, legs crossed and hands resting on his knees, studying the handsome white missionary. Behind him his wife prepared coffee.

Sheffield, with Reena sitting beside him, was dressed in his usual black suit and string tie. He glanced at Reena once before speaking. "Plenty Trees, I thank you for allowing me into your home. It's a very nice home."

Plenty Trees inclined his head.

"I have been with your brothers, the Sarcees, and have taught them many things. I'd like to help your people learn new ways."

"The woman beside you teaches us."

"Yes, she teaches you about God and teaches your people to

speak English, which is well and good. But I'd like to instruct you in something different—agriculture. It will help you greatly."

Plenty Trees' dark eyes were puzzled as he looked at Reena. "Agri—?"

"Agriculture," Reena finished for him. "Producing crops of food. Raising livestock. We call it farming."

"What is . . . livestock?"

"Animals—cattle and goats, which produce milk and may be used for meat. Breeding and raising them can be very helpful to you."

Raindrop served them coffee, then seated herself behind Plenty Trees. She was of medium height, given to pudginess, and her face was open, honest, and pleasing to look at. Like her husband, she kept her eyes on Sheffield.

"Why don't you teach us these things, Reena?" Plenty Trees asked. "Why do we need this man?"

"Because I don't know anything about agriculture. But Jack does." She looked at Sheffield and explained, "He doesn't mean any offense toward you."

"None taken." Sheffield looked Plenty Trees directly in the eyes and said, "Your people depend on the government and North-West Mounted Police for much of your food and supplies. If you let me help you, your people could be self-sustaining . . . um . . . you could take care of yourselves without depending on others. That has always been the Blackfoot way, hasn't it? You are a proud people."

Reena watched Plenty Trees consider this. He possessed a broad, bold face that sometimes hid the kind man inside. She thought that Sheffield was slightly intimidated by him.

Plenty Trees sipped the hot coffee, his eyes not leaving Sheffield's face over the rim of the cup. Slowly he brought the cup down to the ground in front of him and replied, "What you say is true. My people did not need the white man until the white man came here. We were happy and cared for ourselves. It is very strange." He paused and stared wistfully at the ground for a moment, then said, "You can stay, but you cannot tell us the words of God—"

"What?"

"—that is for Reena to do."

"Plenty Trees—" Reena began.

"That is the way it will be."

Sheffield leaned forward and said earnestly, "But I am a man of God, just as Reena is a godly woman—" He stopped when Reena placed a hand on his arm and shook her head. After considering her actions, he sighed and nodded. "Thank you for the opportunity to help you, Plenty Trees. I accept your offer."

After they finished their coffee, Reena and Sheffield stepped outside into the dazzling sunlight. Sheffield raised his hands over his head and stretched. "Well, that could have gone better."

"What are you talking about? You got what you wanted." Reena found herself irritated by his remark.

"I got *part* of what I wanted."

"Then why don't you thank God for that?"

He faced her with a look of surprise painted on his face. "You're upset with me."

"I think you're fortunate to have been accepted so easily. It was months before the Blackfoot allowed me to move into their village. See that stand of cottonwoods over there? That's where I lived for a long time, all alone."

Sheffield's face softened. "You're right, of course. I apologize."

"Apology accepted."

"Really?" he grinned.

"Really."

"You still look angry."

"Well, I'm not."

Reena watched a goshawk in flight over the cottonwoods she'd just pointed out. She wished it would give its unique cry, but it sailed on, oblivious of the village below.

"What's this?" Sheffield asked, reaching toward her.

She took a startled step back.

"What's the matter? I was just pointing to your cross."

Reena looked down at the large hand-carved cross that hung from her neck by a thin strip of leather. "My little brother made that for me before I left home."

"What's the inscription?"

"*Deo Gratias.* 'Thanks be to God.' "

"It's wonderful. He must be very talented."

"Listen, Jack, it's my turn to apologize. I was just . . . I mean, it's your right to be disappointed—"

Sheffield held up a hand. "Say no more. We forgive each other, all right?"

"Okay."

He ran a hand through his red hair and looked sheepish. "I know I wouldn't have had a chance with these people if you hadn't already earned their trust. It's because of your perseverance and faith that you've accomplished as much as you have. I admire that."

Embarrassed, Reena started to brush away his compliment when the thunder of pounding hooves sounded through the village. The Blackfoot who were outside enjoying the day stopped and listened, as did Reena and Sheffield. A few braves armed themselves with bows and arrows, while others brought out rifles. They set up a defensive perimeter around the camp while the women and children moved to the farthest areas of the village, away from the sound. Reena also saw the man who'd stayed the night with them—a half Metis, half Sarcee named Shadow La Belle—cock his rifle. He was dark-skinned, with a black bushy beard and dark eyes.

Plenty Trees suddenly appeared beside Reena, gripping a war club and staring off toward the coming horses. "You go with Raindrop, Reena."

Before Reena could turn and follow the Indian woman, she saw scarlet-jacketed riders burst from the forest. In the lead was Hunter Stone carrying the shiny rifle he always kept with him. As usual, when she saw him she smiled and seemed to warm all over.

Relief washed over Stone's strong features when he saw her, and she wondered what had happened to cause the men to exhaust their horses to reach them.

Plenty Trees raised a hand when the troop came to a halt in front of them. "Stone Man, it is good to see you."

"And you, Plenty Trees. It's a fine day, isn't it?"

"It is."

Stone gave Sheffield a quick, all-encompassing assessment, then looked at Reena with questioning eyes. "Hello, Reena."

"Hi, Hunter. Is something wrong?"

"Not now." He swung off his lathered horse and walked over to them, fingering the reins in his large-boned hands. His eyes were on Reena, a rare, happy light shining from them. "We thought you might be in some trouble." Once again his glance passed over Sheffield, this time with a sudden, palpable suspicion.

"Reverend Jack Sheffield," the man said, stepping forward and holding out a hand. "What sort of trouble, Sub-Inspector . . . Stoneman, was it?"

"Sub-Inspector Stone. Stone Man is what the Blackfoot call me." He looked at Plenty Trees with affection.

"Stone Man," Plenty Trees said, nodding enthusiastically and shaking Stone's hand with vigor.

"I don't know why they call me that," Stone reflected.

"I do," Reena remarked and said to Sheffield, "Do I have some stories to tell you!" She caught a strange look in Stone's eyes when she faced him and was sorry she had said that, for she realized his expression revealed jealousy. She didn't, however, know how to take back her words, so she changed the subject. Waving at the men behind Stone, she called, "Hello, boys! Why don't you step down and have some coffee?"

They looked at Stone hopefully, received a nod, and dismounted. "Thank you, Miss Reena," Boogaard said.

"Now, what trouble, Hunter?" Reena asked.

"There's a gang of men who've been out of control in the Territory. Things have been done—some pretty bad things—and we thought we found some of their tracks leading here."

Reena glanced at Plenty Trees, who shook his head. "We haven't seen anyone except Jack here. Oh, and Mr. La Belle."

"Who?"

La Belle moved toward them and spoke with a thick French accent. "Shadow La Belle, sir. I was passing by here on my way to Old Man's River when it got dark on me. Dey allowed me to stay wiz zem last night."

Stone nodded, barely listening.

La Belle continued with a surprising announcement. "I help you find dese men you after."

"You *know* who they are?"

"Oui. Dey want me to join zem, but I could tell dey were bad men. I not a bad man."

Stone looked him up and down, then asked, "What do you do for a living, La Belle?"

"I trap beaver."

"Beaver's trapped out around here."

"Dat is why I go to Old Man's River."

"Trapped out there, too, I hear."

Reena wondered why Stone was interrogating the man. After all, he'd offered to help catch the men Stone was chasing. She sensed that Stone didn't like La Belle for some reason.

La Belle shrugged but didn't avert his gaze from Stone's direct one. "I trap, Sub-Inspector. It is all I know how to do. I must try wherever I may. You say Old Man's River is no good— I must try anyway."

Stone said nothing, but he still seemed reluctant to trust La Belle.

D'Artigue, a fresh cup of coffee in his hands, had been listening. "This sounds pretty good, sir. The best lead we've had so far."

La Belle caught D'Artigue's accent, grinned, and spoke rapid-fire French to him. D'Artigue bowed slightly, and the two men carried on a short conversation.

Stone interrupted them. "La Belle, you say you were asked

to join these outlaws. Why did they let you live when you said no?"

Reena grew cold. These must be very hardened men if they would kill for such a reason.

La Belle grinned, revealing a gold tooth in front. "Because I had this pointed at dem." He held up his rifle, which looked to be wickedly efficient.

"Is that a Remington?" Stone asked.

"Yes, monsieur. Ten years ago it won ze silver medal at ze Imperial Exposition in Paris as ze finest rifle in ze world. I believe it still is."

"Then you're mistaken. The Henry repeater is the finest."

La Belle inclined his head. "If you say so, monsieur."

Stone seemed to soften just a bit. He reached out and took the Remington and cracked the breech. "Do you know any of these mens' names?"

"No, I am sorry. Dey didn't introduce demselves, nor me to dem." The gold tooth flashed.

"How many?"

La Belle calculated a moment. "Six or seven. But I tink dere were more."

D'Artigue said something in French.

"What was that, D'Artigue?" Stone asked.

"I told him there *were* more."

Reena blurted, "But you've only got five men—"

Stone's eyes cut over to her. "Vic's behind us with more men. Thinking that bunch was somewhere around here, we came as fast as we could."

"How many more men?" Reena demanded.

"Enough," Stone told her curtly. "La Belle, if you were to lead us, how do you know they're where you saw them last?"

"Dey tole me where dey were going, da fools!"

"Where?"

"North of here, at the Bow River."

Becker had been watching quietly, sipping his coffee and chewing jerky. Reena saw that his scar was less visible in direct sunshine. With the same skeptical tone Stone had used, he asked La Belle, "How can you afford to take us? Old Man's River is south—we'd be keeping you from your trapping."

La Belle looked surprised. "Oh, I won't be taking you for free! I am a poor man, and I hear ze Police pay well. Dat is why I offer."

"These are murderers we're after!" Becker exploded. "What are you, some kind of land pirate?"

"Becker," Stone said calmly, "you didn't think he'd lead us out of the goodness of his heart, did you? Wake up." He faced La Belle, unable to disguise his distaste. "You can take us, La Belle. But if we don't find them, you don't get a cent. Understand?"

"Of course, monsieur! Dat is only fair!"

Stone nodded curtly. "Get your mount ready. We leave as soon as the rest of the troop get here."

"What mount?"

Stone looked heavenward.

"He was on foot, Hunter," Reena told him softly.

He was getting angry. She watched him close his eyes for a moment and shake his head. Ever since she'd met him, she'd known him to be an intense, no-nonsense man. It was only lately that he had begun to smile and laugh more. Now, in a matter of minutes, she was beginning to see the old Hunter—the grim-faced, stormy tracker of men he'd been his whole life. She wanted the new Hunter back.

Leaning close to him she said quietly, "Let's take a walk."

———

The small creek that threaded its way through the cotton-woods babbled and gurgled. Every once in a while Reena saw a fish dart away as she and Stone walked side by side. The sunlight danced through the high branches of the trees. He stopped and threw a stone in the stream, and they watched the widening circle of wavelets ripple across the water.

"It's good to see you," Reena said softly.

Squatted down beside her, he looked up and smiled. "It's always good to see you."

They were silent for a while, enjoying the whisper of the wind through the trees and the calming sound of water running over stones. Reena moved behind him and massaged the tight muscles in his shoulders.

"That feels great."

"You're too tense . . . relax."

"I am relaxed."

Reena squeezed the ligaments and tendons just to each side of his neck as hard as she could. All he did was grunt, but the muscles did seem to loosen a bit. "I'm happiest when you're around, Hunter. But you're still turbulent, still unhappy, still savage with yourself. That makes me sad."

He chuckled softly. "Happy yet sad. And you think *I'm* confounding."

"Do you know the reason I brought you out here?"

"I don't suppose it was for this wonderful massage?"

"It was because you were about to dismiss that man, or worse, and you need him to help you find those outlaws."

Stone stood and sat on a nearby boulder. He held a stick in his hand and began idly twirling it through his fingers. "I despise men like that. They have no sense of decency, no idea of what it's like to do something just because it's the right thing to do. All they care about is money."

Reena moved to him, leaned over, and kissed him lightly on the forehead.

"What was that for?" he asked, obviously pleased.

"Just for being you. You have such high standards that not many men can live up to them, and you waste your time worrying about them."

"Am I a hypocrite? Do I expect more from other men than I'm willing to give?" He dropped the stick and took her hands in his, looking as if her answer was very important.

"Absolutely not," she told him firmly, yet softly. "You're the most fair and giving man I've ever known. When I say it's hard for others to live up to your standards, I'm talking about the standards you set by your own actions, not your expectations."

He gazed at her so long and with such intensity that Reena began to get uncomfortable. Then he reached up and lightly ran the back of his fingers down her cheek, his eyes following the imaginary path he was making. "I could stay here with you forever. You are an amazing woman."

Reena took his hand, held it against her face, and sighed.

"I love you, Reena. More than you know."

A small ache bit at her heart when she remembered why he was here. "Please be careful going after those men. They sound ruthless, and I don't know what I'd do if . . . you . . ." She broke off when she felt a sudden, powerful surge of emotion. Swallowing, she finished, "I can't imagine my world without you." She reached out and brushed a lock of blond hair from his forehead.

His gray eyes were only inches away, direct and honest and searching. When he looked at her, he seemed to search every inch of her face with an almost disturbing scrutiny. "I hope I never lose your love."

Slightly disconcerted after his intimate inspection, Reena gave a small shrug and said simply, "That could never happen."

Tenderly, he took her face in his hands and kissed her for a long moment. His hand on the back of her head pressed her lips to his, and the sweet words he whispered resounded in her mind like the soft waves of an echo.

When he pulled away, a fierce emptiness filled her, and with a sigh, Reena gently pressed Stone's face against her shoulder and laid her cheek against the top of his head.

The running brook seemed to murmur its approval.

PART TWO

HUMANITY

Cruelty has a human heart,
And Jealousy a human face;
Terror the human form divine,
And Secrecy the human dress.

William Blake
A Divine Image

CHAPTER SIX

Schoolhouse Blues

When word spread to the settlers surrounding Fort Macleod that a school was to be established, almost everyone pitched in to help build a schoolhouse at the edge of the growing settlement. The North-West Mounted Police donated both money and lumber, and the settlers provided the hand labor and hard work needed to complete the building. The small structure was erected in just two weeks' time.

Jenny Sweet loved the schoolhouse. Sometimes after the children and Megan had left in the afternoon, she would stay behind and sit at one of the desks, as she did now, and just stare at the blackboard or finger the pages of a tutorial. Every once in a while she would lift the book to her face and breath deeply of the pages.

Having grown up with no mother and no schooling whatsoever, Jenny longed for female companionship and thirsted for knowledge. Megan had taught her to read and had shown great compassion for Jenny's struggle to overcome the embarrassment of her ignorance and her difficulty in learning to decipher the strange characters of the alphabet. The two women had developed a close bond that Jenny cherished. Though eight years younger than Megan's twenty-six, Jenny looked upon Megan as a mother, friend, confidant, and confessor. Jenny had never before known even one of these.

Growing up the daughter of a ruthless whiskey runner, Jenny had learned many useful skills. However, though she could skin a deer with surgical precision, she had learned nothing of human kindness. Her ability to harness a team of horses no man could surpass, but she had been denied tenderness and love from the time she was a child. It had been quite a shock for her to learn that the world didn't consist only of unruly men bent on thievery, the pursuit of money, and selfish desires.

Jenny rose from the desk, stretched to her full height of five feet five inches, and emitted a pleasant moan as her spine aligned itself. She was wearing a plain brown cotton dress with white lace at the half-sleeve and hem. Her light brown hair, kept trimmed somewhat short, was tied back with a matching brown ribbon. Before coming to stay at Fort Macleod permanently after her father's death, her frame had bordered on emaciated, and she'd invariably sported a bruise or two on her face or body. Now, with Megan's help and advice about healthy eating, she had added several pounds to her small-boned frame.

The door opened at the front of the school, startling her.

Megan grinned at her from the entrance and said, "Keeping late hours again, Jenny?"

Slightly embarrassed, Jenny laid the tutorial down on the desk and her face colored. "Yes. I hope you don't mind."

"Of course I don't," Megan replied as she came forward. "I must say, though, that I don't see the attraction. You spend all day in here. That isn't enough?"

Jenny shrugged and looked away. "Sometimes."

"I came back for my copy of *Jane Eyre*. Seems I'm getting more and more forgetful these days." Megan glanced down at the tutorial on the desk as she passed Jenny on her way to the teacher's desk at the front of the classroom. "What were you reading?"

"Nothing. I was just . . . sitting, really. Thinking."

"About what?"

"Oh, I don't know."

Megan gave her a mock-pained look. "Come, now, Jenny, you can tell me."

Jenny shifted on her feet, her hazel eyes fixed on the wooden planks of the floor in front of her. "Dirk Becker," she whispered.

"I didn't hear you, dear."

"I said, Dirk Becker."

Megan stopped rummaging in her desk and looked at her. "Oh." Finding the book, she rose and asked, "What were you thinking about him?"

Jenny didn't answer.

Megan came around the desk to stand in front of her. Gently she said, "Look at me, Jenny. Please look at me."

Jenny finally brought her gaze up to Megan's kind brown eyes.

"There's nothing wrong with thinking about him," Megan told her. "Did you think there was?"

"I don't know."

Megan smiled and offered, "Let's sit down." After they were seated beside each other at parallel desks—a tight fit for Megan with her full figure—she said, "You're eighteen years old, Jenny. You *should* be thinking about boys. It's perfectly natural."

"I never had nobody—"

"Anybody."

"Anybody. I never had anybody sweet on me before. How am I supposed to act?"

"Like the young lady you are. How do you want to act?"

Jenny shrugged her small shoulders again. "I get this strange feeling when he's around me. And when he looks at me, I feel kinda . . . nauseated, you know? No, that's not the right word. My heart kinda starts pitter-pattering, and I feel like it's gonna race off to the moon or something."

"Yes, I—"

"And when he smiled and *touched* me the other day, I

thought I was gonna fall down, I felt so weak. Now, what was that all about?"

Megan laughed—another attribute of hers that Jenny liked. Compared to Megan's throaty giggles, Jenny felt as if hers sounded like a donkey braying.

"What's so funny, Megan?"

"Oh, I'm not laughing at you—I'm laughing *for* you! Dear Jenny, you sound like you have a disease that's been afflicting women throughout all the eons of time."

"What disease?" Jenny asked, her brow wrinkling with sudden worry. They'd just studied diseases the previous week in school, and Jenny had been shocked to hear about some of the horrible afflictions that were in the world. She'd decided then and there that she didn't want to die of any disease. She'd rather be shot or fall off a horse—anything but waste slowly away.

Megan placed a well-manicured, warm hand over Jenny's and pronounced, "Love, Jenny. You exhibit all the symptoms of falling in love."

"Love! Uh-uh, I ain't in love. I don't know nothin' about that. I take back all I said."

Jenny started to rise, but Megan put a hand on her arm to stop her. "What's the matter?"

"I don't want anything to do with love. All it does is hurt and kill!"

"Jenny, that's preposterous!"

"Did you love your husband?"

Megan paused. "At first I did."

"And now he's dead, right?"

"But that has nothing to do with—"

"My pa loved me. I see what you're thinkin', Megan, but he *did* love me, and I loved him . . . and now he's dead. Even though I never knew my mother very good—all I got is a drawin' of her by some man in Toronto—I loved her, too. I still look at that drawin', and it hurts to look at it, but I do—every night." Jenny stopped and shook her head firmly. "There ain't *nothin'* good about love. I don't love Dirk Becker, and he better not love me, either!''

Megan was only mildly surprised by this tantrum. Jenny hadn't been exposed to any normal relationships as a youth; instead, she'd lived the life of a nomad, an indentured servant to her father and his men. Every emotion she'd ever felt had been subdued and crushed by Armand Sweet. Every day of her life had been a drab monotony, broken only by brief spurts of danger and worry that when her father left with his men to make deliveries, he might not return.

When Dirk Becker saved her from one of her father's men and brought her to the town, Jenny had been ignorant of civilized life. The children had dubbed her the Black-and-Blue Lady because of the bruises on her face and arms. Reena and Megan had taken responsibility for her and had slowly introduced her to women's clothing and social manners.

Jenny's moods were volatile and varied. At times she would grow quiet and sulky, and occasionally, like now, she would become irrational. Megan tolerated her tantrums sometimes, but she would not on such an important subject as the one that had been broached.

"Now, you listen to me, Jenny Sweet!" Megan declared, grabbing Jenny's arm and turning her around to face her. "You can just stop that kind of talk this instant! You've had a horrible life—a *brutal* life. You've had the kind of life that people talk about in whispers, the kind that some people don't even believe exists in this world. The things we experience while growing up shape us inside. Terrible things have happened to you, Jenny. Whether you know it or not, they've scarred you here." She placed a hand high on Jenny's chest—"and here"—she put her other hand on Jenny's forehead.

Jenny stared at her wide-eyed and open-mouthed.

"Sometimes you don't know what you're talking about," Megan continued in a more gentle tone. "Your logic eludes me, and I think I know you better than anyone. Love with the right person can be the sweetest thing on earth. There's no devastating hurt or fear in real love, and killing has absolutely nothing to do with it. Are you listening to me?"

"Yes."

"Now, I'm sorry to speak harshly to you, but of all the men in the world who will *not* hurt you, Dirk Becker is one of the best. He's a fine, honorable Christian man who probably has never before been in love. Did you stop to think that maybe he's scared, too?"

Jenny pulled a face. "He's a man."

"You think men don't get scared?"

"I've never seen one scared . . . except for Sid when Dirk knifed him."

"Dirk was protecting you and may have even saved your life that day. Are those the actions of a man who would intentionally hurt you?"

"No, I guess not," Jenny responded softly, staring at her hands.

Megan leaned back and smiled gently. "No, it's not. You've been raised around violent men, Jenny. But not all men are like that. You've got to understand there are many good men out there, too."

"Like Dirk? And Hunter?"

"Right. Those are two very good examples."

"And Vic?" Jenny asked with a gleam in her eye.

"Vic's a good man, too."

"Bet you *really* think so."

"What does that mean?"

"You know," Jenny replied with the same sly look.

Megan shook her head, smiling. "We're not talking about me, we're talking about you."

Jenny pressed her lips together firmly, revealing twin dimples. Deep in thought, she stared off in the general direction of the blackboard so long that Megan was afraid she had lapsed into one of her trances. Megan believed that the strange catatonic seizures that gripped Jenny were the by-product of too many blows to the head and of the girl's inner attempt to escape from the world. Over the years, Jenny had developed many reasons to *want* to escape.

To Megan's relief, Jenny brought her gaze around to her and asked, "Why would Dirk like me?"

"What kind of question is that? You're a very pretty young lady, and you have an innocence about you that I'm sure draws him to you. You have many endearing qualities—"

"He's too handsome for me, even with that scar, which I don't think is such a bad thing. In fact, I like it. Do you think that's strange?"

"Not at all."

"Do you like it?"

"I don't think about it as liking or disliking. It's just part of Dirk."

"Yeah. Maybe that's why I like it." Jenny suddenly giggled and said, "He's got scars on the outside, and I've got them on the inside. What a pair, huh?"

Megan smiled, but it was a sad smile.

———

At school the next morning, Jenny met Lydia and her brother, Timmy, at the door. Timmy was eight, Lydia five, and they'd been the first friends Jenny had made in Fort Macleod. The children had immediately sensed Jenny's childlike innocence and taken her into their circle.

Lydia, a tiny girl with blond pigtails, deep brown eyes, and a crimson birthmark on her left temple, looked up at Jenny and gave her a half smile. Jenny knew at once that something was wrong, as was often the case with the sensitive little girl.

"Did you read it?" Jenny asked.

"Yeah."

"Did you like it?"

"I guess."

"Well, you don't sound like it. Here, let's sit down."

Lydia hesitated. "It's almost time for lessons."

"We've got time. Sit down." Jenny sat on the stone steps to

the left of the front door and patted a spot beside herself. "We'll read it together."

With obvious reluctance, Lydia sat down and placed her books on the step beside her. Glumly, she placed her elbows on her knees and her chin in her hands, staring out over the muddy grounds before them. A Chinook had blown in the night before, melting the rest of the snow.

"Lydia, are you all right?"

"Yeah."

Jenny studied her profile for a moment and decided that Lydia would tell her about it in her own time, as was her way. Opening the book she was holding and turning to "The Lamb" by William Blake, she asked, "Did you understand the poem?"

"Not really."

"Let's see if we can figure it out together." Jenny began to read.

> "Little Lamb, who made thee?
> Dost thou know who made thee?
> Gave thee life, and bid thee feed
> By the stream and o'er the mead;
> Gave thee clothing of delight,
> Softest clothing, wooly, bright;
> Gave thee such a tender voice,
> Making all the vales rejoice?
> "Little Lamb, who made thee?
> Dost thou know who made thee?
>
> Little Lamb, I'll tell thee,
> Little Lamb, I'll tell thee:
> He is called by thy name,
> For he calls himself a Lamb.
> He is meek, and he is mild;
> He became a little child.
> "I a child, and thou a lamb,
> We are called by his name.
> Little Lamb, God bless thee!
> Little Lamb, God bless thee!"

Jenny lowered the book and looked at Lydia. "So what do you think?"

Lydia shrugged with disinterest.

"Come on, Lydia—try!"

"I don't wanna try."

Jenny closed the book and put her arm around the girl. "Something's botherin' you. What is it?"

Lydia shook off Jenny's arm with a scowl and stubbornly kept her eyes straight ahead.

"You don't have to be mad 'cause you couldn't figure out the poem. I couldn't either, but I'll tell you a secret if you want to hear it."

Not even the mention of a secret would make Lydia look at her. Jenny *knew* something was wrong now.

"I'll tell you the secret, and then when Miss Megan asks the question, you can raise your hand and take credit for it, okay?"

Lydia shrugged the tiniest bit.

"The secret is, the Lamb who made us is Jesus. Jesus is the same as God. Did you know that?"

Lydia finally turned her eyes on Jenny and asked, "How could Jesus make us? He was just a man, wasn't he?"

"You know, Lydia, I asked Megan the same thing, and she said that He was a man, but that He was also the Son of God, which made Him perfect. There's never been and never will be a perfect man again." Jenny stopped and a wrinkle formed between her eyes. "Or somethin' like that."

"I don't understand."

Once again Jenny put her arm around the tiny shoulders, and this time Lydia relaxed instead of shrugging her off. "I don't either, but someday I will. It's an amazin' story, isn't it? Can you imagine . . . a perfect man!"

"There sure ain't any around anymore," Lydia murmured.

"*Aren't* any around."

"You say ain't, too," Lydia told her accusingly.

"Yeah, but I'm tryin' to stop. It ain't—it isn't ladylike, and I aim to be a real lady like Miss Megan."

From behind them they heard, "Why, thank you, Jenny. But I think you already are a lady."

Jenny and Lydia whirled around in surprise.

"Megan, how long have you been standing there?" Jenny asked.

"Long enough to hear that compliment, no more. It's time for school, girls."

"We'll come in a minute," Jenny told her and inclined her head toward Lydia meaningfully.

"All right," Megan said, "don't be long."

When Megan was back inside, Jenny said, "Now, we don't have much time, Lydia. You look like you're about to bust to tell me somethin'. What is it?"

The defensive curtain fell over the little girl's face again. "I don't wanna talk about it."

"Do too."

"I do not!"

"What are you so mad about?"

"My pa's been gone a long time. He might even be dead for all we know."

"Aw, Lydia, he's not dead."

"How do you know?"

"Hasn't he been gone before?"

"Not this long." Lydia picked up her books and stood. Her lower lip trembled, and Jenny noticed that her hands were shaking, too. "We better get inside."

Jenny had no idea what to say to her. If she told Lydia to stop worrying, that everything was all right, the words would sound hollow and trite. "We'll talk later, Lydia," she said, and then she followed the tiny girl into the schoolhouse.

CHAPTER SEVEN

Dilemmas

In a way, Liam was glad he was blind on the day Meecham felt "bloody" according to Gossett. Following the shots, the screams of the woman didn't stop—they increased in volume. With terrible dread, Liam expected to hear the screams cut off with another gunshot, but none came. Finally the piercing cries trailed off into pitiful wails that reached Liam's ears even from a distance. He wondered if children were present and considered asking Gossett, but two things prevented him: his voice seemed to have left him along with his sight, and he suddenly didn't want to know the answer.

Liam then heard a few shouts, the restless lowing of cattle, and Gossett chuckling beside him. With disgust coating his voice Liam asked, "What are you laughing at? Do you think murder is funny?"

A long silence followed.

"You've got a lot to learn, boy. I don't know why Meecham chose me to wet-nurse you, but I don't like it, so watch your mouth."

Liam didn't speak to Gossett again. When the rest of the men returned, he called out for Meecham over and over until he heard the soft voice right beside him.

"I'm here, O'Donnell."

"Mr. Meecham, I want no part of this." Liam heard a few snickers and snorts from the others, but he didn't care.

Meecham spoke, his easy voice a sharp contrast to his words. "Well, son, you are a part of this whether you like it or not. You wanted to come with us, so here you are."

"I'm not your son."

Liam felt his coat being grabbed roughly, and Coffin's grating voice broke in as he growled, "Why, you little ungrateful pup—"

"Let him go, Coffin. O'Donnell, you've got a choice, of course. Would you like to leave?"

Liam bit his lip, seeing the uselessness of his threat to leave.

"I'm waiting, boy," Meecham warned, "and I don't have time to wait. Give me your answer."

"I'll stay," Liam whispered.

"I didn't hear you."

"I said I'll stay."

"Fine. Then I trust there'll be no more whining? I don't tolerate whining in my men."

"No, sir."

Liam didn't speak another word for the rest of the day. They traveled with the livestock they'd stolen, but in which direction Liam didn't know. Pod was beside him again, talking and talking. He took care of Liam that night, preparing his supper and arranging his bedroll under a tree. Liam slept very little.

The next morning he found that he could make out figures and some landscape, but everything was enveloped in a yellow haze. He decided to wear the bandanna around his eyes all day with the hope of further healing.

The day was warm and the air crisp. Liam tried to enjoy it, but his situation weighed heavily on his mind. They rode all morning over flatland, and when they stopped, Liam was again held back while the other men and the cattle went ahead. This time, the silent Newby was left with him. Liam spoke for the first time in twenty-four hours. "More killing coming up?"

Liam didn't expect an answer and didn't receive one. He heard no shouts or gunfire, though, and the men returned without incident. It was only after they rode a little while that Liam figured out what had happened; the sound of cattle was missing. They'd sold them to someone.

"Pod?" Liam asked, knowing the boy would be close.

"Pod ain't here."

"Who's there?"

"Rodriguez."

"Where are we going now, Rodriguez?"

"North."

Liam waited, but nothing more was said. "That's it? Just . . . north?"

"Yep."

Liam was sick of silent, evil men. He was sick of Pod, who never shut up. He was sick of being helpless and dependent. Suddenly, he ripped the bandanna from his eyes but cried out immediately. The sunshine was a blast of intense, pure light that seemed to go right through his eyes into his brain.

"That was stupid," Rodriguez observed.

Liam squeezed his eyes shut and felt hot tears rolling down his cheeks. The pain was incredible.

"You just might have set yourself back to where you were when we found you," Rodriguez predicted matter-of-factly.

"I don't care!"

"Suit yourself."

Liam replaced the bandanna, tying the knot at the back of his head so tightly and viciously he developed a headache after only a few minutes.

They rode all day. Liam knew they were heading in a northwesterly direction, because in the late afternoon he felt the sun's heat full on his face a few times. He waited until well after dark to remove the bandanna, and when he finally did, it was with trembling hands and a grave fear that Rodriguez had been right

81

in his observations. He kept his eyes squeezed tightly shut after removing the kerchief, then gained the courage to open them.

Liam realized he'd been holding his breath, and his breath exploded from his lungs when he looked around. He could see a fire and figures huddled around it. Surprised, he found someone sitting directly in front of him, watching, his face a round moon by the firelight's glow. "Who's there?"

"It's me—Pod."

"How long have you been there?"

"Just sat down. Saw you were takin' that thing off and thought I'd see how you was doin'."

"Well, say something next time. You startled me."

Pod snickered.

"What is it?"

"You sure talk fancy. You go to some fancy school?"

Liam gently rubbed his eyes, which weren't burning as badly as the previous two nights. "Yes, you could call it fancy."

"Where? What was its name?"

"Um . . . never mind. Just a school back east in the States." Liam didn't want to divulge the school because he didn't know how Meecham or Coffin would react. However, he wasn't aware that Meecham was right behind him.

"What school?" the pleasant voice asked.

A shape appeared in front of Liam. It was lean and wiry and tall, with a large wide-brimmed hat perched on a head too small for his body. Of his facial features, Liam could tell nothing except for a black handlebar mustache.

"What school did you go to?" Meecham repeated.

Liam decided to lie and spoke the first name that came to mind. "Bradford."

"Where's that?"

"Pennsylvania."

Meecham didn't say anything.

Liam used the uncomfortable silence to try to make up more lies. He wanted Meecham to know as little as possible about him.

"Never heard of that school," Meecham finally commented.

"My wife's from Pennsylvania. I'll have to ask her about it. What city would that be in?"

"Philadelphia."

"He's lyin'," a voice broke in.

Meecham asked, "Why do you say that, Todd?"

"Because I'm from Philadelphia. There's not a Bradford College there."

"University," Liam added weakly, stubbornly sticking to his story, though it was surely futile now.

"There's not a Bradford University, either. There's only the University of Pennsylvania."

Liam wanted to smack the know-it-all in the face. Of all the Eastern cities to choose, he'd picked one that was well known to one of Meecham's men.

"Interesting," Meecham commented. "That true, O'Donnell? You wasn't fibbing us, were you?"

"What difference does it make where I went to school?" Liam asked, tired of these men.

"It didn't, really, 'til you lied about it." Meecham's voice, though still soft, had an unmistakable edge to it. "Now I'd sure like to hear the truth."

"What if I think it's none of your business?"

In the silence that followed, the large cook fire popped twice. Liam saw movement, then felt his face slapped so hard that he fell off the stump he'd been sitting on.

"I sure hate to hear ungrateful talk, boy," Meecham told him in a rising voice. "Here I've taken you under my wing like you was my own kin, and all you can do is sass me. That's real sad."

Liam got to his feet but couldn't see where Meecham was standing because of his blurry vision. He'd never been hit so hard in his life, and Meecham had used an open palm, not his fist. Maybe he wasn't as thin as Liam had first thought.

"Now, I do have to apologize for hitting a blind man, O'Donnell. That wasn't a fair shake. Sometimes I lose control of my temper quicker than a mongoose grabs a mouse."

The kindly tone was back, but Liam knew what the man was

about now and wasn't affected. In fact, he pictured Meecham moving in position for another punch.

Pod remarked, "If I'd gone to college, I'd be prouder than a rooster to brag about it."

"Nobody asked you, Pod," came Coffin's voice from Liam's right. "Why are you lyin' about things, O'Donnell?"

Liam was surrounded, and now Coffin's coarse voice caused him to throw caution to the wind and tell the truth. "I went to West Point for two years." Silence met this unveiling, and Liam sensed that they were all exchanging glances.

"West Point," Meecham repeated in a thoughtful voice.

"I told you, Fitz. We shoulda left him to die."

"Why?" Pod asked. "What difference does it make that he went to West Point? What *is* West Point?"

"Shut up, dummy," Coffin growled. "How 'bout it, Fitz? He could be some kinda spy or somethin' sent by the U.S. Army or those pesky Mounties."

"Look at him, James. He's blind. How could he have faked that?"

"How do we know he's blind? He's maybe seen everything."

Liam sat down on the stump, tired of the whole thing. He should have just taken his chances with the snow blindness, but how was he to know these men were what they were? Meecham had sounded so kind and fatherly—

"What would you like to do, James? Shoot him and leave him?"

"That's exactly what I'd like to do."

"But he looks strong. He might be a good hand once we break him in."

"Fitz, you'd think a ninety-year-old grandmother would have potential. That's your weak point—you think too much of people's potential and not enough about their possible backstabbing."

"I've got you around for that, don't I?"

"That you do. So what'll it be?"

"You ain't gonna shoot him, are you?" Pod whined. "He's

the only man that'll listen to me in this whole bunch."

The talk above him was strangely detached, as if they were talking about someone else. The last four days had been the worst of his life, and he wished he'd stayed at West Point to get his education instead of following this ridiculous dream of seeing the continent and his sisters.

He heard Coffin's holster squeak and the hammer of a pistol being cocked. Suddenly Liam didn't want to die. If he stayed alive, there would have to be a way to escape these men. He knew that begging would only bring their loathing, so as calmly as he could manage he said, "I'd be a good hand to you, Mr. Meecham. I expect I could outshoot any man in this outfit, and I've had some experience with livestock. My best friend's father in Chicago was a farmer, and I helped him care for the animals. You won't be sorry you took me on."

"What about that comment that you don't want any part of this?"

Liam gestured toward where he thought Coffin was standing, probably holding a gun pointed to his head. "I don't want any part of that, either, sir."

Meecham chuckled, then laughed out loud. "Yeah, I can see that. All right, put your gun away, James. We've got us a new hand."

"I don't like it, Fitz."

"I didn't think you would."

Liam saw Coffin's form lean toward him, and he briefly wondered if he were going to disobey Meecham outright and shoot him. Involuntarily, he pulled away.

"I'll be watching you, boy. You mess up once, and I'll follow through on this matter. Do you understand?"

"Yes."

Coffin and Meecham moved off, and Liam heaved a sigh of relief.

"You're lucky, son," Pod observed. "Coffin usually has his way with Mr. Meecham. In fact, that's the first time I've ever seen Coffin voted down. Funny."

Liam prayed for the first time in years before going to sleep. "Please let me see in the morning, God, so I can get away from these lunatics."

———

On a clear beautiful morning, the troop of Mounties prepared to head north with La Belle as guide.

When Vickersham and the supply wagon arrived the previous evening, Stone told Vic about La Belle. Vickersham met the man, and with his naturally easygoing nature, he didn't share Stone's distrust.

"It's just what we need, Hunter. Some chap who knows where to find these men. What's wrong with that?"

"I just don't like the man."

"Pardon me, my friend, but like has nothing to do with it. His knowledge is what we're after."

Stone made sure that all the men were ready and their equipment clean and serviceable. When he got to Becker, he asked, "You feeling all right?"

"Yes, sir."

"Don't lie to me, Becker. Your voice sounds like gravel. Do you want to stay here with the Blackfoot while we're gone?"

"Absolutely not, sir," he declared, clearing his throat and tightening the cinch on his saddle.

Stone stared at him, then smiled faintly and moved on. Becker was tough. There was no questioning that. Moving among the men, Stone came to Dr. Carson and said, "I want you to check on Becker and see if he's got a fever."

"Already did that, sir. He's fine except for the sore throat."

"You're sure? I don't want a man coming down with pneumonia out in the middle of nowhere."

Carson, a pleasant, amiable man with handlebar mustache, grinned at Stone. "No guarantees in medicine, Sub-Inspector. I do know that the boy doesn't have a fever this morning. Tonight—who knows?"

"How encouraging."

"Sorry, sir. If you don't mind my saying so, you sure can't control everything, though sometimes it seems like you do."

Stone clapped him on the back and wondered, "I don't know whether to give you a reprimand or a promotion for saying that. Watch yourself, Carson."

"Yes, sir," the doctor grinned.

Stone's smile vanished when he saw Reena talking to Sheffield. They were standing by Buck, Hunter's horse, and Reena stroked the buckskin's nose lightly while they chatted. Sheffield leaned close to her and said something that made her laugh. Stone's big hands closed.

Del and Vickersham appeared at his side. Vic commented, "I say, he's a handsome specimen, isn't he?"

"He's almost as pretty as she is," Del added with a gleam of amusement in his eyes.

"Don't you two have something to do?" Stone asked irritably.

"Nope," said Del.

"Not a thing," Vickersham shrugged.

"Well, find something. You're ruining some perfectly good feelings of jealousy and murderous intent."

Vickersham looked at Del and winked. "Don't kill him, Hunter. He's a missionary. It just wouldn't look right on your impeccable record."

"Look at him," Stone said tightly. "I'm supposed to just ride off and leave him here with her?"

"Well, you could arrest 'im, but that wouldn't look too good, either," Del said. "Hey, maybe you could just wing 'im from afar with that fancy rifle of yours. I won't tell anyone you done it, if you have a mind to."

"My lips are sealed, also," Vickersham agreed.

Del eyed him suspiciously. "That'll be the day. I cain't remember the last time you didn't have a comment on something."

"What good would winging him do?" Stone asked. "Then she'd just have to nurse him back to health, and look what happened the last time she did that."

"The patient fell in love with the nurse," Vickersham stated with a grin. "What a quandary you're in, Hunter."

"What's a quandary?" Del asked.

"A dilemma . . . a state of uncertainty as to what action to take, or whether to take any action at all. It's a bit like—"

"All right, all right, I didn't ask for a speech on the subject."

Sergeant Stride walked up and told them the men were ready.

"Where's that scout?" Stone asked.

"He's ready, too, sir. He's over there by the supply wagon."

"Well, make sure he doesn't take any of the supplies, will you?"

"Of course, sir," Stride returned with a rare smile.

Stone gave him a direct look. "I'm not too sure I was joking about that, Sergeant."

"Sir?"

"I want you to keep an eye on our new friend."

"Hunter—" Vickersham began.

"Just a precaution, Vic. Humor me. Have the men get mounted, Sergeant."

"Still don't see how we need that feller, anyways," Del grumbled. "Ain't I a good enough scout for you?"

"Of course you are, Del. But you don't know where those men are any more than I do. There's a slim chance that La Belle's actually telling the truth."

"Humph. The man's a stone liar. You can tell just by lookin' at him."

"Do tell," Vickersham prompted.

"Yeah, he's just got that skunk look. You know how a skunk seems to kinda slink along like he's guilty about somethin'? That's what that feller reminds me of. He speaks French, too, and that's a mark against him, if you ask me."

"What's that got to do with it?" Stone asked.

Del nodded sagely and ominously. "I never met a Frenchman I could trust."

"Nonsense," Vickersham laughed. "What about Tony La

Chappelle who has the store in Fort Macleod? He's a personable chap."

"Give 'im a chance—he'll do somethin' distrustworthy someday."

"Untrustworthy."

"Whatever. Just keep your eye on 'im."

Stone looked at Vickersham and shook his head. "We'd love to shoot your wisdom full of holes, Del, but we've got to get moving."

"Quite right," Vickersham agreed.

Stone turned to his horse, still with a surprising sense of jealousy inside him. When he reached Buck, Reena looked up at him and smiled prettily.

"You'll be careful?" she asked.

Stone took the reins from her and nodded. "Always."

"Go with God, Sub-Inspector," Sheffield said and held out his hand.

Hunter took the offered hand and found that Sheffield had a strong, confident grip. "Thanks, Reverend." He started to get on the horse, but Reena's hand stayed him. Surprising him, she stood on her tiptoes and gave him a kiss on the cheek. Stone glanced at Sheffield and the mounted men, all of whom were suddenly finding various aspects of nature to admire—all, that is, except for Vic, who grinned at him broadly and winked.

Awkwardly, Stone told Reena, "Thank you," and mounted his horse hurriedly.

"When will I see you again?" she asked.

"I don't know. Soon, I hope."

"Me too."

He smiled at her, admiring the incredible richness of her light blue eyes as they shined up at him. Every time he saw her, it became more and more difficult to leave her.

Stone heard Vickersham give the order to move, and Buck stamped impatiently. Sheffield tipped his hat and moved away. After a quick look around, Stone leaned over, placed his hand on the back of Reena's head, and kissed her solidly on her warm mouth.

"For luck," he whispered.

Reena shook her head. "For love."

CHAPTER EIGHT

Treachery

The same morning that the Mounties set out with Shadow La Belle to find Meecham, Liam found his eyesight. The temptation to jump up and down with joy was strong, but during the night, just before he'd drifted off to sleep, he'd considered the possibility that he might be able to see in the morning and decided that if his eyesight was back, he would conceal it as long as he could. Now that it was indeed a reality, he quickly stifled his elation and, for the moment, tied the bandanna around his eyes again.

"Still blind?" Pod wanted to know.

Just before tying the kerchief, Liam had caught his first glimpse of the boy. His hair was black, of medium length, and was standing straight up on the top of his head in ridiculous cowlicks. Pod looked even more youthful than he sounded, with a small straight nose and full lips. "Yes, I am," Liam answered, attempting to plant remorse in his voice.

"Too bad. Gotta be flustratin'."

Liam secretly grinned at the pronunciation of the word. Pod's speech and thought patterns were that of a small boy.

"Say, what's the last thing you remember seeing?"

91

"I don't know . . . my horse, I suppose."

"Well, that's not so bad. He's a fine mount, anyways."

"Yes, he is."

Pod brought Liam some breakfast, and while Liam ate, the boy saddled his horse. Liam felt a bit guilty about letting the boy wait on him now that he was perfectly capable of taking care of himself. However, there was no way he was going to let anyone know that his eyesight had returned; there just might be a way to escape during the day.

As they traveled that morning, Liam adjusted his bandanna so that he had a sliver of a view beneath it. They crossed a river at noon, and he used that as an excuse to remove the kerchief, dip it in the water, and take a quick look around him. Beside him was a tall, wiry man whom Liam guessed was Newby. He had a flat, square face that didn't match his build and his hands were extremely large. The bay he rode was huge.

When Liam covered his eyes again, he held the mental picture of his surroundings for as long as he could. He counted the men in the picture and came up with twelve. They looked hardened and were tough, capable men who knew nothing of nonsensical actions. Liam now knew it would be a miracle if he were given a chance to escape, and the thought greatly depressed him.

In the afternoon, Pod was riding beside him, chattering about how he loved to touch aspen trees and stare at the chalky residue on his fingers. "I just can't pass an aspen without touchin' it, you know?"

"Pod, do you know where we're going?"

"Naw. Mr. Meecham doesn't tell us sometimes. He just keeps plans in his head. He may look like a farmer, but he's real smart. Oh, you haven't seen him yet, have you?"

"No."

"He looks like a farmer. Tried it a few years back, but he hated it."

"Is that why he shot that farmer the other day?"

"Don't know. He *does* hate farmers for some reason. Mostly he shoots whoever he feels like or whoever deserves it."

Liam felt his heart sink. These men were beyond ruthless if they went along with behavior like Meecham's. "Deserves it according to whom?"

"Whom? What kinda word is that? Um . . . deserves it accordin' to Mr. Meecham, I guess. I'm gonna quit talkin' about him now, seein' as how he just turned around and gave me the evil eye. He's got dead eyes, you know, just about the deadest eyes I ever saw 'cept maybe for Coffin's. Do you think he heard me talkin' about him? He's way up at the front."

"I don't know, Pod. I can't see, remember?"

"Oh, yeah. Sorry."

"Did you ever shoot anyone?" Liam held his breath. If this boy-child riding beside him was a killer, there was no hope for him.

"Yeah . . . once. What are you lookin' at, Gossett?"

"You talk too much, Pod. Was I you, I'd think about gettin' me some packthread and sewin' up that four-cornered thing you call a mouth."

"Well, you ain't me, now, are you?"

"One of these days, Pod, you're gonna catch me in a bad mood, and I'll have to squash you like a beetle."

"You mean you're in a good mood sometimes?" Pod asked, exploding in high-pitched laughter.

"Just keep your mouth shut about your business," Gossett growled.

"I'll say whatever I want," Pod returned petulantly.

After a while, Liam took a chance and tilted his head back for a look around. To his right some men were passing a bottle around as they rode, talking quietly. Wanting a look at Meecham, Liam's eyes went to the front of the group, and he recognized the leader instantly by the handlebar mustache he'd seen the night before. Meecham turned around and scowled at the drinkers but didn't stop them.

Liam put his head down at once in case Meecham should look at him. In the brief glance, Liam had seen the eyes Pod had talked about: dark black dots in a pale face under thin eyebrows that wrapped all the way down to the corners of the eyes. Pod had called them dead, but Liam thought that was too extreme. They shone with a malevolent intelligence that belied the plain-looking, thin appearance of a bookkeeper. Meecham's head swiveled on a slim neck, and his coat hung from what appeared to be a scrawny frame. He was most unimpressive—except for the frosty eyes that seemed to bore into whatever he looked at with penetrating scrutiny.

In his look around, Liam saw that he was alone with Pod, the ominous Gossett absent. Remembering the conversation they were having, Liam asked, "About that man you shot, Pod . . ."

"Yeah?"

"Did you kill him?"

Pod didn't answer for a while, and Liam began to wonder if he was just making it up as he went along. In this rough outfit, Pod may have invented a story just to be included and feel accepted as part of the gang.

"Yeah, I kilt him."

Liam was shocked at the depth of remorse in the simple statement.

"He was drawin' down on Coffin—I had to shoot him." A pause. "Hit him in the belly . . . took him a long time to die. I never heard so much moanin' in my life. It got to where I just wished I could've took back the shot so I wouldn't have to listen to him no more. But that wouldn't have been right, would it? Then Coffin would be dead for sure."

"Maybe the man would have missed Coffin."

"He was only a few feet away . . . had him dead to rights. He would've plugged him without a doubt."

Liam knew it was probably some innocent settler they were talking about who was only trying to protect his family or property. The thought sickened him, but Pod's remorse was so palpable that Liam felt he should say something to help ease his pain. He hated to defend a murderer and regretted the words that came from his mouth. "Then you should console yourself that you saved a man's life, Pod. Not many men have that chance in a lifetime."

"Yeah, I guess," Pod responded glumly. "A man shouldn't have to suffer like that, though. Gossett offered to shoot him to put him out of his misery, but I wouldn't let him. He was only interested in shutting him up, anyways. He didn't care about him sufferin'."

"How did you come to hook up with this bunch, Pod?"

"Didn't have nowheres else to go," Pod answered with a shrug in his voice. "Don't have no schoolin' or education. I was workin' for almost nothin' for a buffalo hunter, skinnin' the hides, when Mr. Meecham came along and asked if I wanted to join him. I was off in a flash."

"Where are your parents?"

"I don't know. I was left at an orphanage in Dufferin when I was a baby. Ran away when I was five."

"Five?"

"Yeah."

"Good heavens." Liam couldn't imagine being on his own at five years old. When he was that age, he was riding horses, learning proper etiquette, and being taught marksmanship with fine rifles and pistols. His only hardship had been having to get up early in the morning.

"It's not so bad, really," Pod stated.

"Not so bad? Pod, do you realize that if you're caught by the Police they'll hang you?"

"We won't get caught."

"How can you know that for sure?"

"Mr. Meecham said he has a plan for them Mounties, a plan that'll keep 'em at bay while we make a whole pile of money. And Mr. Meecham's plans always work."

"Did he say anything else about it?"

"Nope. Like I said before, he keeps stuff in his head a lot of the time. He might tell Coffin about it, but not that I've seen."

Liam shook his head sadly. If he happened to be with the outlaws when they carried out their plan against the Mounties, there was no hope left. He *had* to get away. Briefly he considered asking Pod for help, but Liam wasn't sure he could trust him. The thought of Coffin's pistol to his head again was too much. He'd just have to take his chances.

Meecham stopped the group at dusk. Curiously, there was still enough light left to travel farther, and Liam wondered what was so special about the spot he'd chosen to make camp. He removed the cover from his eyes and tried to keep his gaze straight ahead and glassy as he looked around. The area had good shelter, there was no doubt about that. They were situated in a tiny glade, surrounded by aspens and lodgepole pines. It was beautiful but had a closed-in atmosphere that Liam found claustrophobic.

"No fires tonight," Meecham announced to the men.

Startled, Liam almost looked directly at the man but managed to catch himself.

"What?" a man asked, unbelieving.

"No fires?" protested another. "We'll freeze!"

Meecham locked his dark gaze on the man. "You're not gonna freeze, Ott. You're standing there in your shirtsleeves now, and it's almost dark. It's not gonna get much colder. Anybody else got a complaint?"

There was a general shaking of heads.

"Good. Now listen up. We're gonna have some company real close tonight. I want complete quiet. Do you understand? If any man so much as sneezes too loud, he'll answer to me. I want everyone to bed down early, too."

Liam tried to keep his mind calm that night, but the prospect of what Meecham had in mind the next day kept him tossing and turning fitfully all night.

———————

Dirk Becker came awake with a start, the remnants of a dream about stalking a white-tailed buck floating away. His father had taught him to hunt in Mississippi—the skills of staying downwind of the prey, of staying perfectly still for hours at a time, and of placing a perfect shot. In the dream, however, he'd been impossibly close to the buck—only a few feet away—and instead of holding a gun, Becker was empty-handed and lying on the ground. The buck had wheeled suddenly in a blur and stood over Becker, looking down at him with brown liquid eyes. Becker could only stare back, paralyzed for some reason. The buck had raised up on his hind legs, and Becker saw the black, sharp hooves descending toward him to slash him.

Becker came suddenly awake, holding his hands above his face protectively. *What was that all about?* he wondered in sleepy confusion. Glancing around, he saw that he was the only one awake, and the sky was lightening in the east. Instead of going back to sleep, he decided to get up and stoke the dying fire in preparation for breakfast.

His throat was better, he was glad to discover. Still, he took a long drink of water from the canteen lying beside him before rising. Snores emanated from the sleeping men and rattled the air like droning insects. The night had been so pleasant they hadn't even bothered staking out the tents, and everyone slept in the open. Becker wondered who was on guard duty, but it was still too dark to see the area around the livestock. He thought it was Doe, but he couldn't be sure. Becker smiled to himself, feeling his facial scar stretch unnaturally down his face. He would make some coffee, take some to Doe, and tell him about the buck dream. "Tell Doe about the buck," he chuckled to himself.

After the coffee was made, he carried two steaming cups to the makeshift corral. "Andy?" It had gotten a bit lighter, and Becker could see the horses clearly, but no Andy Doe. He walked around the corral and called to Andy again just as he spotted a figure sprawled on the ground.

Dropping the mugs, Becker raced to him and turned him over. It wasn't Doe; it was a constable named Sanders, and he looked dead. Becker felt his jugular and found a faint beat. After a quick look around to see if the attacker was still in the area, he ran back to the camp and rousted Dr. Carson and everyone else in the noisy process.

Stone stared down grimly at Sanders, waiting for the doctor to give the prognosis. Becker saw him suddenly look up and regard each man gathered around. "Where's La Belle?"

Everyone glanced around at each other, then shook their heads.

"Who had watch before Sanders?"

"I did," D'Artigue answered.

"Was La Belle here when Sanders took over for you?"

"Of course, sir."

Stone's face changed as he looked down at Sanders again. His jaw clenched, and the normally cool gray eyes clouded with anger. Through tight lips he ordered, "Garner, go see if La Belle's horse is in the corral. And while you're at it, check to see that all of our horses are there, too."

Vickersham said, "Sergeant Stride, please go check the supply wagon also."

Stone gave Vickersham a meaningful look that Becker didn't understand. Vickersham only shook his head and shrugged. Vickersham asked Carson, "How is he, Doctor?"

"Concussion most definitely. Actually, he's lucky to be alive. Someone really bashed his head good, probably with that rock over there."

Becker looked to where Carson pointed and saw a rock the size of a pumpkin at D'Artigue's feet. The Frenchman turned the rock over with his foot and they saw blood splashed on one side with dirt clinging to it.

From the corral Garner called, "La Belle's horse is gone, sir!"

"Everyone get mounted *now*!" Vickersham ordered.

"Me too?" Carson asked. "Sanders can't be moved—I guess you know that."

"You stay here with him," Vickersham told him. "We'll be back for you when we've caught that traitor."

Stride marched up and announced, "It looks as if everything in the supply wagon is intact."

"He was trying to be quiet and didn't have enough time to steal anything," Stone offered.

Something occurred to Becker, and he asked, "Sir? Why would La Belle lead us out here and then run off? It doesn't make any sense."

"We don't know, Becker," Stone told him. "Get saddled up, and we'll find out." Stone looked at Del as he approached, his hair wild and long beard sideways, rubbing his eyes sleepily. Del was notorious for his ability to sleep through just about anything.

"What's goin' on?" he asked, squinting at the prone Sanders. "What's the matter with him?"

Vickersham told him briefly what had happened, then placed both hands on the small scout's shoulders. "Listen, Del, you need to wake yourself up and find La Belle's tracks. Right now."

"All right." Del yawned again and scratched his neck, but he headed toward the camp to gather his things.

The troop made hurried preparations and were soon on their way minus Sanders, Carson, and Sub-Constable Simmons. Vickersham had left Simmons behind to assist Dr. Carson and watch over the other two in case La Belle doubled back.

The Mounties rode in double column, leaving Becker riding beside Andy Doe. The youthful-looking man was humming a tune, seemingly happy to be riding on such a beautiful morning. Unfortunately Doe only knew a few bars of the tune, and the repeating monotony was beginning to drive Becker mad. "Say, Doe, don't you know any more of that song?"

"Nope."

"Well, hum something else, then. What you're doing now looks like a complete waste of time and breath in my opinion."

"Yeah, I agree," Garner called from behind Becker. "Better yet, why don't you stop humming altogether?"

Doe was offended. "What's wrong with humming?"

Chuckling, Becker answered, "There's nothing wrong with *good* humming, but I don't hear any at the moment."

"Hey, Becker—sorry, *Constable* Becker—you're from the American South. All you southern gents can carry a tune, can't you?"

"I don't know about that."

"What state was it you're from? Missouri?"

"Mississippi."

"Well, sing us a song."

Behind Becker, riding beside Garner, was a new man named Bollinger who said, "If you're from the South, sing us a rendition of 'Dixie.' "

Becker didn't answer. From the corner of his eye he saw Doe turn around slowly and look at Garner.

"What's the matter?" Bollinger asked.

Whispering, Garner told him, "His pa and brother were killed in the war, fighting for the South. He's never going to sing that song again."

Becker felt his jaw clench. Though Garner was whispering, it seemed as if the whole troop could hear him.

"Oh," Bollinger breathed out lightly. "Sorry."

They rode on in silence, Andy Doe stopped his humming, and Becker was left alone with thoughts of two men who now seemed more a dream than a reality. For years after their deaths, Becker had pushed all thoughts of them and grief for them to the back of his young mind and had concentrated on taking care of his mother. She'd died of fever right after the war, leaving the eleven-year-old Dirk with no immediate family. An uncle had taken him in, and finally Becker had faced the fact that everyone he'd been closest to his whole life had been taken from him. Anger had choked him for months, then despair, and finally he'd attempted to withdraw from the world in general, but was gently brought back by his aunt Charlotte. The introduction of God into his life by his aunt had changed his whole perspective and his personality, as well. Hearing about the suffering Jesus Christ endured for him made his own problems seem as nothing.

Surprising everyone around him, Becker began humming "Dixie" in a slow, feeling manner. Though he still felt an ache when he thought of his family, hearing Garner tell Bollinger that he'd never sing "Dixie" again suddenly sounded silly—like the deliberate action of a bitter man. Humming, he actually started to feel *good*, as if there were a cleansing going on inside of him.

Becker saw Stone turn at the front of the column and look right at him. Just as Becker thought he was going to cut him off, Stone nodded at him and turned forward again. Becker liked having Stone's approval. If there was one man who knew about personal loss, it was Hunter Stone. Becker wondered how Stone had dealt with his doubt and suffering. There was no question that Reena had had something to do with it, but Becker still didn't understand how anyone could come through losing loved ones without God's help.

When Becker finished the song, Doe said, "Hum it again, Dirk. You're a lot better than I am."

Becker started over.

The early morning sunshine broke over them, engulfing them in an orange-tinted glow.

Becker had gotten only to the second line when a gunshot split the air. The whole troop froze for a moment in confusion. Heads swiveled around, looking for the shooter, but the shot had echoed strangely all around them, and they couldn't decide where it had come from.

Another shot followed a few seconds later, and Andy Doe was blown off his horse beside Becker.

CHAPTER NINE

Into the Morning Fire

Liam woke about the time the Mounties discovered the injured Sanders. Groggy, tired, and not thinking clearly, Liam opened his eyes and made a big mistake: he looked directly into the scowling face of Meecham. The dark eyes flickered with a hint of surprise, then recovered quickly.

"So," Meecham drawled, "you can see today. Congratulations."

"Thanks." Liam mentally chastised himself for letting down his guard. Now his chances of escape had been torn in half. For the first time, he had the opportunity to study Meecham directly and openly but found that he couldn't hold the cold gaze.

A man walked up and when he spoke, Liam knew instantly that it was Coffin.

"He's comin'," Coffin growled to Meecham.

"Good. Our new friend here can see now."

Coffin turned his forceful presence on Liam, who remembered the man's gun pointed at his head and felt like cringing. Coffin had a pinched, wedge-shaped face with a full black beard and piercing eyes. *Now, those are dead eyes*, Liam thought with dread. Coffin, too, had a thin neck, but corded muscles stood out like cables.

"You ready to earn your pay today?" Meecham asked.

"I haven't *gotten* paid."

"You will, if you pull your weight. Think you can do that?"

"Of course."

Meecham's inspection bored into Liam with frightening intensity. "Do you remember our deal? You won't be thinking on cutting out in the middle of a scrap, will you?"

"I keep my promises," Liam declared, attempting to display defiance in order to gain the man's confidence. He thought it came out pretty well, but Meecham was solidly inscrutable.

A man rode into the stirring camp, nodding at Meecham and Coffin.

"Any trouble?" Coffin asked.

"None, *monsieur*," Shadow La Belle answered as he dismounted. "Incompetent fools. I don't know why you even bother, Monsieur Meecham."

"That's my business." With a look at Liam, Meecham nodded to La Belle. "Let's talk over here."

Liam stood and stretched, finding himself the same height as Coffin but somehow feeling smaller.

"You might want Rodriguez to look at your eyes. He might have something to put in them to help. Do they still hurt?"

"They're still a bit grainy. Who's that man who just rode up?"

Coffin considered him before answering, "Name's La Belle."

Liam pulled his suspenders over his shoulders and gave Coffin a wry look. "I don't suppose you're going to tell me any more than that, or what we're doing today?"

"You'll find out soon enough."

For the first time in five days, Liam fixed his own breakfast, though he had no appetite. He was glad to have his vision back, but a sick feeling lay coiled in his stomach at having lost his only defense. If he saw someone shot this day, Liam could be considered an accomplice to murder. If Meecham or Coffin told him to shoot someone, could he do it?

"Nope," Liam said to himself in a firm tone as he watched the men clean up their utensils. "There's no way."

"No way for what?" Pod asked. "Hey, you can see!"

"Morning, Pod."

"You don't sound too excited about it."

Liam's eye was caught by Pod's hands shining in the early morning light. He smiled and shook his head. "You've been petting the aspens, haven't you?"

Pod held up his hands, which were covered with the strange chalk from the trees, and grinned broadly. "Ain't they somethin'? Did you know they sing?"

"Sing?"

"Yeah. When the wind moves through 'em just right, the leaves sing. You oughta listen to 'em sometime."

"I will."

"Hey, you got real pretty eyes, you know that? Now, I don't usually tell a man that, don't get the wrong idea. It's just that this is the first time I've really seen 'em. They're about the same color as these suede chaps of mine."

"Thanks, Pod. By the way, those are nice chaps."

"Thanks. They cost me a quarter eagle. They oughta be nice."

Meecham, standing alongside La Belle, announced to the group, "Check your weapons—full loads."

Pod asked Liam, "Is that all you got? That pistol there?"

"Yes. I had to trade in my rifle for that roan and some cash."

"Maybe Mr. Meecham will let you borrow one."

"What are we shooting today?" Liam sincerely wished it were game instead of men, but he knew better than to hope for that.

Pod shrugged. "I don't know. Whatever he says to shoot at."

"What if it's a woman, Pod? Would you shoot a woman?"

" 'Course not!"

"Even if Meecham were going to shoot you?"

"You better get in the habit of callin' him Mr. Meecham. He don't take kindly to being 'ferred to by his last name only."

"What's his first name?"

Pod thought a moment. "I got no idea."

"Where's he from?"

"Somewhere down—hey, why you askin' all these questions? You sure ask a lot of 'em."

"I like to know who I'm riding with." Getting information out of the dull-witted Pod was a natural means of possessing valuable information for the authorities, should Liam ever escape. However, by Pod's very nature he was unobservant and didn't have the sense to ask the others for information that Liam would find useful.

"What about that woman, Pod?"

"What woman?" He was concentrating on checking his rifle barrel for grit and blockage.

"If your life depended on it, would you shoot a woman?"

"I dunno, Liam! Why are you always askin' hard questions that I don't wanna answer?"

"It's part of making friends. You *do* want to be my friend, don't you, Pod?"

"Yeah," Pod responded glumly. "I just like to do the talkin' and askin', that's all. I ain't used to no one else wanting to know what I think. In fact, everbody else thinks I *don't* think." He chuckled at this, then a sad seriousness came over his young features. " 'Course, they're right about that, mostly."

"Nonsense, you think just as much as any other man."

"You really think so, Liam?"

"Yes, I do. You just do it differently, that's all. There's nothing to be ashamed of in that." Liam threw his arm around the boy's shoulders and gave him a brief squeeze.

Pod, obviously touched, looked away shyly. "You're turnin' into the best friend I ever had, Liam. I'm stickin' right by you today, boy. You can count on that."

Gossett passed by them and commented, "You ladies gonna get saddled up or just admire each other all day?"

The ride was short—Liam estimated it was about two miles. They stopped on a small mesa overlooking a dry riverbed and a prairie that stretched as far as the eye could see. Meecham ordered a man to stay with the horses while the rest of them headed toward the edge of the mesa. Before they reached it, Meecham told everyone to dismount, draw their weapons, and crawl the rest of the way.

Liam found himself between Pod and Gossett, with Newby on the other side of Pod, and Rodriguez beside Gossett. Liam, with the smell of dirt and grass in his nostrils, looked around desperately for a way out, but there was none. He found himself sweating despite the cool morning air. Just as they reached the edge of the mesa and looked down, the sun rose behind them and cast an orange glow over the land, except for the valley in the shade of the mesa.

"When is he going to tell us what we're looking for?" Liam whispered to Pod.

"Are you still blind?" Gossett growled. "Look down there."

Liam followed his pointing finger and froze. He'd never seen a Mountie before, but he'd heard of their scarlet coats and white helmets. A column of them was emerging from a small stand of cottonwoods and rode along the rim of the riverbed. The sun was in their eyes, and Liam saw a few of them reach up and pull the brims of their helmets down.

"What . . . what's . . ." Liam stammered.

"Be like shootin' fish in a barrel," Gossett stated in a low voice as he took aim.

"Range is too far, you dummy," Rodriguez informed him.

"I know that! I'm just gettin' ready."

"You . . . you're just going to shoot them?" Liam asked in shock. "Just . . . shoot them down?"

"No," Gossett said, "*we're* gonna shoot them." He turned a malevolent eye on Liam. "Aren't *we?*"

Liam swallowed, but his mouth was as dry as the dirt upon which he was lying.

"Draw that pistol, boy. Why didn't you get a rifle? You can't hit anything from here with that peashooter. Go on—draw it!"

Liam found himself numb and couldn't have drawn the pistol even if he'd wanted to.

"Newby, we may have to persuade O'Donnell to join the fun with a little creative reasoning," Gossett drawled. "Switch places with him, Pod."

"Nope, I'm stayin' by Liam . . . promised him I would."

Rodriguez told Gossett lazily, "If you start moving around, Mr. Meecham will shoot you himself and save the Mounties the trouble of it."

Gossett leaned toward Liam until he was right in his face, his blue eyes blazing. "You draw that piece right now."

"Get out of my face, Gossett!" Liam hissed harshly, jabbing him with his elbow.

They all heard the hammer of a gun being cocked behind them and turned to find James Coffin looking thunderous. "All you boys better button those lips, or I'll do it for you!"

Gossett motioned to Liam. "What do you wanna do about him? He won't even draw his gun!"

"That true, O'Donnell?"

"We can't just ambush Mounties, Mr. Coffin! It's wrong!"

"Are you going to help, or do I need to take care of this problem like we talked about the other night?"

Angrily, Liam drew the pistol and checked the load. Through tight lips and desert-dry throat he declared, "I'll do my part."

Coffin watched him a moment, then moved to the other side of Rodriguez at the end of the line.

Liam was furious. There was no way he would stand by and watch the slaughter of the helpless Mounties below without at least giving them a warning, no matter the consequences to himself. If he died this day, at least he would die trying to help the good men instead of the bad.

The Mounties were almost in range, and Liam still felt sick about the slaughter that was sure to happen in the next few minutes. *Here goes. . . .*

With a quick look around, he saw that every eye was trained on the men below. Liam moved his pistol hand between Gossett and himself, pointed it straight into the air, and fired. Gossett jumped, then gave Liam a deadly look.

"I know what that was for, boy—"

"Who fired that shot?" Coffin hissed.

"Was that you, Liam?" Pod asked beside him.

"It's done now!" Coffin growled, and Liam saw him take aim and fire at the Mounties. Liam looked down and saw a scarlet shape turn a backward somersault over the haunches of his horse.

More shots followed as the whole line of Meecham's men opened fire.

As the Mounties began to run for cover, some of them dropping to the ground and writhing in pain, Liam wondered if his warning shot had done any good at all. *At least I tried*, he told himself, but he derived no comfort from the fact.

He stared at the scene in horror.

––––––––––

When Becker saw Andy Doe jerk and disappear behind his horse, he could only gawk dumbfounded. In the split second afterward, he had the crazy thought that this was no time for theatrics and foolishness. Then he heard the sound of many shots echoing from a mesa to his left, and the reality of what was happening hit him full force.

"Cover!" Stone screamed.

Becker saw him and Vickersham making for the dry riverbed they were following. Somehow Stone already had his rifle out and seemed to be guiding Buck with his knees, because he was furiously laying a covering fire toward the top of the mesa. In the confusion and shock of attack, Becker had no idea where the shots had come from, and he lacked the instinct to return fire.

Becker saw another man cry out and fall from his horse. As a group, all the Mounties except Becker poured into the riverbed and dismounted, trying to control the maddened horses that smelled blood in the charged air. Becker looked down at the unmoving Doe and the other man he recognized as Sub-Constable Garrett, and his instincts returned.

Jumping down from his horse, Egypt, Becker ignored the whizzing of bullets in the air and the dirt kicking up around him and went to Doe. Garrett was writhing on the ground and moaning, but Doe seemed to have the most serious injury. Becker saw blood around Doe's head; a huge amount of it had already soaked the earth rye-colored. Becker knew instantly that Andy Doe would never rise from his awkward position.

A singing bullet tugged at the collar of his coat. He scooted over to Garrett and dragged him to the riverbed, thinking that the grazing bullet had very nearly taken his head off, just as one had Doe's.

Stone was beside him instantly in the riverbed, shouting, "What about Doe?"

Becker only shook his head as he drew his Adams revolver and began firing up at the mesa. The noise of the Mounties firing and loading and firing as fast as they'd been trained was deafening. When he'd emptied his gun at the puffs of smoke drifting off in the dawning sunshine, he looked at Stone. He was staring at Doe's corpse, and Becker saw his jugular vein throbbing heavily in his neck, his jaw clenching and unclenching. Becker heard Vickersham screaming something at them and realized Stone was totally exposed to the firing from above. He reached out and grabbed Stone's arm but was thrown off immediately as the piercing gray eyes locked on his.

"Are you sure he's dead?" Stone demanded.

"I'm sure!" Becker shouted.

"Where's your horse?"

Becker looked around, suddenly afraid he'd find Egypt shot, lying outside the riverbed. Relieved, he saw that D'Artigue held Egypt's reins with his own horse's while firing his Adams. "Over there—"

Stone suddenly lunged at him, crashing into him, and Becker thought that he'd lost his mind until he saw Vickersham over Stone's shoulder.

Very nearly screaming and as wrought up as Becker had ever seen him, Vickersham shouted, "Would you two like to have a tea party out in the open? Stay under cover!"

A horse screamed, wheeled, and almost fell on Boogaard.

Another man went down, holding his arm.

"I'm going up there!" Stone told Vickersham.

"How?"

Stone pointed. "Back through the riverbed, then up. The mesa levels out to the ground back there. You stay here and keep them occupied."

"You're taking some men with you, Hunter! You're not going alone!"

"I'll take Becker and D'Artigue."

"Take more."

"No. We don't want to attract too much attention by having our rate of fire diminished from here. Help the wounded, Vic!"

Stone grabbed Buck's reins and nodded at Becker, who was crouched down behind the tall wall of the riverbed. Stone tapped D'Artigue on the shoulder, and without a word D'Artigue fell into step behind them, bringing the horses.

After walking about two hundred yards, the riverbed deepened even more, and they mounted the horses and took off at a run with Stone in the lead.

Liam could only lie there, watching the battle through sunlit gun smoke that stung his eyes and nose. He heard a man scream once and saw him go limp, and Rodriguez scooted around their rear to him. No sooner did he reach them than the man on the other side of Gossett suddenly cried out and actually sat up, holding the side of his face, inadvertently making himself a prominent target. More bullets instantly thudded into his chest, and his body was driven back forcefully. The Mounties were making more than a stand—they were well-trained and accurate shooters, Liam thought with a twinge of satisfaction. He wondered if Meecham had counted on losing two men in the first minute of the battle.

As if to give credence to Liam's admiration, his gun was

suddenly torn from his hand in a shower of broken metal. He didn't know if the shot was lucky, or if someone had taken aim at his silhouette and barely missed. He ducked his head down into his arms protectively, seriously considering making a run for it in the confusion and gunfire.

"Liam! Are you hit?" Pod shouted from beside him.

"No!"

"Then what are you doin'?"

"Hiding, you fool! They shot my gun out of my hand!"

"Here—take my pistol!"

"I don't want it!"

The firing seemed to wane for a moment, and Liam raised his head to see that another man was wounded. Meecham definitely was getting more than he was giving out, and the Mounties had less cover. Liam was elated. He saw Coffin and Meecham discussing something in heated tones, and Coffin shook his head in seeming frustration. Meecham's eyes locked on Liam's, and Liam suddenly didn't want to know what Meecham was thinking. Meecham made his way toward Liam, keeping his head down and issuing commands to each man as he came. One by one the men listened, some nodding with ill-hidden relief as they began running back toward the horses.

When Meecham reached Gossett, Liam heard, "Gossett, you and these boys cover our retreat!" He said something else that Liam couldn't hear, but Gossett nodded and looked to the north part of the mesa.

Meecham's black eyes came to Liam, and he shouted, "Make me proud, boys!" Then he was gone, running after the other men.

Gossett said, "Pod, go get our horses and bring them back here."

"Right."

Gossett watched Liam a moment, then said, "I know what you did with that warning shot. I may be the only one, but I'll see to it that Mr. Meecham finds out."

Liam swallowed, then said defiantly, "I don't care. This was wrong." The thought of being executed by Meecham was a nightmare, but he really *didn't* care. At least he would be rid of these lunatics.

The shooting from the riverbed had stopped, but the lawmen had made no move to charge.

"Why don't they come after us?" Liam asked.

"They are," Gossett answered mysteriously as he reloaded. Jerking his head to the north, he continued, "Probably from that direction."

"Who?"

Gossett gave him a withering look. "Mounties, you fool. We're gonna take a few shots at them, scare them off and send them on their way back to their buddies, then we follow our boys."

"A few shots? How many are coming?"

"I don't know. Meecham said a few, which probably means three or four." He gave Liam a sour look. "I'm gonna have to keep one gun on you during the fight. If you try anything—I mean anything at all—I'll shoot you down."

Newby stood beside the body of the man who'd sat up and been shot many times. One of his legs was twisted double underneath him, and the front of his shirt was tattered from bullet holes. Liam hated to think what the back of his shirt looked like.

"Clem always had bad luck," Gossett told him. "Do you know he actually fell off a cliff once and lived to tell about it?"

"Those shots weren't luck," Liam maintained.

Gossett's face darkened, and his lip curled in a sneer. "You sound like you admire those Mounties."

"More than I do any of you."

"Why, you little—"

Pod arrived with their horses and shouted, "Come on!"

"You'll pay for that remark, you little runt!" Gossett shouted as he mounted his horse.

Liam watched Newby jump into his saddle without the use of stirrups, then saw the tall man's eyes widen. Turning to the north, Liam saw three white helmets coming over a small rise, then red coats—then everything happened so fast Liam could barely believe it even as he saw it.

Out of the corner of his eye he saw Gossett, Newby, and Pod fumble for their rifles. Gossett grunted in surprise, the last sound he would ever make.

The lead rider of the Mounties had a red plume flashing from his helmet, and Liam just had time to register rage in the approaching face—a rage that seemed to emanate from his whole body and being, frightening in its intensity. The sun glinted off the barrel of a shiny rifle, and then the Mountie fired with incredible speed and accuracy. Liam sat frozen in his saddle.

Beside him, Gossett pitched backward in the saddle and slid to the ground without a sound. Newby had just raised his rifle to his shoulder when he cried out, dropped the gun, and slumped to the side.

The Mounties, charging at full speed, were nearly on them.

Liam finally found the sense to raise his hands high in the air, showing that he was unarmed. Pod managed to get one shot off but missed. The lead Mountie fired again, and Pod grabbed his arm with a small scream.

The Mounties pulled up directly in front of Liam, and he saw ice-gray eyes aiming down the barrel of the gleaming rifle. *I'm unarmed, and he's going to shoot me anyway,* Liam thought with a strange calmness and certainty. One of the gray eyes closed as the man aimed, and Liam braced himself for the bullet.

"Hunter, no!" shouted a scarred young man to his right, grabbing the barrel of the rifle and tilting it upward just as it went off.

Liam's insides felt watery and heavy, and he found that he'd suddenly broken out in a cold sweat. He'd been that close . . . that close to dying.

The man called Hunter kept his strange, cold eyes on Liam. All of them were breathing heavily, and Pod moaned on the ground to Liam's right.

The man with the scar looked from Pod to Newby to Gossett, amazement on his face. "You got them all, sir! D'Artigue and I didn't even get off a shot. D'Artigue, look at this!"

"I see very well," D'Artigue answered in the same awed tone of voice.

"Are you armed?" Stone asked Liam.

Liam tried to speak but found that he couldn't and cleared his throat to try again. "N-n-no, sir!"

Stone wheeled his horse and rode to the edge of the mesa. Raising the rifle high in the air, he waved it three times, then returned. "Get those men on their horses. We're leaving." Once again he pierced Liam with his gaze. "How old are you, son?"

"Twenty."

"Do you realize that you probably won't see twenty-one? There's another boy down there in that riverbed who won't see his next birthday, either, and he's your age. How do you feel about that?"

Liam could see the rage bubbling just below the surface, waiting to boil over and scald again. Liam swallowed but didn't answer. There was so much to explain that he didn't know where to start, but he really didn't think this man would either care or believe him right now, anyway.

Without another word, Stone wheeled his horse and rode off in the direction Meecham had taken.

Liam wondered if he was going to take on the rest of the gang by himself and decided that it would probably be fair odds for both sides.

CHAPTER TEN

Reena's Request

Jack Sheffield was both astonished and fascinated by Reena.

He watched her teach the children of the Blackfoot, giving love and gentle care to every one of them as if they were her own. He watched her read the Bible to the adults and patiently answer every question that was asked of her. He watched her work tirelessly, often until late at night, yet upon rising, she looked as refreshed as if she'd had nine hours of uninterrupted sleep. Sheffield observed her and, though disturbed, found himself admiring her wholehearted dedication to these people.

At the moment they were sitting on a blanket outside her tepee, and Reena was kneading dough to make bread. The flour covered her small hands up to her slim wrists. She wore a blue dress, capped at the shoulders, with half-sleeves that ended in white lace. Sheffield noticed the stains on the well-worn dress and wondered about the life she had given up.

"Do you miss Chicago? The fancy clothes, the balls, the concerts?"

"Not really." Reena blew at an ebony lock of hair that had fallen in her face, but the strand only returned to the same position. She reached up and pushed it back with her arm, and some of the flour brushed against her temple.

Sheffield considered telling her about it, but found it rather quaint and appealing. "You don't miss it even a little bit?"

"Well . . . maybe a little bit. How about you? Wait a minute, I don't even know where you're from."

"Back east—a tiny town called Worthington on the shores of Lake Ontario."

"So we both grew up near lakes."

"I believe we did." Sheffield found this fact to be highly significant and charming, but he didn't say so.

"What did your father do?" Reena stopped for a moment and sat back on her feet, massaging her hands.

"He was a fisherman."

Reena smiled. "And now so are you."

"I am?"

"A fisher of men."

"Oh yes," Sheffield laughed. He realized that his laugh sounded like a high giggle, and he wondered what was happening to him.

"Are your parents still alive?"

"Yes, still going strong, thank the Lord. My father is sixty and still takes his fishing boat out every morning—except Sunday, that is. And yours?"

"My mother died last year."

"I'm sorry."

"It's all right. She was a Christian and ready to meet her Lord."

Sheffield nodded slowly and said, "That helps the grieving, doesn't it?"

"Without a doubt."

He watched her begin kneading the dough again and looked at the flour smudge on her forehead. The white stood out starkly against her olive skin and dark hair. She was looking down, but he could still see her fine nose and high, prominent cheekbones. Her skin was unblemished and looked as smooth as the side of a Ming vase.

She looked up, and Sheffield glanced away quickly, certain that guilt was written all over his face.

"What are you thinking?" Reena asked.

Surprised, Sheffield thought quickly and said, "About Ming vases."

"What? Why on earth were you thinking about that?"

"I don't know, really. I just was."

"I saw a Ming once. It was indescribably beautiful and looked so . . . delicate. I remember thinking that if you thumped it with your finger it would probably crumble into tiny little pieces."

"Yes, that's what I was thinking, too."

"It was? About thumping one with—"

"No, no. About indescribable beauty and frailty."

"You must think some nice thoughts."

"On occasion." He built up his courage and asked something he'd wanted to know ever since the day before. "So, this Hunter fellow . . . are you two . . . um. . . ?" He saw a strange look come over her face and said immediately, "I'm sorry if that was too personal. I didn't mean to—"

"No, it's all right." Reena smiled. "It just took me by surprise, that's all." She took a deep breath and let it out slowly. "Hunter and I are very good friends. We've been through a lot together."

"He seems to be a fine man. He's a fine *specimen* of a man, anyway."

"Yes."

"I'd hate to have him after me for some crime."

"Mm-hmm."

Sheffield looked at her closely. "You're worried about him, aren't you?"

Smiling faintly, Reena didn't meet his eyes when she murmured, "It's inevitable, isn't it?"

"I suppose so." Sheffield was disturbed to find that he didn't care for her thinking about another man. *What's the matter with me? I barely even know her!* Alarmed, he heard himself asking,

"Do you love him?" As soon as it was out of his mouth, he wanted to reach into the air between them and snatch the words back.

Reena looked up at him with her clear blue eyes, no longer smiling. "You're very direct, aren't you?"

"Yes, too direct sometimes, and I apologize."

"So you've figured out that the answer to your question is none of your business."

"Absolutely. Next subject."

"What about you, Jack? Have you ever been in love?"

"Once," he replied, looking away. "I was engaged before I came out here, but she drowned."

"I'm sorry—"

"It was years ago." He grinned. "We seem to be apologizing a lot, don't we?"

The strand of hair was back in Reena's face, and she brushed it back, leaving another smudge on her face. "You know, Jack, occasionally time doesn't heal our wounds. Are you okay with it?"

"Reena, it was over ten years ago, and yes, I'm fine with it. Actually it was sort of an arranged marriage. We knew each other from the crib, and there was a general agreement that we'd know each other to the grave. That was the plan, anyway."

"It sounds romantic."

"Excuse me, but you have a smudge on your forehead. May I?" He produced his handkerchief and reached out hesitantly.

"Oh my, I must look ridiculous!" Reena exclaimed.

She leaned forward and Sheffield wiped the flour away gently. "There."

"Thank you. How embarrassing."

Sheffield picked up a pine needle and idly chewed on it. "You're not at all what I expected, you know."

"What did you expect?"

"Older. Bigger. More matronly."

"Glad to disappoint you."

"You're really good with the Indians. They seem to trust you, and I know how difficult it is to gain their confidence."

Reena displayed a flash of even white teeth.

Suddenly a group of braves appeared and ran by them. One of them took the time to call, "Stone Man coming!" as they disappeared.

"What did he say?" Sheffield asked.

"The Mountie troop is coming," Reena told him, unable to hide her excitement and relief.

———

Stone led the horse that carried the body of Andy Doe, wrapped in a blanket and tied over the saddle.

"It's not your fault he's dead, Hunter," Vic had told him before they left the ambush site. "You're not responsible for everyone."

"Then who is?"

"What do you mean?"

"We're officers, Vic. We *are* responsible."

Vickersham had shaken his head. "Men die in this line of work, Hunter. We can't stop that from happening."

Stone hadn't answered. He had just returned to the riverbed after restraining himself from going after the band of outlaws single-handedly. The temptation had been great, but then he'd remembered that he no longer was a bounty hunter, as he'd been in his younger days. He was now an officer in a territorial police force and had his men to think about. He had jerked the reins hard, twisting Buck's head with more force than he'd intended and had gone back to the rest of the troop.

He'd found the men gathered around the body of Doe, staring down at it with hollow eyes. Ken Garner cried openly, his sobs echoing strangely off the walls of the riverbed.

They'd buried the bodies of Gossett and the other outlaw Meecham had left behind. Becker crudely dressed the wounds of Pod and Newby, being none too gentle. They'd picked up Dr. Carson, Simmons, and Sanders, who had a monumental headache but was otherwise all right.

Now, as he rode into the Blackfoot camp and glanced over Doe's body to the boy he'd nearly shot point blank, the consuming anger surfaced again. The boy looked back at him, then quickly brought his gaze back to the front. Stone wondered how a wholesome-looking boy like that could have fallen in with the likes of Meecham. A few times along the way he'd been tempted to ask, but the thought of carrying on a conversation with the man who might have fired the bullet that killed Doe was too much.

Looking ahead, he saw Reena and Sheffield coming with some braves to meet them. He'd forgotten about the visiting missionary until now, and his mood only darkened further.

Reena was looking at him as they rode up, then she saw the body laid neatly across the horse and frowned deeply. After saying a few words to Vickersham at the head of the column, she moved by Becker and Garner to Stone.

Hearing a choked sound from his right, Stone turned to find the boy gazing in absolute shock and disbelief at Reena.

"Who is it, Hunter?" she asked in a hushed voice, touching Doe's horse.

"It's Andy, I'm afraid," he answered, looking over at the boy again. He finally found his voice.

"Reena?"

She turned, and from the view of her profile, Stone saw her match the boy's confusion and surprise. Her mouth literally fell open. "Liam?" She ducked under the head of Doe's horse and moved to the boy.

"Wait, Reena!" Stone cried, dismounting at once and going to her.

"Why are his hands tied?"

"Reena, it's so good to see you, " Liam said, his voice choking. "You have no idea—"

"Get away from him, Reena!" Stone told her, grabbing her arm. He didn't want anyone close to the killers.

"Let go of me! Do you know who this is?"

"Yes—an outlaw. Maybe a killer."

"He's no killer. He's my little brother!"

Stone held his breath, stunned.

"What is this, Hunter?"

"Reena—" Liam began.

"Untie him, Hunter. Please?"

"I can't, Reena."

"Nobody understands," Liam said in frustration.

Stone looked up at him. "I understand perfectly. You were with a group of men who ambushed us, killed this boy here, and wounded three others. I understand very well what you are."

Reena looked back and forth at the two men, her mouth still open. "What are you—? How—?"

Stone felt sorry for her, but it didn't matter who Liam was. "I'm sorry, Reena, but he was with Meecham's gang when we arrested—"

"I wasn't *with* them. Not really!" Liam pleaded. "I didn't shoot anybody!"

"See, Hunter?" Reena asked. "Now, will you untie him? He's not going to run off or grab a gun and shoot someone."

"How do you know that, Reena?" Stone watched anger touch her eyes, but before he could say anything else, Vickersham stepped between them.

"I'll untie him and watch him."

"Thank you, Vic." Her eyes were still on Stone, disbelieving and hurt. Finally she looked up at Liam and asked, "What are you *doing* here? Why didn't you tell us you were coming?"

Liam grinned crookedly. "I wanted to surprise you. I guess I did."

Vickersham cut his bonds, and Liam slid off the horse to take Reena in his arms.

Now that Stone saw them so close together, he could see a definite family resemblance. His mind whirled at the coincidence of it all and at the situation under which he'd found the boy. Stone had hated Liam for two days, barely able to keep himself from striking him out of anger over Doe's useless death. Now his feelings were completely confused.

"Did they hurt you?" Reena asked, pulling away from Liam and inspecting his face for marks.

"Reena!" Stone protested. "Of course we didn't hurt him!"

"I'm sorry, but . . . oh, I'm so confused!"

"You wanted to hurt me, though," Liam accused. "You, especially."

"You watch your mouth, or I'll tie you up again."

Liam faced him fully. "You nearly killed me in cold blood. I wasn't even armed!"

"What are you talking about?" Reena asked.

Stone said nothing.

"You heard me, Reena," Liam continued. "He came riding up to me, my hands were in the air, and if that fellow with the scar on his face hadn't stepped in, I'd be dead now. Because of him," he finished, nodding at Stone.

"Is that true, Hunter?"

Hesitating, Stone told her, "It was the heat of the battle, Reena. You wouldn't understand—"

Reena's eyes narrowed. "I understand that I don't know you like I thought I did."

"Andy had been killed, others were wounded, and—"

Vickersham took Reena's arm. "Reena, it's difficult to explain."

Taking Liam's arm, Reena started to guide him out of the middle of the crowd that had gathered around them. "Come on, Liam."

"Whoa," Stone argued, taking Liam's other arm. "Where do you think you're going?"

"To my tepee so we can talk, if you don't mind," Reena replied icily.

"He's not leaving our sight, Reena."

Taking a deep breath, Reena closed her eyes and visibly took control of her emotions. "Can we just have a moment together, Hunter? Liam says he didn't shoot anyone, and I believe him."

Stone considered her for a moment, then let go of Liam's arm and nodded. "All right, but just for a few minutes." He watched them walk away, stop after twenty yards, and talk earnestly. Sometimes they touched each other as people do who haven't seen each other in a long time, as if they couldn't quite believe they were actually together.

Vickersham appeared beside him and smiled weakly. "Hunter, this is incredible."

"I know."

"What are we going to do?"

"We're going to take him in for trial, that's what we're going to do."

"Reena won't like it. Neither will Megan, come to think of it."

Stone felt a baffling, unreasonable anger fill him. Instead of banishing it, he let it take him. "I don't care who doesn't like it, Vic. It's the right thing to do. Come on." He strode over to Reena and Liam, sure that Vic was following. They looked at him in surprise when he reached them.

"That wasn't very long, Hunter," Reena said.

Stone ignored the comment and looked directly at Liam. "I don't want to hear any fairy tales. If you were with that gang, admit it like a man and take your punishment."

"Hunter," Vickersham said beside him, "maybe you'd better let me handle this."

"Why? Are you pulling rank on me?"

"You're just not yourself right now, my friend."

"Sure I am, and I'm still waiting for an answer," he stated, glaring at Liam.

Liam tilted his hat back and met Stone's gaze squarely. "I was snow-blind. They came across me and offered to take care of me until I regained my sight. I swear I didn't know what they were when I joined them." He turned to Reena. "I had no idea."

"Will you let him go now?" Reena asked Stone.

"Nope."

"Why are you being so stubborn?"

Vickersham said, "It's not that, Reena."

"Then what is it, Vic?"

125

"It's the law, actually. We have to take him to the fort for questioning, debriefing—"

"A trial?"

"Probably."

Reena looked at Hunter, then nodded to the side. "Can I talk to you, please?" Stone followed her a small distance away, and she turned to him and said, "I'm having a very hard time understanding this."

"Don't look at me like that," Stone said in a low voice. "You have to let us do our job, Reena."

"He's my *brother*. Don't you understand? He could no more be a part of this than I could. There has to be an explanation."

"I saw him riding with three other men who were aiming rifles at Becker, D'Artigue, and me. I didn't see him trying to stop them from blowing us out of our saddles. I could be dead right now, shot by a man your brother rode with. How do you feel about that?"

Reena looked away.

Watching her delicate profile, Stone realized that they'd never been at odds before with each other, and the thought depressed him.

Her eyes came back around to him. "What if I asked you to let him go? For me?"

The question stunned him, and he bit back his first reaction of anger. "That's not fair, Reena."

"Why not? I've never asked one thing from you. Now I'm asking."

"I can't."

"You won't even consider it?"

"Look around, Reena. There are a dozen other lawmen here who wouldn't stand for that, and you know it. They all loved Andy Doe and want to see the ones responsible for it punished."

"Liam wasn't responsible for it."

"But we don't know that, Reena. He was with Meecham's gang when they attacked us." Beyond frustration, Stone spotted the tall man he'd wounded standing off by himself, waiting to

126

leave. Stone shouted, "Becker! Bring that man over here!" Taking Reena's arm, he led her back to Vickersham and Liam. "Let's get this cleared up right now."

Becker brought Newby over, both of them looking puzzled.

"What's your name?" Stone asked.

Newby didn't answer.

"His name's Newby," Liam offered. "He rarely talks."

"Well, I don't need a speech," Stone informed them. "In fact, I just need a yes or no." He looked at Liam and said, "I'm going to ask him something, and I don't want to hear one word out of you, do you understand?"

"Yes."

"I mean it."

"Okay. I've got nothing to hide."

Stone turned to Newby. "On that mesa, did this boy fire down at us?"

Newby looked at Liam, expressionless, then answered, "Yep."

"I fired over your heads!" Liam reasoned. "Do you remember that shot, the one before all the real shooting started? That was me, trying to warn you!" He turned to Newby. "Tell him, Newby. Tell him how Coffin threatened to shoot me in the head if I didn't go along with everything."

Newby shrugged lazily. "Dunno."

"You were there!"

Stone cut them off. "Get him out of here, Becker."

"Yes, sir."

"Do you have your answer now, Reena?"

She looked at her brother in obvious discomfort. "It doesn't look good, Liam."

"But I'm telling the truth!"

Stone nodded to Vickersham and told Reena, "You've got five minutes alone. We've got to get back to the fort, drop off these prisoners, and resupply before we head out again." He waited for her usual, "Be careful," but it didn't come. "Goodbye, Reena."

Reena turned to Liam after they left and watched him shuffle his feet nervously.

"Don't look at me like that, Reena."

"Why not? You've done some pretty stupid things in your life, but this is—"

"All right, I'll ask *you*. What was I supposed to do? When I could see again, they said, 'You ride with us, or you're dead.' They threatened me with a cocked pistol pointed at my head. Would you like for me to have answered, 'Sorry, I'd disappoint my sister too much, just pull the trigger.' Is that what you would have wanted?"

"Of course not!"

"Then tell me what I was supposed to have done."

"You couldn't escape?"

"I never had the chance."

Reena bit her lip, then threw her arms around him. "You're right. I'm just glad you're alive."

Liam patted her back gently, then asked, "Is there something between you and Stone?"

After a brief hesitation, Reena said, "Yes."

"Whew! You sure can pick 'em."

"He's really a nice man. He just . . . gets intense sometimes."

"Intense! Yeah, you could say that. You wouldn't believe what he did . . . I can't even believe it."

"What was it?"

"Your intense friend shot the three men I was riding with before any of them could pull a trigger. I never saw anything like that in my life."

"Did he really almost shoot you?"

Liam pushed her back to arm's length and locked eyes with her. "I thought I was dead, Reena. But I have to tell you, he was telling the truth about it. He was just . . . *wild*, you know? The heat of battle was in his eyes and face like I've never seen. It was like he wasn't in control . . . like something dark inside him was pulling his strings. I never want to see that again."

Reena knew exactly what he was talking about. When Hunter

had saved her from the renegade Red Wolf, she'd seen the same look on his face and had wished the same thing her brother wished for now: to never see it again.

"What do I do, Reena?"

"You cooperate in any way you can. Give them names, descriptions, habits, what you heard them talking about—anything you can think of. It'll be all right, Liam."

"I sure hope you're right."

Reena hugged him again, partly because she wanted to, and partly to hide the doubt in her eyes.

PART THREE

THE POWER

Those have most power to hurt us that we love.

Francis Beaumont and John Fletcher
The Maid's Tragedy

CHAPTER ELEVEN

Colonel Macleod's Decision

Colonel Macleod, accompanied by an honor guard for Andy Doe, met the troop at the gate of the fort. Vickersham had sent a man before them with news of the disastrous campaign.

Stone considered Macleod's stormy expression and dreaded the debriefing. Though he was slow to anger, Macleod could exhibit a blistering temper. The colonel's eyes softened considerably, however, when his gaze shifted to Doe's body.

Stone handed the reins of Doe's horse over to Becker, and he and Vickersham dismounted before Macleod and saluted. Macleod nodded curtly but didn't return the salute.

"I'm very sorry, sir," Vickersham said. "I take full responsibility for this fiasco."

"You both take it equally," Macleod returned, watching the men file by him on their way to the stables.

The honor guard behind Macleod snapped to attention as Doe passed by them. Stone noticed that most of the men followed the body with their eyes, some of them inscrutable, some looking ill.

Stone felt as if he should say more to his commanding officer, but he had no idea what. The evidence of the failure of their mission was passing right in front of them.

Macleod continued to gaze at the column of men after they'd gone by, his lips tightened and his eyes narrowed. "Such a tragedy. Such a waste of a fine young man. What did those devils hope to accomplish by this? Do they think we'll be too cowed to send out another detail? How many of those blackguards did we get, Vickersham?"

"Two dead, plus those three prisoners, two of them wounded."

"I think there were more wounded who got away," Stone added. "There was an impressive amount of blood on that mesa."

Macleod grunted. "Well, there's some consolation, I suppose. But it won't bring that youngster back. Did the men account for themselves well?"

"They performed in exemplary fashion, sir," Vickersham informed him.

"Let's walk, gentlemen. Tell me about it."

Between Stone and Vickersham they told Macleod the events of that day. Macleod asked a question here and there, but mostly he only nodded and grunted from time to time.

Stone finished the account. "So Becker, D'Artigue, and I flanked them, but the majority of them had already left, leaving behind four to cover their retreat."

"I might add," Vickersham said, with a glance at Stone, "that Sub-Inspector Stone cut them to pieces before either Becker or D'Artigue could fire a shot."

Stone gave his friend a withering look.

"In my opinion," Vickersham continued, ignoring the look, "Hunter should be up for some sort of commendation."

"Vic, that's enough," Stone pleaded.

Macleod stared at Stone for a moment, then said thoughtfully, "I'll see what I can do. Well done, Stone."

"Thank you, sir."

"There is another rather touchy matter in the midst of all this, Colonel," Vickersham said.

"What's that?"

"One of the prisoners may not be a part of all this. Did you see the young boy who wasn't wounded?"

"I saw him."

"He's . . . um . . ." Vickersham looked at Stone.

"Well, what is it, Vickersham?" Macleod demanded.

"His name is Liam O'Donnell."

"So?"

"O'Donnell, sir. Reena's little brother."

Macleod nodded slowly as this information sank in, then he shook his head quickly as if trying to wake himself up. "That we do not need."

"No, sir."

"What was her reaction?"

"I think you can imagine, sir. She was very upset."

"What did she expect, that you would just let him go?"

"It was requested, sir."

"Mmm." Macleod stopped and picked up a small rock. Pitching it in the air over and over he said, "I suppose I should expect her to react that way, but still it disappoints me. The lad will stand trial just like the others; you both know that, don't you?"

Vickersham and Stone exchanged glances. Stone said, "We've been discussing it, Colonel, and—"

"I sincerely hope you're not going to ask what I think you're going to ask."

"May I finish, sir?" Stone asked, more sharply than he'd intended.

Macleod stopped pitching the rock into the air and gave him a penetrating look. "I'll allow that insolence to pass since you've had a rough time of it, Stone. Next time, I may not be as lenient. Now, continue."

"Sorry, sir," Stone said tightly. "What I was going to say was that the boy claims he was snow-blind and had no choice but to join them. He's pretty convincing."

"Did he fire on you?"

"We don't know for sure," Vickersham answered. "One of the men says he did, the other doesn't know. O'Donnell claims he fired over our heads."

"So he had a gun?"

"Yes, sir, no one denies that."

Macleod let the rock fall from his hand, and they all stared at it for a moment. "Then he'll stand trial," Macleod announced. He was the ultimate authority in the Territory, and once a man's guilt was proven in his court, he wasn't known for leniency.

Suddenly Stone didn't like Liam's chances at all.

"What are they gonna do with us, Liam?" Pod asked from the cell next to his. Newby was on the other side of Pod, lying on his bunk, which was a foot too short for him. Liam sat on his bunk and rubbed the back of his neck.

"What do you think, Pod?"

"You think they'll hang us?"

"I'm pretty sure of it, actually." The cells were small but clean. Liam rose and went to a tiny washstand to splash water on his face. He'd been in jail once before at West Point, but it had turned out to be a gag pulled on all the underclassmen at one time or another. A fake arrest summons had been delivered in the middle of the night to his room, and he'd been hauled off by men he thought were police. Actually, they'd been civilians hired by the upperclassmen to impersonate policemen. They'd had the cooperation of the local police, though, since they placed Liam in a real cell. They'd let him stew for two hours before some of his older friends had shown up, practically choking with laughter.

With water dripping from his face as he leaned over the washstand, Liam smiled faintly as he thought of that night. When he thought of the difference between that situation and his current one, his smile turned down into a frown.

"Liam?"

"What?"

"I don't wanna hang."

Liam looked over at Pod. His wounded arm was in a sling, and his shirt was tattered from the bullet's entrance and exit. "You should have thought about that a long time ago, Pod."

"I know I deserve to die, but I just don't want them to hang me. I've heard that . . ." He stopped and swallowed with a gulp.

"Heard what?"

"That sometimes a man's head comes off," he answered with haunted blue eyes. "I don't want my head comin' off, Liam, I really don't. Could you maybe ask 'em to shoot me instead?"

"What makes you think they'll listen to me?"

"Well, you know, I saw you talkin' with 'em back at that Injun camp, and I thought maybe they considered you somethin' special since you talk fancy and all that."

Liam barked a humorless laugh as he went to the front of his cell and gripped the iron bars. "I've got news for you, Pod. They don't consider me special at all."

"Who was that woman huggin' all over you back there? She sure was pretty."

"That was my sister, Reena."

"Your sister! I didn't know you had a sister around here."

"I didn't want anyone to know," Liam murmured. "None of your bunch, anyway."

"Why not?"

"Oh, wake up, Pod!" Liam exploded, leaping over to Pod's side of his cell. "Use your head! You ride with killers and thieves. Do you think I want them to know where my family is?"

Pod stared back at him with round eyes and mouth open.

Newby lazily turned his gaze on Liam, his eyes unreadable.

Liam felt the urge to reach through the bars, take Pod by the hair, and bang his head against the iron. The rage inside him was hot and barely controllable, stunning him. "What did you think, Pod, that you were playing some kind of childhood game while you were running with those men? Well, I've got news for you. Those were real guns and real bullets you shot, and people *died* because of you. They're gone forever."

Pod began to cry silently, great tears gathering in his eyes and rolling down his cheeks, creating clean paths in his dirty face.

"It's a little late for that, isn't it?" Liam stalked back to his bunk and threw himself down. He glanced over at the Mountie guard at a desk by the door. He was a stern-looking man who was staring at Liam with a faint smile on his face. "What are you laughing at?" Liam shouted.

He didn't answer, but the smile stayed in place.

"I don't belong here, you know," Liam declared.

"Son, if I had a dollar for every time I've heard those words spoken in here, I'd buy Parliament and legalize polygamy."

"What's that?" Pod asked through his tears.

"Never mind, Pod," Liam sighed. "You just cry it out. I won't bother you anymore. Sorry I yelled at you."

Pod went to his own washstand and found it empty. "Hey, redcoat, can I have some water over here?"

The Mountie acted as if he didn't hear.

"Hey!"

Liam jerked the bandanna from his neck and went to his washstand, dipped it in the water and handed it to Pod. "Here. Don't call them names, and it'll go easier for you."

Pod accepted the kerchief and wiped his face. "I ain't never been in jail before. If what you said earlier is right, this'll be my first and last time." He handed back the bandanna. "I seen a man hang once, Liam. His head didn't come off, but it still wasn't pretty. Why do people come to watch that?"

"I don't know, Pod. I really don't."

"Will there be a bunch of people watch us hang?"

"I don't know that, either."

"Maybe the Mounties don't let civilians watch. I sure would hate for my head to pop off in front of a woman or child, wouldn't you? I don't suppose I'd mind if it was only men who saw—"

"Would you stop talking about heads coming off? Why don't you take a nap or something?" Liam was tired of talking and tired physically. He stretched out on his bunk and pretended to sleep to discourage Pod from asking any more questions or from talking about his head coming off.

After only a few minutes, Liam heard the boy snoring softly.

———

After supper that night, Liam had a visitor. Hunter Stone strode in, having to duck under the door header, and brought a chair over to Liam's cell. The top three buttons of his tunic were unfastened, revealing a white cotton shirt underneath. Liam had the feeling that he rarely looked as casual as he did right now.

Stone crossed his legs and arms, and the gray eyes fastened on Liam, performing a slow inspection from Liam's head to his feet. His thoughts were hidden; he might very well have been gauging the worth of a horse. Stone glanced over at Pod and Newby, who both stared at him and waited to see what would happen.

Liam was sitting on his bunk against the wall, his knees raised in front of him with his arms encircling them. He watched Stone dismiss the other two with his strange eyes and bring them back to Liam with an almost physical force.

"You're in a spot, O'Donnell."

"How observant," Liam replied with a turning up of his lip.

"You know, your arrogant attitude is only going to dig you deeper. I would have thought you were smarter than that."

Liam didn't answer. He knew Stone was right, but he couldn't seem to shake the self-pitying feelings inside him.

"Guess not. Megan and Reena got all the smarts in your family, didn't they?"

"Did you come here to taunt me?"

"No. Actually I came here to see if I wanted to try to help you. Needless to say, your stock is sinking fast."

"I'm sure my sister can change your mind for you."

Something slithered behind Stone's eyes, and he rose from the chair.

"Wait," Liam said. He hung his head for a moment and took a deep breath. "I'm sorry. I'm just tired of this whole—"

"Don't give me an excuse for being an idiot. It ruins the apology." He sat back down, leaning forward and resting his elbows on his knees. When he looked up, Liam was surprised to see a softer light in Stone's eyes.

"Then let me just say I'm sorry."

"That's better."

"Sir?" Pod broke in from his cell.

Stone looked at him as if he'd forgotten he was even there. "What?"

"Are y'all gonna hang us?"

"There's a good chance of that, son."

Pod looked at Liam, who shook his head and said to Stone, "Pod doesn't want to be hung. He wants a firing squad."

"Any particular reason?"

"Don't ask him that question, please."

"I don't want my head comin' off when you pull that lever on the trapdoor," Pod said.

"See, I told you," Liam commented.

"Your head won't come off," Stone told him.

"How do you know?"

Stone leaned back in his chair and crossed his legs again. "I'm trying to have a conversation with Liam here. Do you think we could talk about your decapitation later?"

"De . . . what?"

"I'll tell you later, Pod," Liam assured him.

Disappointed, Pod sat on his bunk with his back to them, mumbling to himself.

"How did you meet my sister?" Liam asked Stone.

"I'll let her tell you about that, if she wants to. I'm here to inform you that you're going to be tried along with these other two."

Liam's gaze fell to the floor between them. "I thought so."

"I explained to my commanding officer, but the fact that you fired a weapon during the fight swayed him."

"I shot in the air," Liam whispered. "I'm going to die because I fired a pistol at the sky."

"You're not dead yet, so let's dispense with the self-pity."

"That's easy for you to say. You're sitting out there, and I'm in here." The shadow fell across Stone's eyes again, and Liam sighed and rested his head against the wall behind him. "Sorry."

"What's the real reason you didn't contact one of your sisters to tell them you were coming?"

"I just didn't, that's all."

"You're a very bad liar. That's why I tend to believe your story, because I don't think anyone would make up such a bad excuse and stick to it. Don't start lying to me now."

Liam stretched out his legs and laced his fingers together behind his head. "Do you ever make a mistake?"

"Of course."

"I'm starting to wonder. When you look at people, I'll bet they react like me."

"How's that?"

"I feel guilty, even though I haven't done anything wrong. Did you know you have that effect on people?"

Stone shrugged slightly. "Never thought about it."

"I can see why Reena's in love with you."

"Did she tell you that?"

"No. I could just tell. She's always been attracted to straight-forward people. Except for Louis, of course. I've never figured out why she gave that fool the time of day. Reena loves honesty and has always dreamed of a knight in shining armor coming to sweep her away to his castle. Why haven't you swept her away, Sub-Inspector Stone?"

"I guess my armor's not shiny enough."

"Could have fooled me." Liam chewed on a fingernail, then said, "I dropped out of West Point. I've traveled two thousand miles thinking about it, and I still don't know why. If I'd contacted Reena to tell her I was coming, she would have known that something was wrong and might have cabled my father. I couldn't have Dad sending a posse out after me."

"How do you know he hasn't? He surely has been contacted by the school."

141

"He may have—who knows? But I didn't tell a soul where I was going, so Dad doesn't have a chance of finding me."

"Do you want me to cable him, considering your position?"

"No. I'll get enough lectures from my sisters before I die."

"Stop talking like that."

Liam chuckled and spread his hands. "Look at me. How can I *not* talk like that?"

The front door burst open, and Megan charged in with Vickersham in her wake. As she passed by the Mountie at the door, she ordered curtly, "Open my brother's cell, please."

"Hello, Megan," Stone said.

Totally ignoring him, Megan said, "Hello, baby brother."

Liam went to the bars and thrust his arms through to take her hands. "Megan, it's good to see you."

"It's good to see you, too, though it's difficult through iron. Come unlock this cell!" she cried to the guard, who was standing behind the desk looking from Stone to Vickersham.

Vickersham nodded at him. "It's all right. Open the door."

The man did as he was told, and Megan hugged Liam fiercely. Stone and Vickersham stepped back, with Stone asking, "I guess I'm in trouble with her, too, huh?"

"Not nearly so much as me, old chap."

"She didn't say a word to me."

"Hunter, take my word for it. You don't want her to. After viewing the tempers of the two O'Donnell sisters in full force, I must say the edge goes to the eldest. Her ears go back flat against her elegant head, and claws emerge in an alarming fashion. Is my face blistered?"

"Blistered?"

"From the verbal thrashing that was so skillfully hurled in my direction earlier."

"Now that you mention it, your features are a bit ruddy."

"Quite right."

Megan turned to them and asked, "May we go for a walk?" She glanced over at Pod and Newby. "For privacy?"

"Megan, my dear," Vickersham began.

"Never mind," she said frostily, plopping herself and Liam down on the bunk. "I should have known better than to hope for leniency from you two."

Stone and Vickersham started out the door. Vickersham said, "I say, I know what we can do now."

"What?"

"Go find two holes jolly well large enough to accommodate our insensitive hides and crawl into them. What do you say?"

CHAPTER TWELVE

Saying Good-bye

Lydia Meecham sat in the living area of her cabin, listening to her mother and father argue in their bedroom. Actually, she was listening to her father rave about one of the cows dying in the snowstorm of a week ago. Catherine Meecham, as far as Lydia knew, had never raised her voice to her husband.

The cabin was small but clean. Lydia sat on a worn brown sofa and rocked her doll in the cherrywood cradle Megan, Reena, and Jenny had bought for her. The doll inside had one arm missing and was dressed in threadbare clothes. Her name was Winnie.

Timmy came in, looking warily at his parents' bedroom door. He was holding a wooden rifle cradled in his arm and wore a coonskin cap and buckskin clothing.

"Are you hunting pretend bears again?" Lydia asked.

"Yeah. How long they been in there?"

Lydia shrugged. "I don't know. A while."

Timmy went into the kitchen and got himself a cookie. "What's he hollerin' about?"

"The cow that froze."

"Well, why's he screamin' at Mama? It was my fault."

Lydia took Winnie out and began changing her diaper. "If it

145

really was your fault, you better go hide. He sounds awful mean today."

Timmy sat down in a rocker by the sofa and said around a mouthful of cookie, "He just got home after being gone for weeks, and I'm supposed to go hide from him?"

Lydia shrugged. "Suit yourself."

"It got quiet in there. You think he's through?"

Fitz Meecham emerged from his room, hatless and shirtless. His eyes came upon Timmy, who stopped eating the cookie and seemed to shrink back in the rocker. "How many times have I told you, boy, to watch for those storms and gather the livestock before they hit? How many times?"

"I don't know," Timmy answered in a small voice. He looked down distastefully at the half-eaten cookie in his hand.

Meecham moved around the rocker slowly, keeping his eyes on his son. "That all you got to say?"

"Sorry, Pa."

"You're lucky I came into some money while I was gone. Otherwise we'd take a trip to the barn to talk about it some more."

Lydia concentrated on Winnie's diaper, trying to make herself invisible. When her father was in a mood, which happened more and more before he went on his long trips to wherever, she tried really hard to become invisible. It never worked, but she kept trying.

Timmy asked the question that Lydia wanted to, but didn't dare. "Where you been, Pa? Where'd you get some money?"

Meecham brushed both sides of his thick handlebar mustache with the back of his index finger before answering. "Never you mind—neither of you. You hear me, Lydia?"

"Yes."

Meecham sat down on the sofa and rested his arm on the side of the crib. Lydia stared at his hands, continually amazed at the size and strength of them.

"I tried trapping, and I tried farming," her father told them. "You know that. And you know it didn't work. I'm no more a farmer than I am a politician." He looked over at Timmy. "You will understand when you grow into a man that you'll do anything to care for your family—whatever it takes. And that's what I've done."

Timmy again avoided the heavy gaze, but his mouth worked briefly.

"What is it, boy?"

"Um . . . aw, it's nothin'."

"Say it."

"I've just heard some things, that's all."

"What things?" Meecham asked sharply.

"I don't wanna tell you, Pa. You might hit me. They're probably lies anyway."

"I ain't gonna hit you, son. Now, what things?"

Timmy shifted in the rocker, the forgotten cookie still clutched in his hand. He glanced at Lydia, who held her breath, wondering if he would say it. Timmy bit his lower lip a few seconds, then said, "There's been some people killed by some bad men in the Territory. Josh Kennedy's pa was shot by them—in cold blood, is what Josh says."

Meecham waited, then prompted him. "Why are you telling me this?"

"'Cause those men started their stealing about the time you left."

"Doesn't mean it's me. You think it's me?"

Timmy didn't answer.

Meecham looked over at Lydia. "Do you think I'm a part of that?"

Lydia shrugged and smoothed out Winnie's tattered dress.

"You think I could kill someone, Lydia? Do you, Timmy?"

"No, sir."

"I didn't hear you."

"I said, no, sir."

"Lydia?"

"No, sir."

"You ain't just saying that, now, are you?" he asked and put his large hand on Lydia's knee.

Lydia shook her head and managed a smile. Sometimes her father's tone took on a kindly manner, and sometimes he even touched her like he was now, and she never failed to warm to it. Rare times they were, to be sure, but she enjoyed them while they were taking place.

To her disappointment, her father withdrew his hand, and his face changed to the one that he wore when something was *really* bothering him. The look vanished as soon as she saw it. Fitz Meecham wasn't one who let his feelings show much.

"I want you two to do something for me," he told them.

"What, Pa?" Lydia asked, ready to do anything for him if he would just touch her again as he just had.

"I want you to go out to the barn and saddle my horse."

"Where you goin'?" Timmy asked.

"We'll talk about that when I get out there. I'm gonna tell your mama good-bye."

Lydia slammed Winnie back into the cradle angrily, then was immediately sorry for the doll. What if she'd hurt her?

"Hey, hey," Meecham growled, "I don't want any of that. Just do what you're told."

"But you just got here, and now you're leaving again!" Lydia cried as she stormed by him. She was close enough for him to reach out and grab or spank her, but he did nothing. This, for some reason, made her more angry.

Meecham jerked his head at Timmy, and the boy followed Lydia outside. Then he rose, stretched, and went back into the bedroom.

Catherine Meecham had been a beauty in her younger days. Now she was prematurely gray and haggard. Her nose was still fine, and her cheekbones soft in her oval face, but lines around her eyes and mouth gave her a slightly unhealthy look.

She was sprawled across the bed, one forearm over her forehead, her nearly white hair tied up in a tight bun. Beside her was a thick wad of bills bound with a string.

Meecham went to the chest of drawers and withdrew a red bibbed shirt.

"What are you doing, Fitz? Why won't you tell me?"

"Best you not know."

"Is it illegal?" Catherine asked, rising to a sitting position. "Just tell me that."

"Why?"

"Because it's . . . *something*! I don't know anything anymore, much less my own husband. What happened to you?"

Meecham buttoned the cuffs on his shirt silently, staring down at her. The shirt hung on his slim frame like a tent. Catherine had bought it for him nearly five years before, but he'd rarely worn it. She wondered about the significance of his choosing it now.

"I have a right to know something!" Catherine stated firmly. She had never raised her voice to him in that way, and she watched his eyes narrow slightly and his fingers stop their buttoning, but still he didn't respond. "You aren't coming back, are you?" she asked, sure that she was right.

"I don't know that."

"I do. It's why you've been acting so strange since you walked in that door last night." Catherine scooted to the edge of the bed and stood. She was almost as tall as he was, and usually she kept her gaze averted slightly so that he wouldn't feel short. Now she didn't care and went over to him to face him eye to eye. "What is it, Fitz? Another woman? Or are you just tired of having the responsibility of coming back here to pretend you're a husband and a father?" Catherine winced, sure that a blow was coming; it didn't.

"You wouldn't understand, Catherine. You're a woman."

"What kind of answer is that?"

Meecham pulled his suspenders over his shoulders and reached for his gun belt. Catherine grabbed his hand, jerking it away from the gun. Meecham looked at her, anger rising in his eyes—the eyes she'd once thought were so caring and deeply lined with love for his family. Lately they were just black dots to fill out the rest of his face.

"Let go of me, Catherine," he told her in a near hiss.

"You didn't even know how to fire a gun a year ago. Now it's your most important possession, isn't it? Even more important than your family."

Meecham twisted his arm, and she lost her grasp. "Nothing's more important than my family!" He went over to the bed and scooped up the wad of bills. "Do you see this? Do you think I don't care what happens to you and them kids?"

"What's going to happen to *you*, Fitz?"

"How can anybody know what's gonna happen to them?"

Catherine couldn't shake the feeling that this was the last time she'd see him. Her love for him had vanished over the past few months since he'd changed into a quiet, bitter man who was never home. Still, she didn't want to lose him.

Suddenly melancholy, she stepped up to him and put her arms around him. He tensed, probably surprised, then wrapped his arms around her.

"Don't you worry, Catherine."

"I don't know who you are anymore."

"What do you mean?"

"It was the farming that killed you inside, wasn't it?"

He pulled back to arm's length, his face unreadable.

Catherine nodded. "I thought so. It wasn't your fault we had a flood and lost the crops. Don't you know that? We could have gone on, rebuilt, and planted again the next spring."

Meecham was shaking his head before she even finished. "We were dead broke, Catherine. You know that. Something had to be done." He glanced out the window at the late afternoon sun and shook his head. "I've got to go."

When he reached for his gun again, Catherine didn't stop him. She watched him strap it on, her anger gone, replaced by a sad resignation. He picked up his saddlebags, kissed her on the cheek and, starting toward the door, turned after only a few steps.

"I done the best I could, Catherine. No one can say I didn't."

"And no one will."

After he left, Catherine sat on the bed and cried silently.

———————

The children had Meecham's horse ready when he got to the barn. He threw his saddlebags behind the saddle and turned to face them. "I know I just got home and haven't had any time for you. But I've got to go now. There's no doubt of that."

Lydia wouldn't look at him. He removed his hat and squatted down in front of her.

"She's still mad, Pa," Timmy informed him.

Meecham looked up at him. "And you?"

Timmy hesitated, then shrugged. "I don't care anymore. You've been gone so much, it don't really matter that you're leavin' again."

Meecham considered this, then nodded slowly. "That's fair enough, I guess." He looked at Lydia—the liquid brown eyes, the crimson birthmark on her forehead, and the full lower lip like her mother's. "I know you're mad, little girl. But you're gonna get over it and wish you'd hugged me."

Lydia's eyes welled with tears, and she threw her arms around her father's neck. "Please stay for a while, Pa. Please?"

"Gotta go, Lydia. You take care of your ma for me while I'm gone, eh?"

The little head nodded against his shoulder.

Meecham broke their embrace and stood. "Timmy, do you at least want to shake my hand?" He held it out, but his son only stared at it. Meecham nodded curtly. "Good-bye, son." He turned and took the reins of the horse, neither surprised nor bothered.

"Pa?"

Meecham swung into the saddle. "Yeah, Timmy?"

"I won't let no more cows die. I promise."

For the first time that day, Meecham smiled. "I know you

won't." He tipped his hat to Lydia, then spurred the horse out of the barn.

Just before he rode out of sight of his house, Meecham stopped the horse and turned for one last look. He didn't think he'd never see it again.

———————

It snowed the day they buried Andy Doe.

Jenny Sweet stood beside Dirk Becker and watched the fat flakes fall on the pine coffin. She hadn't known Andy, but from the reaction of some of the Mounties around her, she knew he was well liked. One man wept openly, and every once in a while Jenny saw a white-gloved hand travel up to an eye and wipe at it.

The minister who performed the ceremony was the new man with Reena, Jack Sheffield. Jenny thought him handsome, but not as handsome as the man who stood beside her. Becker had come to the boardinghouse in a wagon to get her, and his re-splendence had dazzled her momentarily. He'd made a joke about losing the whole morning spit shining his boots, but she thought the truth may have been hidden underneath the bluster. The boots were so shiny they'd looked wet. Thinking of it made her look down at them, and with a strange sadness she found them snow- and mud-spattered.

"I didn't know this man," Sheffield told the onlookers, "but since his death, I've talked to those who did, and I find myself sorry that I didn't come to this place sooner to get acquainted with Andy. I feel as if, by my ignorance of his existence on this earth, I've somehow missed out on something—a blessing, maybe—a chance to enjoy one of God's exceptional creations."

Reena and Megan stood behind and to the side of Sheffield. Jenny couldn't help noticing Stone and Vickersham across from her, well away from the women. Megan had told Jenny of her brother's surprise appearance and the ensuing bad feelings that had surfaced. Jenny would never tell it to either of the sisters, but she thought that there was nothing wrong with the Mounties' insistence on trying Liam. He'd been caught with a ruthless gang of outlaws. The court would have to determine his guilt or innocence, just as it did for anyone else.

She looked over at Hunter. Every time her eyes had come upon him he'd been in the exact same stance: helmet held in his hands in front of him, heedless of the snow, gazing steadily downward at the coffin. Jenny couldn't see his eyes, but she could tell from his posture that he was sad. Dirk had told her that he was like a ghost around the fort, even more silent and brooding than usual. Dirk was worried about him.

Sheffield read from the Bible, then gave way to Colonel Macleod, who said a few words. The coffin was lowered into the snowy ground, and Andy Doe was gone.

After the final prayer, Jenny looked up at Becker and was surprised to find his cheeks wet. She smiled weakly at him, unsure of how to react. Until this day, she'd never seen a man cry in her life.

The mourners began to drift back to the fort for refreshments. She and Dirk weren't the only ones to stay behind; Stone, the crying Mountie, and Vickersham remained on the other side of the grave.

"I just can't believe he's gone," the crying man said. "I just can't believe it."

Becker whispered, "That's Garner. He and Andy were practically brothers. They even looked alike."

"Why'd it have to be Andy, sir?" Garner asked, but Jenny wasn't sure if he was asking Stone or Vickersham. "He never hurt anyone. Why him?"

Stone's jaw clenched, but he only continued staring down into the grave.

"We don't know the answer to that, Ken," Vickersham said.

"But . . . why did God take him? He was only doing good on this lousy earth. He'd cheer people up who were feeling low, and everyone liked him. So why?"

"I don't believe God necessarily takes people. I think sometimes He allows things to happen for the benefit of us all. I know you don't think Andy's death is to our benefit, but we can't know God's all-encompassing plan."

In the silence that followed, Jenny whispered, "Is that true, Dirk?"

"Yes. It's just hard to comprehend."

Stone made a sound that could have been interpreted as either a snort of derision or a sniffle. Vickersham looked at him, but Stone didn't move, look up, or speak.

Garner must have thought it was a snort, for he said, "I'm with you, sir. God's plan doesn't make any sense at all—if that's what it is." He wiped his face, shook his head and, with one last look at the coffin in the ground, replaced his helmet and left.

Becker took Jenny's arm, and they moved around the grave. Vickersham nodded to them, but Stone didn't look up. Becker said, "That's something that will haunt me for the rest of my life. I was riding right beside him. Why did the man who shot Andy zero in on him instead of me? Or either of you, for that matter?"

"It should have been me," Stone muttered. "I was in the lead, obviously an officer, and that fool picks off Andy right in the middle of the troop."

Vickersham looked at them, then started toward the fort. Over his shoulder he said, "I think it's time for everyone to accept the fact that it was Andy who was killed and to stop trying to take his place. You're all alive—be thankful."

Jenny watched the two men in front of her. They were almost the exact same height, with Dirk a bit more heavily muscled, but not by much. Jenny, standing only to their chests, felt like a little girl among men.

Stone turned and looked at her as if noticing her for the first time. "You didn't know him, did you?"

"No, but Dirk's told me about him."

Stone nodded, melting snow dripping from his blond hair, and put on his helmet. With the tall helmets on, the two men looked like giants. To Becker he said, "Vickersham's my best friend, but I don't care what he says. It should have been anyone but Andy. Look down there." He pointed into the grave. "In there lies the proverbial lamb, and who led him to the slaughter?"

Becker shifted his feet and looked uncomfortable. "Sir, you really have to stop blaming yourself for this. What could you have done differently? Nothing."

"I should have trusted my instincts and not even considered trusting La Belle. I believe that was the stupidest mistake I've ever made. Am I the one to pay for it? No, *he* did." He jerked his head toward the grave, his lip curled.

Becker took Jenny's arm and turned toward the fort. "Let's go, Jenny."

"Yes, you two go eat, drink, and be merry with the others at the party," Stone said bitterly.

Becker stopped and turned back. "Would you rather we stay here and cry over that grave?"

"Anything wrong with that?"

"Permission to speak freely, sir?"

"Yes."

"Everyone's about tired of your wallowing in self-pity."

Jenny looked up at Becker in shock.

Stone's eyes narrowed as he came toward them slowly. Jenny took Becker's arm and pulled at him to try to back him away, but he stood his ground solidly.

Stone stopped in front of Becker, almost nose to nose. "Because I gave you permission to speak your mind doesn't mean you can say anything you want. You have no right to pass judgment on me."

Becker took a deep breath and broke eye contact. "You're right, sir. I apologize."

Stone turned and went back to the graveside.

Jenny asked quietly, "Do you think we should ask Reena to come out here?"

"I think we should stay out of it. Let him do his own asking." Becker took her arm again, and they started back to the fort.

CHAPTER THIRTEEN

The O'Donnells Make a Trade

At the reception following the funeral, Reena watched as Becker and Jenny came inside and shook the snow from their coats and boots. She wondered where Hunter was.

She stood sipping hot tea with Sheffield and Megan. Vickersham orbited them like a moon but apparently didn't have the courage to approach. Reena couldn't help but feel sorry for him. Jaye Eliot Vickersham was one of the nicest men she'd ever known, and he had no more ability to intentionally hurt anyone than a rabbit. His hurt over Megan's snubs showed in every part of his face and posture. Reena had asked Megan to reconsider her stand, but Megan was like Reena. The thought of their only brother having a possible date with the hangman's noose was too much for them to bear, and they considered the Mounties to be a collective hangman.

"Do you want to go now?" Sheffield asked Reena, breaking into her thoughts. "To see Liam?"

Reena thought of Hunter at the ceremony. She'd never seen him so grieved, and every instinct told her to take him in her arms and ease his pain. But she'd avoided him, trying not to look at him, and she wasn't even sure if he knew she was there. On

157

the walk to the mess hall she had decided to wait for an opportunity to speak to him before going to see Liam. "No, not just yet."

Sheffield nodded but watched her closely. He had a direct gaze that sometimes made her uncomfortable, much like Hunter's often did. Whenever either had looked that way at her, she got an eerie feeling that they could read her thoughts. Coming from Hunter, it was frightening yet romantic; coming from Sheffield, it was merely unsettling.

"That was a nice service, Jack," Megan told him.

"Thank you."

"Andy would have liked it," Reena added.

"I sincerely hope so."

Jenny came over while Becker went for coffee. "Hi," she said shyly, glancing at Sheffield.

"Hello, Jenny," Reena smiled. She introduced Sheffield to Jenny and told her that he would be helping with the Blackfoot tribe.

"That's nice," Jenny told him, then whispered to Reena, "Can I talk to you?"

Sheffield must have heard, because he said, "I'm going to talk to Colonel Macleod. Would you ladies excuse me?"

After Sheffield moved away, Reena asked, "What is it, Jenny?"

"It's Hunter. I'm worried about him. Ain't—aren't you?"

"What's wrong?"

"He and Dirk just had a fight, and he's still out there by the grave. He's just not actin' like himself."

"A fight?" Reena asked, alarmed.

"Well, an argument. Not a real fight. Why don't you talk to him, Reena?"

"Because I don't have anything to say to him."

"Make something up."

Reena took a sip of the tea, which had turned tepid, and thought about it. "Whatever I say won't help him, Jenny. He's just really sad right now and has to get over it himself."

Jenny looked away in disgust. "I didn't think you'd do it. If you don't mind my sayin', I think you and Megan are wrong. Those men are just doin' their jobs, and you act like they've got leprosy." She marched off to join Becker, leaving Reena and Megan to stare after her in surprise.

"Do you think she's right?" Megan asked.

"I don't know," Reena answered, her tone coated with frustration. "This is the most horrible situation in the world. How could Liam have been so stupid?"

"Do you think we should cable Dad?"

"I don't know the answer to that, either. What do you think?"

Megan shrugged. "I guess not. The trial's in two days, and he wouldn't have time to get a good lawyer up here, anyway."

Reena's eyes kept going to the door, looking for Hunter. Was he still out in the snow?

"What about Jenny's observations?" Megan asked her. "Are we that stupid, or is she overreacting?"

"Why are you asking me all these hard questions? I don't know any more than you do."

"Sorry."

"No, *I'm* sorry. I'm feeling very irritable these days."

"Look," Megan said, pointing toward the door.

Reena lifted her gaze and saw Stone coming in. When he removed his helmet, she saw his damp hair lay plastered flat to his head. "He's going to catch his death of cold. I'm going over to talk to him. Why don't you let Vic talk to you, and we'll see how things go?"

"All right."

Stone saw her coming and waited by the door. Reena couldn't read his expression—it was blank and indifferent. "Hello," she greeted.

He looked over his shoulder, then back to her. "Are you talking to me?"

"Aren't you cold?" she asked, ignoring his sarcasm.

"A little bit."

"You need to change into another tunic and dry your hair."

"I will."

Reena waited to see if he would say more, but he only watched her calmly. "You're not making this easy, you know. Can I get you some coffee?"

"No, thanks. I'll get some when you're through talking to me."

"Don't you have anything to say to me?"

His eyes softened a bit, then the reticence returned. "Unless you've changed your mind about me, I don't see what we have to talk about. I've done all I can for Liam, except let him go, of course. It's up to you how you choose to feel about that."

Reena pulled her coat tighter around her shoulders. The cold air seemed to be seeping through the cracks in the door. "I didn't have a chance to tell you how sorry I am about Andy."

"Thank you."

"Can we move away from the door?"

"Sure."

She led them to the other side of the large hall toward a wood stove, noticing that Megan and Vic were talking by the punch bowl. They looked as strained as Reena felt.

Holding her hands over the stove, Reena asked, "Are you going out again? After those men?"

"Yes."

"Can you give me something other than one word answers?"

"Of course. There's two words."

"You're really angry with me, aren't you?"

He glanced away, and she saw a vulnerable look pass over his face—a look so alien to him that she could only stare in surprise.

Shifting his feet, Stone murmured, "I'm not angry at you. Or . . . I don't know, maybe I am a little. We've never had a crisis before where we weren't behind each other one hundred percent. I don't know how to act, or what to do when we're at odds like this."

"Neither do I."

"You and Sheffield seem to be getting along."

She heard the questioning tone in his voice and said, "You don't have to worry about him."

"It's not him I'm worried about."

"You don't have to worry about me, either." She moved away from the hot stove and stood with her back to it. Looking over at Megan, she noticed that Vickersham wasn't with her anymore. She scanned the hall and saw him talking to Macleod by the snack table. Was he called over, or did he and Megan find themselves unable to communicate? As she watched, Vickersham looked directly at her and walked over to them.

"The colonel doesn't want to waste any time going after those men," Vickersham told Stone. "He wants to meet in an hour to discuss plans for the next patrol."

"All right."

Vickersham nodded at Reena and walked away.

"I've got to go get cleaned up," Stone told Reena. "You're going to see your brother?"

"Yes."

He nodded. "I'll see you later, then."

Reena watched him leave, then walked over to Megan. "No luck with Vic?"

"It was . . . strained."

"Same here."

"You know, Reena, something occurred to me just now when I saw you two talking."

"What?"

"You're angry at him for one of the very reasons you love him—his uncompromising devotion to duty and justice. I have the same feelings about Vic, and it bothers me. Maybe we *are* wrong."

The truth of what her sister said hit Reena hard. It was their brother's stupidity that had placed everyone in an uncomfortable position, not the Mounties. Thinking of Hunter's distant attitude, she wondered if it was too late for everyone involved.

———

"What do you mean I'm not going?" Stone asked Macleod.

"I mean just what I said. You're not going on the next patrol." He looked at Vickersham. "And neither are you."

"Why?" Stone asked, unable to grasp the idea. "We have a *right* to go."

"Stone," Macleod said with exaggerated patience, "your tone is bordering on insolence. I think you're forgetting yourself. You might remember to throw in a 'sir' every once in a while also."

"Sorry, sir, but I just—"

"You just can't believe it, I know. But you know good and well that I need you both here for the trial."

They were in Macleod's office, along with Del Dekko and Sergeant Stride. The presence of so many bodies in the relatively small office had raised the temperature to a stifling level. Macleod went over to a window and lifted the sash a few inches. The cool air from outside washed over them nicely.

"What about me?" Del asked the colonel.

"You stay, too."

"Who's taking the next patrol, sir?" Vickersham asked.

"Inspector Walsh. Listen to me, gentlemen. We can't make a move until those men strike again. I know it's difficult to wait for another attack, but there it is. We have to know their location."

"Why can't we just go back to that riverbed and pick up the trail from there?" Del asked.

"Because it has probably snowed up there and covered their tracks."

"And maybe it hasn't," Stone suggested.

Macleod sat down heavily behind his desk. "It's three days away, Stone. I won't have a patrol travel that far on a mere possibility. Then if the gang did raid again, the patrol might be a week away from the site." He shook his head. "We wait."

Stride asked, "Excuse me, sir, but have any of the prisoners talked?"

Macleod looked at him, surprised, then put a hand to his

forehead. "I must be losing my mind. The O'Donnell boy requested a meeting with me. Run and fetch him, Stride."

"Yes, sir."

"How stupid of me," Macleod commented in a tired voice.

"You're just upset today, sir," Vickersham told him. "We all are."

Stone went over to the window and gazed out. His conversation with Reena had been strained and had left a lump deep in his belly. He supposed he'd been very lucky with women in the past; in his marriage to Betsy they'd never had so much as a disagreement. Reena's Irish temper directed his way was disturbing and unsettling, and he didn't know what to do about it. If he left her alone, she might cool off and see his side of things. On the other hand, her anger might just grow to larger proportions.

While growing up, Stone had been molded by his mother's practical and aggressive nature. He liked the idea that the sun rose in the east and set in the west. It was reliable and never needed to be worried about. He liked the clumps of snowflakes that landed on his sleeve and broke apart to reveal each six-sided particle of perfection. Never five sides, always six. Perfection.

When he'd left home and become a bounty hunter, he'd never left a job undone. Only two times had he gone after a man and hadn't caught him. Both times it had grated against him like sandpaper, but it made the satisfaction sweeter when they'd each turned up again, and he'd been able to catch them on his second attempts.

His whole life had been fashioned and tempered by practicality, coupled with a fierce sense of responsibility. Staring out the window, he supposed the reason Reena's anger vexed him so much was that there wasn't a place for it—it didn't fit anywhere in the scheme of things that made up his life.

He heard the door open behind him, and in marched Stride, Liam, Reena, and Megan. Reena's eyes were luminous with anxiety when she looked at him, and the whole group stepped in front of Macleod.

Standing and clearing his throat uncomfortably, the colonel

glanced from one woman to the other, then said, "I'm sorry, ladies, but this is a private meeting."

"You're a public servant, Colonel, so there *are* no private meetings if citizens wish to attend," Megan said calmly.

"My dear Mrs. Goldsen, excuse me for pointing out that neither you nor your sister are citizens of this country."

"It doesn't matter. We're the public, and this matter is of grave interest to us."

"What could you possibly say in here that would be private? Liam is our brother and has told us everything," Reena added.

Macleod looked at Stone, who shrugged, and Vickersham, who smiled. Taking a deep breath, Macleod said, "I must insist—"

"Colonel," Megan interrupted with a knife-edged tone, "I really don't see why you want to ban people from this meeting who are only looking out for a prisoner's interests. I'd heard you had a reputation for fairness and impartiality."

Macleod locked eyes with her, and Stone saw his famous temper just below the surface. *Uh-oh.*

"Sir," Vickersham said tentatively, "there's really no reason they can't be here, is there?"

"I'll be the judge of that, if you please!" Macleod stated, his face reddening. He glared at Vickersham fiercely for a moment. Visibly calming himself, he forced a smile and gestured to the chairs in front of his desk. "Ladies, if you'll have a seat."

"Thank you, Colonel," Megan returned, managing to keep the gloating of victory out of her voice.

"Now—Liam, is it?—what was it you wanted to see me about?" Macleod asked.

"Don't answer that," Reena told her brother.

Macleod's head whipped around. "What?"

"We want your word on something."

Stone watched Macleod stare at her in disbelief, and everyone in the room knew what was coming.

"Liam knows the names of the leaders. He'll give them to you in return for his freedom."

Macleod slammed his hand down on the desk, his face livid. "Under no circumstances is that going to happen! He'll tell us because it's the right thing to do, not as some sort of ruse!"

Megan touched Reena on the arm and said, "Let's go."

"This is preposterous!" Macleod cried.

"Colonel," Reena said, "if you know the names of those men, then half your search is over, and it may very well save more lives if these men are caught before they strike again. Please reconsider." She gave Megan a warning look; this was Liam's only chance.

Macleod thought about the sensible outlook Reena had expressed. Idly he twirled the inkwell on his desk as he reconsidered. "I can't just excuse him, Miss O'Donnell. That's impossible. I can, however, make sure that he avoids execution for his cooperation."

Reena and Megan exchanged relieved glances. Liam took a deep breath and let it out slowly. Stone thought it probably wasn't the most they'd hoped for, but hearing that Liam would at least cheat the hangman was overwhelming.

"Now, Liam," Macleod said, "may I have some names?"

"There's one more thing, sir," Liam said, then braced himself for another outburst from Macleod. When he received only a look of displeasure and a curt nod, he went on. "If word of my cooperation gets out before you catch those men, my life won't be worth that ink you're holding. If the colonel and everyone in this room could . . ."

"Yes, I think you may be assured that the information given in this meeting will be held in the utmost confidence of those present." Macleod scanned the room to plant an exclamation mark after what he'd said, then nodded. "*Now*, may I have the names of those responsible for these outrages?"

"Of course," Liam nodded. "The leader's name is Fitz Meecham, and his—"

"What?" Reena asked. She again exchanged glances with her sister, but this time in absolute surprise. "Did you say Meecham? Fitz Meecham?"

"Yes. Why?"

"What is it?" Stone asked.

"Hunter . . . Vic . . ." Reena stuttered, "that's Lydia's father's name."

CHAPTER FOURTEEN

A Futile Ride

Early the next morning, Sergeant Stride drove the wagon with Reena, Megan, and Jenny as passengers, while Stone and Vickersham rode alongside with a troop of twenty men. The men had been hastily gathered and were more than willing to take the job. Andy Doe's death was still heavy on everyone's mind, and the mound of freshly turned dirt that covered Andy's coffin outside the fort was the object of many a glance as they pulled out of Fort Macleod. Colonel Macleod had made it clear he wanted no vigilante action or anything remotely close to it.

Stone and Vickersham had been allowed to lead the troop since the Meecham farm was only a few miles away. The news of Meecham's identity had spread rapidly through the fort, and the Mounties couldn't believe that the outlaw's home had been practically under their noses while the carnage had taken place. This knowledge rubbed salt in the festering wound caused by the death of Doe, and there were rumblings of revenge as they neared the Meecham farm.

Becker moved silently among the men, listening to their whispered comments and watching the surreptitious glances they aimed toward the officers in the front. Casually he guided his

167

horse in line with Stone, Vickersham, and Del. In his soft south-ern accent he murmured, "The men are really talking it up." Stone's reaction was just the opposite of what he expected.

"Let them talk. Can't say I blame them."

"You don't think there's anything to worry about, then?"

Del spat a long brown stream of tobacco juice, wiped his mouth, then offered, " 'Bout half of 'em are all talk all the time, anyway. The other half—"

"I'm serious, Del. This could be something more," inter-rupted Becker.

Del's jaw clamped around the wad of tobacco in his leathery cheeks as he cast an eye in Becker's direction. "Ain't you the smart snapper? Pardon me fer chewin' tobacco in your pres-ence."

"Del . . ." Vickersham sighed.

"Think about it, Bear Cub," Del continued to Becker, not unkindly, "do you really think any of those dandies back there are gonna go against what the colonel said, especially with Hunter and Vic here to make sure it don't happen?"

Becker shrugged his broad shoulders. "I guess not."

"You *know* not. End of conversation. And don't look at me like that, or I'll pin your ears back for you."

In the buckboard, Megan and Jenny sat in silence on the bench facing the rear of the wagon, gazing back the way they'd come. Reena rode in front beside Stride. Jenny was fidgety, shift-ing her weight and keeping her hands busy by toying with her fingernails. The day was cold and overcast, but no snow had fallen yet. Jenny's nose was red from the raw wind despite the fur-lined hood of her coat.

"Put your gloves on, Jenny," Megan told her. "Your hands are turning blue."

An argument came to Jenny's mind, but she realized that her hands *were* cold. Slipping on her gloves, she asked, "What are we gonna do if Lydia's father has done something crazy?"

Megan's eyes cut over to her, and Reena half turned her head back in their direction. Stride carefully kept his attention straight ahead. "Like what?" Megan asked.

"Like kidnapped them . . . took them away with him on those raids." Her face darkened. "Or worse."

"We don't know that, Jenny," Megan said. "There's no use worrying about things like that. Besides, I don't see how a man can harm his own family—" Megan stopped short, realizing her mistake. Jenny's hazel eyes swung around her way knowingly.

"I do."

Both Megan and Reena cringed inwardly. Jenny's father had had no qualms about harming his only daughter. Of course Jenny would worry about the same thing for Lydia.

"Timmy would try to protect her, but what can he do against a grown man?"

Megan patted her arm. "Let's just wait and see. Lydia and her brother are probably at home, safe and sound."

Jenny looked skeptical but didn't say anything more.

They traveled over gentle, snow-covered hills for another hour before Del stopped his horse at the front of the column. "Meecham's place is just over that rise."

Vickersham nodded, then sent five men back to stay with the wagon while they went forward to the edge of the rise. Stone, Vickersham, and Del dismounted and crawled to the edge until they could see the farmhouse and barn down below. Vickersham produced a spyglass and scanned the area for a full minute before handing the glass to Stone. "It looks deserted."

"Can't be," Del observed. "Who's taking care of that livestock and those horses down there?"

Stone tensed and said, "Someone just moved a curtain in the side window."

Vickersham turned and motioned for Becker, who crept forward. "We're splitting up. Divide the rest of the men. Sub-Inspector Stone will take one group around that way"—he pointed east—"to flank the house, and I'll take the other directly forward after Hunter is in position."

"Yes, sir."

"Becker, you go with Hunter."

"How close do you want me to get?" Stone asked.

"We'll converge in a pincer move. If one of us takes fire, the other gives the house everything they've got."

"There could be children in there, Vic."

Vickersham nodded, then said thoughtfully, "We've got to protect ourselves, Hunter. There's no other way."

"You boys don't worry," Del told them, "if there was a bunch of bushwhackers in that house, there'd be more than two horses. I think it's just the missus and the younguns."

The two units came closer and closer to the house with rifles at the ready. Upon seeing the approaching patrol through the window, Catherine Meecham came out on the porch with her two children, one under each arm.

With one last look around the landscape, Stone spurred Buck forward and both details met at the same time in the front of the house. Stone and Vickersham dismounted and walked to the porch steps, removing their helmets. Becker turned to the rise and waved Stride and the wagon forward.

"Good morning, ma'am," Vickersham greeted. "May I presume this is the Meecham residence?"

"You may," Catherine answered stiffly.

"May we have a word with you?"

Lydia had already spotted the women in the approaching wagon and suddenly ran into the yard among the stirring horses.

"Lydia, you come back here this instant!" Catherine called after her, but Lydia kept running. Among the horses and big men, she looked like an ant. "Timmy, go get her."

Timmy ran through the mounted troops slower than Lydia had, because he took time to admire the stamping horses, bright weapons, and scarlet uniforms.

"Hurry, Timmy!" Catherine watched him speed up, then looked at the Mountie officers. "What's this all about? If you're needing to confiscate cattle, help yourself."

Vickersham looked at her, surprised. "We're not the militia, ma'am. We're the Mounted Police, and we don't do that sort of thing."

"Then what do you want?" Her eyes skittered between them, then fell somewhere to their feet as she swept hair from her face.

"Is your husband around, Mrs. Meecham?" Vickersham asked.

"No." She didn't raise her eyes.

"May I ask where he is?"

"Why?"

"Because we're interested in talking to him," Stone informed her.

"About what?"

Stone shifted his feet impatiently. "I'm sorry, ma'am, but we're going to have to search your house." He turned and signaled Becker, who in turn nodded to three other men. Together they climbed the steps and moved past Catherine.

"I just cleaned today," Catherine told them, "please take care with your boots."

The men stopped and looked at her, then at one another. Becker nodded, and they stamped their feet before entering.

Vickersham asked, "Your husband is Fitz Meecham?"

"Yes."

"I'm afraid we have a warrant for his arrest. The charge is larceny and possible murder."

Catherine paled beneath her olive skin, swayed slightly, and gripped the porch frame.

Stone asked, "Have you ever heard of a man called Shadow La Belle?"

Catherine shook her head, suddenly looking very tired.

"James Coffin?"

"No."

"Rodriguez?"

She looked up briefly, then gripped the post harder. "I've heard the name."

"From your husband?"

"Yes."

"Mrs. Meecham, would you like to sit down?"

171

"Excuse me a moment," Catherine whispered, then went back inside.

Vickersham and Stone exchanged glances. "You don't think she's going after a gun or anything silly like that, do you?" Vickersham asked.

"Not with those men in there."

The men soon reappeared with Becker in the lead and Catherine behind. Becker shook his head. "He's not here."

Catherine marched up to Stone and held out a tin box stamped "Flannagan's Shaving Lotion." She stared at it like it was a coiled snake.

"What's this, ma'am?"

"Take it. What's inside doesn't belong to me."

Stone opened it and withdrew a roll of tightly tied currency. "I don't understand."

Lydia, Timmy, and the women walked up to the porch, and Timmy's eyes grew round as he spotted the roll of bills.

"My husband left that with me. If what you say about him is true, then it belongs to someone else. I don't want it in my house."

"You don't want the money, Mama?" Timmy asked. "Why not?"

Catherine gave Megan a pleading look.

Megan understood at once. This conversation was not for little ears. "Come on, kids," Megan told them, shooing them toward the corral, "show me your cows."

"But, Mama—"

"Go with Miss Megan, Timmy."

The boy went reluctantly, unable to take his eyes from the money until they'd rounded the corner of the house. Reena and Jenny went with them.

Stone handed the tin of money over to Vickersham. "Mrs. Meecham, do you know where your husband is? He's in very serious trouble."

"He went that way day before yesterday," she revealed, pointing to the northwest. "That's all I know."

"Is there anything else you can tell us? Anything at all that would be helpful?"

Catherine took a deep breath, then straightened to her full height. "I didn't know about this, but I suspected he got the money dishonestly. Does that make me guilty of what he's done?"

Vickersham said softly, "Of course not."

"I don't mean legally, sir. I mean morally."

Neither Vickersham nor Stone had an answer for that.

———

Fitz Meecham had set a meeting place for the gang after the battle with the Mounties on the Bow River. It was the day of Andy Doe's funeral—but he didn't know that, and if he had, he wouldn't have cared. He'd lost men, too. He just didn't know how many until he met up with Coffin and the others under a large, snowy embankment.

When Meecham saw Coffin, he knew the news wasn't good. Coffin's usual stony stare was flickering and unsure, as if he wasn't sure whether Meecham's appearance was good or not.

"Coffin," Meecham greeted as he got off his horse.

"Fitz."

Meecham nodded to a few other men before getting right to the point. "How many?"

"Gossett, Timerson, and Ott are dead. Newby, Pod, and O'Donnell are in jail and stand trial Monday."

Meecham swore under his breath and looked away. *Six men.* "Hear anything about the Mounties' casualties?"

"One dead and a few wounded, but not bad."

Shadow La Belle rode up and dismounted from scouting the area around them. After shaking Meecham's hand he said, "It didn't go as we planned. The Mounties are too well trained."

Coffin grunted. "It's no secret they'll come after us again, Fitz. Are you sure you want to—"

"It's the only thing I'm good at, Coffin. Why wouldn't I want to go ahead?"

173

"Because you're the only one with a family. The rest of us—nobody cares what happens to us."

"Do the Mounties worry you, James?" Meecham asked pointedly.

"Well, yeah. Don't they worry you? There's no telling how many they'll send out this time. Could be fifty."

"Fifty?" La Belle blurted.

"Or a hundred. Who knows? We killed one of theirs, and there ain't gonna be any mercy from now on." Coffin looked at Meecham, hesitated, then offered, "We could go down to the States for a while and let things cool off here."

"You running scared, aren't you, James?" Meecham asked with amusement in his eyes. "You afraid of dying? You don't think we can run circles around those Mounties for as long as we want?"

Coffin shrugged his shoulders. "We follow you, Fitz. What do you think?"

Meecham didn't answer immediately. Scanning his men—most of them were lounging around telling stories or playing cards—he set his lips in a tight line and nodded once. "I think we can do pretty much anything we please if we play our cards right."

"What about the boys in jail?" Coffin asked.

"What about them?"

"We gonna try to bust them out?"

Meecham smiled faintly. "James, sometimes you annoy me with your shallow thinking. You want to walk into a Mountie *fort* and try a jailbreak?"

"Well . . ."

"Well, nothing. That's insanity! Those boys are just going to have to fend for themselves."

"They'll hang, Fitz."

Meecham's cold black eyes fixed on Coffin. "Then they hang."

Liam and Pod played checkers on a table the guard had set up for them just outside their cells. It was awkward reaching through the bars to move the pieces, but they managed.

Pod was being uncharacteristically quiet. His movements were wooden, and his checker moves unthinking. Liam had already won three straight games. Even though Liam knew he was thinking about the trial in the morning, he couldn't stand the boy's silence.

"You're awfully quiet, Pod."

A pause. "Yeah."

"It makes me wonder what you're thinking. I usually don't have to ask, you know," he added with a grin.

Pod didn't see the smile because his eyes remained glued to the checkerboard. "It's your move."

Liam jumped one of Pod's black pieces. Jokingly he asked, "You can't play and talk at the same time?"

Without warning Pod sent the checkerboard flying with a quick upheaval. The pieces clattered against the far wall, and the Mountie guard looked up sharply. Pod glared at Liam. "I'm dumb, but I ain't stupid!"

"That's not what I—"

"Just because you got some fancy education don't mean you spit on other people, Liam! You ain't God, you know." He got up and paced the small cell in agitation. In the far cell, Newby sat on his bunk and watched in his usual silent fashion.

"Pod, I didn't mean—"

"When was you the happiest, Liam?" Pod asked, the anger suddenly gone. He stopped pacing and rubbed the back of his neck, waiting with alarming anticipation for Liam's reply.

"Well . . . I don't know," Liam stammered. "I haven't really thought about it."

"I have. I had a dog once—just a mutt. He showed up one day at our house and decided to stay there. I named him Soggy 'cause he loved for me to throw a stick into our pond, and then he'd go get it. He'd have done it all day if I'd had the time and energy. Even when I wasn't throwing the stick, I'd see him swimming. He was wet all the time, so I called him Soggy."

Liam waited for him to go on, but Pod had stopped to stare dreamily into empty air. To Liam's relief, they'd been let out of their cells and allowed a bath that afternoon. Pod had apparently forgotten about combing his thick hair, and now, after it dried, it stood out in every direction.

"You know," Pod continued, almost in a whisper, "I loved throwin' the stick for that dog."

Liam nodded but said nothing.

An hour later Reena and Megan came to visit Liam. They both looked tired, and Liam noticed smudges on their dresses— an unheard-of thing for Megan. He told them, "You two need to get some rest."

The Mountie brought them chairs and, with a scowl at Pod, began picking up the checkerboard and scattered pieces. He growled, "You can forget about the use of my board again."

Pod gave a half-laugh. "It don't matter. You're gonna hang us anyways."

Megan and Reena looked at him, shocked.

"Well, it's true, ladies! Ain't that right, Liam?"

"I said they *might* hang us, Pod."

"You said—"

"Pod, why don't you let me visit with my sisters, all right? Try to get some rest."

"Well, if they *don't* hang us, we'll be put away for so long that I won't have any teeth when we get out. That may be worse than having your head pulled off in a noose."

Megan gasped and Reena put a hand to her breast, looking sick.

"I'm sorry," Pod amended, then went to the far corner of his cell away from them and stared at the wall.

Liam shrugged and grinned crookedly. "Pod's a little . . . different." He watched his sisters exchange uncomfortable glances and said, "Reena, are you staying in town tonight?"

"Yes, at the boardinghouse with Megan."

"You don't have to, you know. What's going to happen has been predestined."

"Don't say that, Liam! You of all people should know that with God all things are possible. It may not be in His plan for you to go to jail."

Liam dropped his gaze. "I hope you're right."

"Doesn't he ever sleep?" Megan whispered, nodding at Newby.

Liam glanced over at the silent man who lay on his bunk staring at the ceiling. "I've never caught him at it. He's awake when I go to sleep and awake when I get up. You can't ask him about it because he never answers questions." He brought his gaze back to them. "Speaking of sleep . . ."

"Oh, are you tired?" Reena asked. "We can go. . . ."

"I was talking about you two. You both look exhausted. Why don't you go back to the boardinghouse? I'll be all right here."

"Will you really? You'll be able to rest?"

Liam chuckled without humor. "I doubt it. But I'm fine, really. I've come to terms with my stupidity, and I'm ready to face whatever comes."

Megan shifted in her chair, watching his face closely. "That's admirable, but I still see a frightened little boy in front of me."

"I'm not afraid, Megan. I'm sad. And I love you both dearly for being with me. I don't know what I'd have done if I'd had to face this alone. It's . . . it's unthinkable."

They were silent for a while, and Liam saw a tear roll down Reena's cheek. Chagrined, Liam remembered that there was more at stake here than his trial. "I'm sorry, Reena—and you, too, Megan—about the trouble with the men in your life. That shouldn't have happened, because I can see their point in all this. Why don't you give them another chance? They're just doing their job."

"We've talked about that," Reena told him noncommittally. "Oh, I almost forgot—we went to the Meecham farm today." She told him about missing Meecham himself and the horror

Catherine had felt when she had discovered her husband's criminal activities.

"You mean she didn't know?" Liam asked. "How can that be?"

"Some men are just good at deceit, I suppose."

"I can attest to that," Megan countered, referring to her own deceased husband's past actions.

"So Meecham's still out there," Liam said thoughtfully, nodding toward the window.

"Do you have any idea where he is, Liam?" Megan asked. "It would help your case if you could tell Colonel Macleod where the gang was going, or give their meeting place."

"No, I know nothing of their whereabouts." He looked over at Newby and asked him the same question, with predictable results: Newby turned away from them without a word. "I don't think Newby cares whether he lives or dies. I've never met anyone like him before."

Reena asked hopefully, "Do you think Meecham has left the country for good?"

Liam shook his head firmly. "Absolutely not. And even if he has, there's Coffin and the others to worry about. They're all the same—they like the money they make from selling that stolen livestock."

Megan sighed. "So the Mounties just have to wait?"

"Yes."

"Hunter and Vic aren't going to like that." She looked over at Reena. "Maybe you *should* go see him before he deserts and rides off with guns blazing."

Reena managed a smile. "If he does, Vic will be right behind him, trying to catch Buck's reins. I think Hunter would have been thrown out of the Mounties, or worse, if it weren't for Vic."

Liam noticed the animation that came into his sisters' eyes and voices when they talked about Stone and Vickersham. All at once, he knew that whatever happened to him, his sisters would be all right.

Surprisingly, he slept well that night.

CHAPTER FIFTEEN
The Trial

On the wall behind Colonel Macleod's balding head hung a portrait of Arthur French, commissioner of the North-West Mounted Police. French possessed a flowing mustache, heavy jowls, and a stern countenance. However, his likeness couldn't compare with the three-dimensional Macleod who had just taken his seat in his court to pass his judgment on the three men who sat in front of him.

Reena and Megan had hired an attorney from Fort Macleod to represent Liam. His name was T. Edward Malone, and the closest he'd ever come to a trial was to read about them in law school. His expertise lay in writing up wills, titles, and other incidental legal papers. Liam had laughed when he'd heard the man's credentials, but he had nodded and cooperated with Malone as much as possible. Despite Malone's inexperience, Reena and Megan felt better knowing that someone was watching over Macleod's rulings. Malone had been delighted to hear that Liam had cooperated with the Police and promised to push that to the limit in his defense.

After a constable read the declaration of the Mounties' right to hold court and to pass judgment in the Territory, he announced, "This court is now in session. The defendants, whose names are Jeffrey Newby, Liam O'Donnell, and Andrew Podolnaya, are hereby charged with assault and murder."

The attorney for the Police was a sub-inspector named Hall, who had the annoying habit of popping his knuckles. He was of medium height, with piercing blue eyes and black hair. He stood now and said, "Sir, I would like to call Sub-Inspector Jaye Eliot Vickersham to the stand."

Vickersham, sitting with Stone, Stride, Del, and Becker, stood and made his way to the witness chair. His hair was slicked back neatly, his dress uniform spotless. He sat down, glanced briefly over to Megan and Reena across the room from the Mounties, then fixed his gaze on Hall.

"Tell us, Sub-Inspector, of the events on January 31 of this year."

In a calm, precise voice Vickersham explained what had happened, from their finding Sanders gravely wounded at dawn to the Meecham gang attack on the Mountie troop. Not once did he take his eyes from Hall to look at the defendants or at Megan. Reena had never seen him so methodical and wooden.

When he was finished, Hall pointed to the defendant's table and asked, "Do you recognize those three men?"

"Yes. They're the ones Sub-Inspector Stone arrested following the engagement."

"Excuse me, Colonel," Malone interrupted, rising to his feet. A bookish-looking man, Malone was milking the moment of his first objection with glee. He gave Hall a condescending look, adjusted his glasses, and said, "This man isn't the arresting officer. Why are we hearing him speak and wasting the court's time?"

Macleod, who'd been listening intently to Vickersham, even though he knew every detail as well as anyone who'd been at the battle, pierced Malone with an incredibly intense gaze. "Mr. Malone, since you haven't been in court—" He paused ever so slightly. "Excuse me, in *my* court at any rate, I'll exercise my right to inform you that I do not allow objections in my court.

You may question the witness after Sub-Inspector Hall is finished. Until then, you will make notes and keep your mouth shut. Is that clear?"

Malone swallowed, the bravado gone. "Yes, sir."

"Sit down. Now, continue Sub-Inspector Hall."

"I have no more questions for this witness, Colonel. If the court pleases, I now call Sub-Inspector Hunter Stone."

Reena saw Stone's lips tighten. Her attention had been spotty and uneasy thus far, and as she'd listened to Malone's chastisement, she had looked over at Hunter. He sat ramrod straight, his eyes straight ahead. For all Reena could tell, he might have been sitting in a room all by himself, with no more noise around him than a fly might make. Sunlight streamed through a window on the other side of him, and Reena saw dust motes swirling around his head.

Macleod said, "Mr. Malone, *now* you may question Sub-Inspector Vickersham."

Malone stared back at the colonel with a blank look.

"Anytime, Mr. Malone. I believe you were concerned a moment ago about wasting this court's time. That, too, is my concern."

"Yes, sir," Malone stuttered, managing to gain his feet. "Um . . . what was it? Oh yes . . ." He again dug up that clever look from somewhere inside himself and pasted it on his face. "Sub-Inspector Vickersham, did you see this man firing a weapon?" He pointed at Liam.

"No. When I first saw him he was tied up."

"Unarmed?"

"Correct."

"No weapons of any kind?"

Macleod barked, "Mr. Malone, the definition of unarmed is 'having no weapons.' Move on!"

"Okay . . . I mean, yes, sir. Um . . . so . . . Sub-Inspector, did you see this young man firing down at you from that mesa? This man right here, sir."

"No, we were too busy dodging bullets to see who was firing

at us from above, one hundred yards away."

"So your answer is in the negative, is that right?"

Something flickered behind Vickersham's eyes but was gone quickly. "My answer is no."

"Thank you, sir. No more questions, Colonel." Malone beamed at his client as he sat down.

Vickersham and Stone nodded at each other as they passed. Stone took the chair and stared straight ahead. Hall had him confirm Vickersham's story, then asked, "Would you tell us what happened after you took Constable Becker and Sub-Constable D'Artigue and left the main troop?"

"We skirted the mesa through the riverbed, found a way to the top, and scattered the gang."

"All except these three men?"

"Yes, and one other."

"That man was killed in the ensuing skirmish, is that correct?"

"Correct."

"And you arrested these men, who were armed at the time, I imagine? Otherwise, you wouldn't have arrested them." Hall gave Malone a withering look but managed not to smile.

"They were armed. May I say something?"

Hall looked surprised. "Of course."

"The O'Donnell boy wasn't armed when I arrested him. He may have had a weapon during the skirmish and dropped it, but I never saw him aim a weapon at me."

Liam looked relieved.

Malone beamed.

Reena glanced at Megan, then dropped her head and put a hand to her mouth. Hall was so surprised at the ad lib, Reena was sure that Hunter had thrown the comment in without Hall's permission. When she raised her head again, Stone was looking directly at her, then he glanced away. In that moment, Reena thought she saw sadness in his eyes, though she didn't know why.

Hall finally found his voice. "Thank you, Sub-Inspector. Now, moving along . . . obviously, since the other two men were wounded and one of the group killed, you and your men were forced to deal with them in the strictest manner when apprehending them. Is that correct?"

Stone hesitated and looked over at Vickersham, who gave a nod of encouragement. Staring steadily at the back of the building, Stone said, "I felt there had been enough bloodshed for that day and wanted to put an end to it as quickly as possible."

"Very good, sir. I'm sure you and your men are to be commended for putting a stop to that action. That's all the questions I have for you, Sub-Inspector Stone. Mr. Malone?"

Malone rose, adjusted his glasses again, and asked, "Sub-Inspector, is it true that you almost killed Mr. O'Donnell in cold blood in his unarmed state?" Malone suddenly jerked back into his chair as if he'd been shot. Liam had gripped a handful of his coat and jerked with all his might. Malone looked at Liam in utter fear. Liam whispered something without moving his lips. Malone stared at him for a moment, then got to his feet again. Sheepishly he said, "I'd like to withdraw that question, Colonel. I have no questions for this witness."

Liam grabbed Malone's arm, pulled him down toward him again, and whispered something else.

Malone looked at Stone and gave him a sickly smile. "I would also like to apologize to the witness himself. I meant no dishonor to Sub-Inspector Stone, whose record is impeccable and speaks for itself."

"Very admirable, Mr. Malone," Macleod returned. "But it's been my experience that one's tongue is best kept in one's mouth rather than being trampled on. Next witness, please."

Dirk Becker was brought forward. To Reena he looked uncomfortable, and she wondered what he would have to add that Hunter and Vic hadn't already established.

"Constable Becker," Hall began, popping a knuckle, "you were riding beside Sub-Constable Andy Doe on that day, were you not?"

"I was, yes, sir."

"Would you describe what happened?"

Unlike Stone and Vickersham, who'd carefully avoided looking at Reena or Megan, Becker kept his eyes on Jenny Sweet, who was sitting beside Megan. Jenny smiled at him with encouragement, and Reena admired their simple communication.

"Andy was humming a tune, and the rest of us were getting on him pretty good. I started singing, and the next thing I knew Andy was shot. One second he was there beside me, the next . . . he was gone."

"And you were the first one to get to him in all the confusion?"

"Yes, I was."

"Was he still alive?"

"No. His wound was . . . was massive."

Hall moved to stand by the defendant's table. "Constable Becker, is there any doubt in your mind about where that shot came from?"

"Came from? It came from the mesa."

"You're sure of that?"

"Of course I'm sure!"

"There's no possibility that someone in your troop accidentally discharged his weapon before the attack?"

"That's ridiculous! Absolutely not."

"Thank you, Constable Becker. Your witness, Mr. Malone."

"I have no questions, Colonel."

Hall said, "I rest my case, sir," and sat down.

Macleod donned a pair of glasses and looked over his notes. With a cough, he peered over the glasses and asked, "Mr. Malone, do you have any witnesses before I pass judgment?"

"I have one, sir. I call Andrew Podolnaya."

Pod, looking so frightened that he appeared sick, took the witness chair. He licked his lips nervously, and his eyes skittered around the room constantly.

"Mr. Podolnaya—may I call you Pod?"

"Sure. Everybody does."

"Very well, Pod, I want you to know that you're not here to incriminate yourself. Do you understand?"

"Yeah."

"Now, you know Liam O'Donnell, don't you?" Malone asked, placing a hand on Liam's shoulder.

"'Course I do. He's my best friend."

Malone's face split into a grin. "That's wonderful. Could you tell me how you met him?"

Pod explained the story to the court of how Liam came to join Meecham's gang.

"And when Liam regained his eyesight, what did he want to do?"

"He wanted to leave."

"Leave the gang, you mean?"

"Yeah."

"Why didn't he?"

"He said that one of the men threatened to kill him if he left."

"Did you hear this threat?"

"Nope. But if Liam says it's true, it's true. You can count on that."

"So in your opinion, Mr. Podolnaya, Liam O'Donnell was forced to be there when this attack took place?"

"Yeah."

"Thank you. You may step—"

"I have a question, Colonel," Hall announced.

"Very well," Macleod nodded.

Without even bothering to rise from his chair, Hall asked, "Mr. Podolnaya, did Liam O'Donnell fire a weapon during the engagement?"

Pod looked over at Liam quickly, his mouth working. Liam nodded to him. "Well, yeah, but I don't think he was—"

"Thank you, Mr. Podolnaya."

"Wait a minute, I didn't finish—"

"I said, thank you, sir!" Hall cried.

"I don't think he was *aiming*—"

Macleod roared, "You may step down now, sir, with a closed mouth!"

185

Pod looked at Liam helplessly as he stood.

"Is that your only witness, Mr. Malone?" Macleod asked.

"Yes, sir."

"Very well. There will be a short recess while I make my decision. Sentencing will be in fifteen minutes."

The temperature outside hovered around the zero mark, so most of the spectators stayed inside. Megan, however, wanted some air. "It's probably just nervousness, but let's step outside, anyway."

Reena pulled her coat around her tightly as the chilly wind hit her. The activity level in the fort was almost nil, but two unlucky Mounties were struggling with a stubborn mule by the stables.

"What do you think, Reena?"

"About Macleod's decision?"

"Yes."

Reena shrugged, then shivered. "He's such a strict man, I don't even want to think about it. Maybe I'll be pleasantly surprised."

"Me too."

The door opened, and Vickersham came out. He glanced up at the gray sky and smiled. "Beautiful day for catching some air, eh?"

"Hello, Vic," Megan said.

"I'll make this quick, since we don't have much time. I'd like to have dinner with you tonight, if possible."

Megan hesitated. "Well . . ."

"Or would you rather wait until we hear the colonel's judgment?" he asked, not revealing whether he was joking or not.

"Vic, that's not fair!"

"Then what's your answer?"

"My answer is yes. I will have dinner with you tonight."

"Thank you. Six o'clock, then." He glanced at Reena and touched the tip of his hat. "Reena."

After he'd gone back inside, Megan gave Reena a puzzled look. "Was I just tricked into having dinner with him?"

Reena smiled. "I think so, but have a good time, anyway."

"Would you have said yes if Hunter had asked?"

"I don't know. It would be . . . awkward." Truthfully, Reena was hoping for that exact thing: to have the opportunity to make a choice if he asked to see her. However, knowing Hunter the way she did, Reena knew she would probably have to go to him.

"We'd better go back inside," Megan told her.

Reena looked for Hunter and saw him standing with Becker and Jenny. He might as well have been standing alone for all the attention he was paying to them. Reena watched his strong profile for a moment as he gazed out the window and wondered what he was thinking. Suddenly he turned and looked right at her. For some reason, Reena blushed and averted her gaze, then Colonel Macleod entered the room.

Without looking at Hunter again, Reena went back to her seat and sat on the edge of it. She tried to read Macleod's face, but it was stoic as usual.

"Will the defendants please stand?" he asked, removing his glasses and fixing them with an unwavering stare. After a pause, he said, "Jeffrey Newby, did you think this court wouldn't find out that you are an escapee from the United States prison system?"

For once, Newby's expression registered something other than boredom and sullenness. His mouth dropped open, and a noise escaped from him that was a combination grunt and gasp.

"Your real name is James Niles, and you, sir, are a convicted murderer. I sentence you to hang by the neck until dead."

Newby's gaze fell to the floor and locked on it in shock.

"Andrew Podolnaya," Macleod continued, "you are a young man who has made some very bad choices. Due to the seriousness of this crime, I have no choice but to sentence you to the maximum penalty of twenty years hard labor, to begin immediately."

Pod didn't move, and his face was completely neutral.

"Liam O'Donnell, due to your friend's testimony, which I've taken under consideration in my deliberations, I have to say that

I'm disappointed in you. I doubt that means much to you, but I feel the need to say it. The word foolish comes to mind, mixed with a little bad luck. However, I would be remiss if I didn't mete out some sort of punishment since you fired your weapon in the engagement. Although there is still the shadow of a doubt that you *were* firing at my men, I sentence you to five years in the penitentiary."

Reena and Megan both gasped. After Pod's testimony, Reena was almost certain that Macleod would let Liam off with a warning or a short stay in jail. But five years!

Liam turned and looked at them, and Reena saw the saddest expression she'd ever seen on his face. Hunter, too, was looking at her. Reena didn't know what her countenance told him, but his face softened.

Reena watched her brother being led away. Megan asked her something, but the blood was rushing through her ears so loudly she didn't hear it.

————

Late that night, Vickersham woke Stone when he came in after seeing Megan. Stone rolled over, squinted at the lamplight he'd left burning, and asked, "How did it go?"

"Very well, actually," Vickersham replied as he got undressed. "Megan's an understanding woman—when she wants to be."

"Did she say anything about Reena? How she's taking the judgment?"

"She says Reena didn't say much. They went to see Liam after the trial, then Reena went back to the Blackfoot."

Stone sat up on the edge of the bed and rubbed his face. He had wanted to say something to Reena, but after the verdict she had appeared unapproachable. Something in her face . . .

"You should have talked to her, you know," Vickersham said. "It wouldn't have hurt to just talk. Maybe she would have been as understanding as Megan."

"Megan's not angry?"

"Oh, I'd say she is a bit, but she knows five years in prison is a whole lot better than what Newby's getting."

"Newby's a murderer."

Vickersham's eyebrows raised. "You don't agree with our distinguished colonel's decision?"

"Not really. I think Macleod went overboard on this one."

"Megan told me that Liam wasn't sad so much at his sentence, but that he would have a criminal record and could never get back into West Point, which is what he wants. A little late for that now."

"Vic?"

"Yes?"

Stone looked at him, hesitated, then said, "I've been thinking all night. I've got an idea."

"Oh no."

"Oh yes."

Vickersham said hopefully, "But I have no responsibility in this idea whatsoever, right?"

"I need your help."

Sighing deeply, Vic murmured, "That's what I was afraid of."

PART FOUR

THE NOBLE HEART

The noble heart, that harbours virtuous thought, and is with child of glorious great intent, can never rest, until it forth have brought th' eternal brood of glory excellent.

Edmund Spenser
The Faerie Queen

CHAPTER SIXTEEN

Strength in Weakness

The next morning before sunrise Del burst into Stone and Vickersham's room carrying a lantern that was much too bright for the sleepy officers.

"They struck again! Let's go after 'em!"

Vickersham rubbed his eyes. "What?"

Stone bounded out of bed and immediately began dressing.

"Meecham's gang has gone and—"

"Del, where are your pants?" Stone asked suddenly.

"Forgot 'em." Del had on his bearskin coat, but underneath he wore only his underwear and boots. "Git up, Vic! It takes you forever to wake up."

Vickersham managed to sit up. When he placed his bare feet on the floor, he gasped. "What time is it?"

"Dark thirty."

Stone finished dressing and asked, "Does the colonel know about the attack?"

"Does he know? He came into the barracks screamin' for Stride and Becker about thirty minutes ago. You know him—he never sleeps, anyway."

"Why didn't he wake us?"

"Told me to. Wants you in his office as soon as Sleeping Beauty here can manage it."

Stone was already heading for the door. As he passed Del he said, "Put your pants on, Del."

"I intend to! Just got in a hurry, that's all."

Vickersham snickered as he pulled on his boots.

"What are you laughin' at?"

"Nothing."

Del continued to watch Vic suspiciously as he tucked his shirt into his trousers. "I'll bet it galls you that you don't have time to shave, huh?"

"It's most uncivilized."

"Thought so."

"There's a touch of glee in your voice, Del."

"No, there's a whole passel of glee in it."

Vickersham quickly ran a comb through his hair and turned to Del. "Do I look presentable?"

"Oh, you're pretty as a peach. Let's go."

Macleod's meeting didn't take long. He was excited and wanted a troop to leave as soon as possible. Vickersham looked questioningly at Stone, who shook his head slightly. Now wasn't the time to put forth his idea.

While preparations were being made and dawn was breaking in a cloudless sky, Vickersham saddled his horse and rode to the boardinghouse. He didn't know if Megan was awake, but he wanted to see her before they left.

Mrs. Howe, who ran the establishment, answered the door when he knocked. She grinned, revealing bad teeth, and said, "Why, Vic, what are you doing here so early in the morning?"

"I came to see Megan. Is she up and about yet?"

"I'm right here," Megan said, appearing behind Mrs. Howe. "Come in, Vic."

She led him to the parlor off the main hallway, and they sat down. Vickersham admired the fact that she was already prepared for school, even though it was still two hours away. Her dark brown dress was freshly pressed, and her hair was tied back with a ribbon like a little girl's.

"What are you smiling at?" Megan asked.

"Just the world in general, and you in particular," he replied, sitting beside her on the sofa.

"You're much too happy for this time of morning."

He rubbed the whiskers on his face and told her, "I have to make up for my shoddy appearance by grinning, I suppose."

"Vic, you're not growing a beard, are you?"

"What if I were?" he teased.

"I'd make you shave it off, that's what."

"You don't like beards?"

"No."

"Why not?"

"I just don't."

Vickersham nodded slowly, scarcely breathing. She was so beautiful—the very essence of loveliness. On impulse, he took her chin in his hand and turned her face toward him. Gently he kissed her and was pleasantly surprised when Megan put a warm hand against his face. Vic felt a powerful sense of joy rising inside him. When she pulled away, he softly planted one last kiss on her cheek. "I thought about you all night. I don't think I slept an hour."

"I thought about you, too."

"Did you?"

"Yes."

Vickersham looked out the window at the daylight growing steadily stronger and reluctantly told her, "I really need to go. I just wanted to see you before I left."

"Where are you going?"

"Meecham's struck again."

"Oh no!"

"We leave within the hour."

"Where? Was anyone hurt?"

"No. Thank God there were no casualties this time. They just ransacked a house and stole some valuables somewhere around the Belly River."

Megan laid her head against his shoulder. "Be careful, Vic."

"As careful as I can be on this kind of mission. You can pray that we catch these scoundrels before they strike again."

"I will, and I'll pray for your safety, too."

"Thanks." The lovely fragrance of lilac rose from her hair, and Vickersham wished he didn't have to leave.

"Are Hunter and Dirk going?" Megan asked.

"Yes. Will you tell Jenny and Reena?"

"Of course," Megan answered, walking him to the door.

Turning and taking her hands in his, Vickersham looked into her beautiful brown eyes and said, "I'll miss you."

"And I you," Megan whispered.

Vickersham's horse must have sensed his master's elation, because he galloped swiftly back to the fort.

———————

When Reena woke that morning, her first thought was of her brother. She'd never known anyone doomed to a prison sentence, much less one of her own family. The thought sickened her, leaving her no appetite for breakfast. The knowledge that she had to write their father that day with the news didn't help her queasy stomach in the least.

She wondered if Hunter was feeling as bad as she, and with a twinge of guilt found herself hoping for just that. "Forgive me, Lord," she whispered as she boiled some water for coffee. "And forgive me, Hunter."

Jack Sheffield had been asleep when Reena returned the night before. He'd wanted to stay for the trial, but Reena had begged him to return to the Blackfoot village the day of Doe's funeral. She didn't want to be out of touch with the tribe for more than a day, and it had already been two. It was strange but encouraging that lately the Indians had been so inquisitive about the Bible that they came to her with questions nearly every day.

When she'd seen that Sheffield had gone to bed for the night, she'd found herself disappointed. He was easy to talk to and a great listener, and Reena had felt the need to talk about the horrible day. Instead, she'd gotten ready for bed and prayed until she'd fallen asleep. Somehow her prayers had seemed unimaginative and wooden, which disturbed her so much that she shed tears before drifting off. Now, this morning, she didn't feel much better.

Shaking her head and slapping her face lightly, she told herself, "I will *not* get depressed," over and over again until she heard Sheffield call her name outside the tepee. Moving to the flap, she opened it to bright sunshine and a smiling, handsome man.

"Good morning, Reena. I saw that the wagon was back and wanted to see how things went yesterday." His smile vanished as he spoke, and with concern he asked, "Are you all right? You look exhausted."

"Come in, Jack. I've got coffee on."

He came inside and sat against a backrest by the fire. Somehow Jack's clothes always managed to appear spotless, even though he sat on the ground much of the time.

Sheffield accepted the mug of coffee she offered. "The news about your brother must not be good."

Reena told him.

"Five years? As a lesson? That Macleod doesn't show much mercy, does he?"

"I'm writing my father today, and I'm sure he'll send one of his attorneys up here to straighten things out. There must be an appeal process."

"I'm sorry, Reena."

"Thank you."

"What about the other two men? Or should I say the other man and that poor boy."

"Newby is going to hang. It turns out he's a fugitive from the States and wanted for murder. Pod gets twenty years hard labor."

Sheffield sipped his coffee thoughtfully. "Twenty years," he breathed. "Poor kid."

Without warning, Reena began crying. Sheffield watched her helplessly for a moment, then moved around the fire and tentatively put an arm around her shoulders. Reena let her head rest against him as she asked tearfully, "Why did this happen, Jack? Liam never hurt anyone in his life!"

Sheffield didn't answer. He gently stroked her arm, then took her hand with his free one.

"It's not fair!" Reena cried, lifting her face. She was shocked to find Sheffield's concerned features only inches away. Amazed and unable to move, she watched as he covered the short distance slowly. "I . . . wait. . . ." She felt his lips on hers and froze. "No!" she pronounced, leaping to her feet.

"Reena, I'm sorry, I—"

"You *should* be sorry!"

"I . . . I don't know what came over me! You don't have to ask me to leave, I feel . . . terrible!" He stood and hastily brushed off the seat of his pants.

When he looked at her, Reena saw that he really was repentant. In his eyes was a mixture of fear and disbelief.

"Jack . . ."

"I'm sorry, Reena. I'm so sorry. Can you please forgive me?"

"Yes."

"I know you just needed a friend, and I've gone and spoiled it. Now you've lost trust in me."

"Jack, it's all right."

"It makes me sick, knowing that . . . that you think I would take advantage of you, because I assure you I'm nothing like that—"

"I know, Jack."

"However, I do care deeply for you. I know that may come as a shock, since we haven't known each other that long, but I do care for you, and I can't hide it anymore."

Reena stared at him, speechless.

"I don't *want* to hide it anymore. It's too painful." He stuck his hands in his trouser pockets and glanced away. Reena was reminded of a little boy.

"Well, Jack, I . . . I don't know what to say."

"You don't have to say anything."

An uncomfortable silence ensued, until Sheffield finally asked, "Is there anything I can do about your brother's predicament? Write a letter . . . something?"

Reena sighed heavily. "How are you at jailbreaks?"

"Sort of rusty."

"Seriously, I don't know what you can do, Jack, except pray."

"That I can do, and will."

They talked for a while more, the awkward moment filed away in both of their heads to think about later.

———

Del had no trouble finding the farm in question on the Belly River late that afternoon. What made him angry was that the tracks leading away from the farm completely scattered about a mile from it.

"They went off in all different directions, Hunter," Del mumbled. "They split up and left, every one of 'em."

Stone, hatless, with the strong wind blowing his hair, looked at Vickersham with a frown. "I can't believe this."

"Any suggestions, Del?" Vickersham asked.

"Yup. We go back to the fort."

"What?" Stone asked. "Are you out of your mind?"

"Hunter, listen. Those tracks go off in ten different directions. Now, these boys"—he nodded in the direction of the thirty-man troop—"are all good men in a scrap, but most of 'em couldn't track their way to their own shadows, much less to these wily scoundrels we're after. What do *you* wanna do?"

Stone looked at Vickersham. "I think it's time to implement my plan."

Vickersham nodded.

"What plan?" Del asked.

"We'll tell you about it later," Vic told him. "Right now it's too late to head back. We'll make camp here. Go tell the men, will you?"

Stone looked out over the rolling river beside them. Here and there he saw fish darting about beneath the surface. He realized he was chilly, since the sun had gone behind the Rockies, and he put on his helmet.

"We'll catch them, Hunter," Vickersham assured him. "It's just a matter of time."

"It's *been* a matter of time already. We've just got to be waiting for them the next time; there's no other way."

Later that night, after Stone had taken a walk along the river, he returned to find Vickersham and Becker talking by one of the fires. Between them was an open Bible. Stone had often found them studying together, and he felt a pinch of jealousy that his best friends shared something in common that he had no knowledge of. He thought about trying to find something else to do, like check on the rest of the men, but most of them were already asleep. So slowly he sauntered over to the fire.

Vickersham was saying, ". . . so I had this huge resentment against my older brother because—sit down, Hunter. You look as if you could use some cheer."

"Always. What was that about your older brother? He's the one in line for your father's earldom, isn't he?"

"Yes. I was just telling Dirk how much I despised the fact that he would inherit all the lands, property, and titles just because he was born two years earlier than me."

"Doesn't seem fair, does it?"

"Well, in all honesty it *isn't* fair. But the point is, I thought I'd left my resentment in England when I came here. Seems that wasn't the case, though."

"What do you mean?"

Vickersham thought about it, sucking on his lower lip. "I mean, since I've become a Christian I've found myself thinking back on the matter, and not fondly. It's like a rat sitting inside me, gnawing the injustice around until it's back into my head. I've had to rely on Christ's help to get rid of it."

Stone hesitated, then asked, "And have you?"

"I think so, yes."

As they'd been talking, Stone noticed that Becker was staring at him intently. "What is it, Becker?"

"Vic and I were discussing resentments. I was just wondering . . . how do you . . . um . . . how do I ask this?"

"Just ask."

Obviously reluctant, Becker shifted his position and finally asked, "Do you still feel resentment over your wife's death? Toward Red Wolf, I mean?"

Stone looked away, unwilling to meet either man's scrutiny. The question had totally surprised him.

"Because you see, I think I know how you feel. I was thinking about it a few days ago. I lost my father and brother in the war, then my mother so soon after that it seemed she might as well have been killed in it, too. I was so angry at the circumstances— I even think I was angry at them, too, as unfair as that sounds."

Stone stared into the fire as he heard the pain in his friend's voice. He knew exactly what Becker was talking about.

"So," Becker continued, "I was just wondering how you handle all those horrible feelings? I have the love of God to lean on, and I can truly say that I've come to terms with the loss of my family and its consequences. Can you?"

"I don't want to talk about this," Stone said in a clipped voice.

"Why not?" Vickersham asked. He leaned forward until the firelight was full on his concerned face. "We're friends here, Hunter. No one's going to judge you—"

"Look, I'm not part of your camp meetings, or whatever you call it when you two sit down around a fire with your Bibles." Stone could hear the petulance in his tone, and it disgusted him. "It's not me."

"It could be," Becker pointed out simply.

"Give it a try, Hunter," Vickersham urged.

"Give what a try?"

"The Christian life."

Stone looked away quickly and stretched out his legs in front of him. Their strange, intense looks were making him more and more uncomfortable. So did the question. "Oh, I don't know, Vic. What would God want with me?"

"That's not the question, Hunter," Vickersham said gently. "You need Him a lot worse than He needs you."

Stone shook his head slowly. "It's time to turn in, gentlemen."

"Come on, Hunter," Becker pleaded. "You can't keep avoiding it."

"I said it's time for bed, Dirk," he shot back more roughly than he'd intended.

Becker hesitated, nodded to himself, and stood. "Good night, then." As he passed Stone he patted him on the back good-naturedly.

Stone glanced across the fire at Vickersham. "What are you looking at?"

"A very stubborn man."

"Oh, not you, too!"

"We're just concerned about you, Hunter. You're in a dangerous job, and you could get killed at any time. I don't think you'd like where you go afterward."

"Let it go for now, Vic."

Vickersham nodded, got to his feet, and headed for their tent. At the flap, he turned and said, "You're going to let it go one day too many, my friend. God can't help you then."

Stone stayed up another hour, staring into the purple night around him.

CHAPTER SEVENTEEN

Escape

Colonel Macleod almost fell out of his chair. "You want me to what?"

Stone cleared his throat. "I . . . we"—he glanced pointedly at Vickersham beside him—"request that you—"

"I *heard* you, Stone. That was a figure of speech. Do you think I'm daft or something?"

"Absolutely not, sir."

"Well, you must if you think I'll go along with that idiotic plan of yours."

Stone's hopes were sinking fast. He'd expected resistance but nothing like what Macleod was exhibiting.

"Sir, may I say something?" Vickersham asked.

"Speak!"

"If I may be so bold, Colonel, we can't see any other way to catch Meecham. If he's going to pull this tactic of splitting up after every raid, there *is* no other way."

Macleod rose slowly from his desk chair, his face thunderous. "In case you gentlemen have forgotten, I sentenced those two boys to prison time. There's no way I'm going to revoke my judgment and set them scot-free!"

203

"But you see, it's not scot-free, sir," Vickersham explained. "It's a second chance for them, not to mention that it's also dangerous. If Meecham finds out that Pod and Liam are there only to lead the gang to us, he'll kill them without blinking!"

"Which part of the word *no* do you not understand?" Macleod demanded.

Stone made a disgusted sound and spun for the door.

"You haven't been dismissed, Stone! Come back here!" Macleod placed his hands on his desk, palms down. "Now listen to me, gentlemen. This may very well be a good idea, but so far I can't see it. What makes you think those boys *deserve* a second chance? Maybe the O'Donnell boy does, but that other one—he's bad news waiting to happen. Podolnaya's too dumb to have enough sense to stay out of trouble. If I let him go, he'd light out for the border so fast he'd leave burn marks in the snow!"

"With all due respect, sir, I don't think that's so," Vickersham argued. "He's infatuated with Liam and wouldn't leave his side unless Liam told him to. Maybe not even then."

"How do you know Meecham will take them back?"

"Why wouldn't he?" Stone asked. "If we stage a jailbreak and let out the news that they outsmarted us, Meecham would hear about it."

Macleod winced. "Podolnaya outsmarting us? I can't think of a more noxious piece of information to release to the public, Stone."

"We could say Liam did it, and Pod followed along, sir. The point is, would you just consider it for more than a heartbeat? There is honestly no other way to catch these men."

Macleod slowly sank back into his chair with a sigh. Stone sensed an opening and decided to play his last card. "Colonel, Vic and I would stake our reputations on those boys doing the job. You could hold us personally responsible and deal with us in any way you wish if they run off."

Macleod's dark eyes went from one of them to the other in surprise. "You really *don't* see any other way, do you?"

"No, sir. That's what we're trying to tell you."

"Give them a chance, sir," Vickersham asked. "If this all worked out, wouldn't it be nice to have the satisfaction of knowing that you helped two young men to the right path in life?"

Stone struggled to keep from smiling. James Macleod was a good man overall, but he did carry around a very healthy ego. Vickersham was playing on that, and Macleod didn't even know it.

Macleod made a face. "But there's no precedent for this! If something went wrong, how would I justify my actions to the Commissioner? Or to the Canadian government, for that matter?"

"It won't go wrong," Stone said slowly with confidence.

Macleod tapped his finger on the desk over and over, then scratched his balding head. The agony on the man's face made Stone feel sorry for him. But then he remembered Reena, and how he'd never seen such a look of sadness and despair cross her face as when Macleod read Liam's sentence. Liam seemed like a good sort, and Stone wanted him to have a way out of the next five dreary years behind bars. Pod was another matter; Stone only wanted him free so he could watch Liam's back.

Macleod looked up. "Word of this fake escape must be kept only in this room."

Stone and Vickersham nodded eagerly, relief washing over them.

"I don't want to be signing those boys' death warrants by someone letting the plan slip to the wrong ears."

"How do we go about accomplishing the escape, sir?" Vickersham asked.

Macleod held up a hand. "That's your problem. By looking at Stone's face right now, I'd say he's already got a plan, and I don't want to know about it."

Stone looked at Vickersham and winked.

Liam and Pod stared through the bars of their cells in disbelief. Stone would have been amused at the twin open mouths if the situation hadn't been so serious.

Vickersham, standing beside Stone, tapped the bars with his knuckles. "Don't you chaps have anything to say to our offer?"

"How come you trust me?" Pod asked.

Stone stepped right up to Pod's cell and locked eyes with him. "I don't like it, but we have to. Do you understand the gift we're giving you, Pod?"

"You're givin' me a present, too?"

"No, Pod. The gift is your freedom if you can give us Meecham. Also, you wouldn't be thinking about running away when you get out of here, would you?"

Pod's eyes grew round, and he swallowed with an audible gulp. "No, sir!"

"Because if you do, I'll hunt you down—and I *will* find you—and then Colonel Macleod would hang you for sure. So don't disappoint us."

"I won't. You can count on me. Can't he, Liam? He can count on me!"

"Sure, Pod."

"You can count on ol' Pod."

Stone smiled at him briefly, then said, "You need to take care of Liam, Pod. Do you understand? You say he's your best friend, and best friends always watch each other's backs."

Pod's face split into a grin. "Oh, don't worry about that, Mr. Stone. I won't let anything happen to Liam. Remember, you can count on ol' Pod."

"Good." Stone turned to Liam. "It's the best we could do for you."

"May I ask *why* you're doing it?"

"Well, it's not just to get back in your sister's good graces, I can guarantee you that."

"I'm sorry. I didn't mean to imply that."

Vickersham explained, "It's the only way to catch the gang. You're our only hope, actually."

Liam nodded slowly. "I really appreciate it—I mean, I really want the chance to make amends for not doing more that day to stop them." He looked at Stone. "And I'm sorry that my coming here has caused trouble between you and my sister. I never meant any harm to anyone."

"I know."

"So what do we do now?"

Stone explained their plan.

———

Early the next morning as Jenny and Megan were getting ready for school, Megan was unusually quiet. Jenny watched her brush her hair in front of the dressing table mirror, then asked, "Is something wrong, Megan?"

"No, not really."

"You can tell me. I won't tell no one."

"Anyone."

"Sorry—*anyone*."

Megan stopped stroking her hair and considered the brush. "I wish you'd look at this. I'm losing my hair faster than a middle-aged man."

"No, you're not! I mean, there's some hair in that brush, but look at what you have left. Your hair's so beautiful, Megan. I wish mine were that pretty."

Megan looked up at her. "Yours is growing out nicely—it's practically the same color as mine—so your compliment is appreciated and can be turned right back around to you."

"Now, see, you did it again!" Jenny claimed. "When I asked if you were all right this morning, you changed the subject then, too. I told you what was bothering me in the schoolhouse the other day. Now it's your turn."

Megan smiled and resumed brushing her honey-colored hair. "Have you ever had something hit you with such clarity that it—"

"What's clarity?"

"Clearness . . . purity in its truth."

"Okay."

"With such clarity that it astounds you? Something that . . .

that hovered just outside your realization, and then suddenly makes itself known out of the blue?"

Jenny stared at Megan's reflection in the mirror, her brows beetled.

"I'm not making any sense, am I? How about if I just say it— I'm in love with Jaye Eliot Vickersham."

Jenny let out a whoop and flung her arms around Megan's neck from behind. "That's wonderful, Megan! That's so . . . *right*. Everybody thinks so."

"What? What do you mean everybody?"

Jenny looked away sheepishly. "You know—everybody. Everybody who knows you two, anyway. You're just perfect for each other. When are you getting married?"

"Married! Why, Mr. Vickersham doesn't even know about this."

"So tell him."

"Jenny, you can't just tell a man that! He has to say it first."

"He does?"

"Yes."

"Why?"

"Well . . . that's just the way it is."

"Says who?"

"Why . . . it's just . . . everyone just *knows* that, Jenny."

Jenny thought for a moment, then announced, "It sounds like a stupid rule to me."

Megan laughed. "Nobody said it was a smart one."

"What happened, Megan?" Jenny asked excitedly. "When did this *clarity* hit you? I like that word."

Megan put down the brush and pulled her hair back to tie it.

"Leave it down today, Megan. It's so pretty when it's down."

"All right." Megan turned her chair around, and Jenny sat on the edge of the bed a few feet away, her eyes shining. "You know Vic and I went to dinner the other night. I was feeling so down about Liam and was really sorry I'd agreed to see him. But as we talked, he kept the conversation away from the trial. He talked about beautiful things like England, his family, anything but what had happened that day. It was just what I needed at the time."

"It sounds wonderful!" Jenny breathed.

"Then, the next morning after you'd already left for school, I was thinking about him and wishing I could see him *right then*. And you know what? Within a few minutes he was knocking on the door."

"No!"

"Yes. It was like he knew what I was thinking, and there he was."

Jenny put a hand to her neck. "How romantic! Is that when you knew how you felt about him?"

"No," Megan grinned, blushing slightly. "It's been something that's been growing for a long time, but I didn't recognize it. Then he kissed me in the parlor."

"In the parlor!" Jenny gasped. "Of this house? Mrs. Howe would throw you out if she knew!"

"Well, she's not going to know, is she? Anyway, when Vic kissed me, it suddenly hit me that this was where I belonged. This was a man with whom I could trust my love and my life. That's when I knew that I loved him."

Jenny suddenly fell back on the bed with a deep sigh. "A knight in shining armor. You're so lucky, Megan."

"And your bloomers are showing—but thank you, Jenny. Your knight will show up one day, you can be sure about that." Jenny didn't answer. "Or maybe he already has?"

Jenny put a hand to her mouth and giggled. "Oh, Megan, you never give up—"

The door burst open and Reena stepped through. Her hair was a tangled mess, her face flushed, and she was out of breath.

"Reena!" Megan cried. "What are you doing in town?"

"Haven't you heard?"

"Heard what?"

"Liam and Pod escaped last night!"

"Escaped! How?"

"I don't know the details. One of the Blackfoot braves heard

209

about it early this morning while getting supplies. Oh, how could Liam be so stupid?"

"This is bad," Jenny murmured. "This is *real* bad."

Megan shot out of her chair. "Come on. Let's go to the fort and find Vic."

————

Liam and Pod had been furnished with mounts, pistols, and coats by Vickersham. D'Artigue had the unfortunate luck of being the one humiliated and tied up to lend credibility to the escape plan.

The two young men rode along the rolling prairie toward the Milk River Canyon where Meecham had found Pod in the first place.

"Mr. Meecham likes to travel through there whenever he can," Pod had informed Liam. "If there's one place we can meet up with him, it's there."

Liam listened to Pod's usual banter, which seemed to be coming at an even more rapid-fire pace since he was so excited about being free. But Liam's mind was on the mission ahead—a very dangerous mission, he knew. Liam didn't fool himself into thinking that his chances were good in coming out alive. Meecham and Coffin were the most feral men he'd ever come across, and he mentally calculated that his probability of survival was fifty-fifty at best. The necessity of his having to lie and deceive weighed gloomily on his mind—not because it was immoral, though that did bother him, too, but because he knew he was so poor at it. Convincing Meecham and Coffin that he really wanted to lead the desperado life was going to be difficult and would require all of his acting skill. The coiled nest of nerves in his stomach was growing with every mile. For relief, he tuned into Pod's chatter.

"That French Mountie sure was nice, wasn't he, Liam? He didn't even act like he minded being tied up."

"Oh, he minded all right."

"Really? How do you know?"

"Until this whole thing is settled and the truth of the matter comes out, he'll be treated as having been incompetent."

"What's in—incom—"

"Incompetent. The other men will think that he's not very good at his job."

Pod looked horrified. "Why, that's not right! He didn't do nothin' wrong."

"That's just the way it is."

"Poor feller."

"Pod, listen to me. Are you sure you understand everything we're supposed to do? It's very important that you ask me questions now if you have them. Our lives may depend on it."

"I think I got it, Liam. We're supposed to pretend, right?"

"That's right. You've really got to fool everyone into thinking that we really escaped by ourselves and want back into the gang. Can you do that?"

"Sure I can. I like playing pretend."

Liam glanced over at him, saw his simple smile, and said sharply, "This isn't a game, Pod! Don't you see? If we can't convince them, they'll kill us!"

"All right, Liam. I won't smile no more."

"You can smile if you want to," Liam said, shaking his head.

They rode all day and into the night. Pod knew the countryside better than Liam had expected and had no problem guiding them to the canyon. They made camp under the same outcropping where Liam had awakened to snow blindness, which had set into motion the devastating events that had landed him in this predicament today.

Pod grew quiet after their supper. The night turned cold, and they huddled close to the fire, using the horse blankets for covers.

Something occurred to Liam, and he said, "Pod, I never thanked you for your testimony at the trial. That meant a lot to me."

"Aw, it was nothin'. Besides, all I done was tell the truth."

"Still, it was nice of you."

After a small silence, Pod asked, "Liam?"

"Yes?"

"Do you think they've hung Newby by now?"

"Probably. It was scheduled for today."

"Funny how he never talked, huh? I wonder if he had any last words before they sprung the trap?"

"I don't know. They say some pretty hard men break down like babies at that moment."

Pod stirred the coals in the fire with a stick. "I don't think Newby would, though. He always seemed like he was somewhere else other than where he was at the time. Does that make sense?"

"I think that describes Newby pretty well."

"I expect he went to that place in his mind and never felt that noose jerk."

"Maybe so."

Liam grew tired soon after that and stretched out by the fire. Pod continued sitting cross-legged, staring into the crackling flames. Just as Liam felt sleep tugging him down, Pod said wistfully, "Ol' Newby's dead. I'll always wonder if he had any last words."

CHAPTER EIGHTEEN

Reunited With Danger

Vickersham was leading a troop of thirty men out of the fort when Megan, Reena, and Jenny arrived in a wagon. Surprised, he nodded at Sergeant Stride to take over and rode over to the women.

"Good morning, ladies—" he began.

"Tell us, Vic," Megan said abruptly.

Vickersham didn't have to ask what she was talking about. However, he was unprepared to give an answer, and Macleod's warning about keeping everything a secret flashed through his head.

"Vic?" Reena prompted.

To stall for more time, Vickersham casually dismounted, removed his helmet, and smoothed back his hair. With a heavy sigh he said, "Liam and Pod bashed D'Artigue in the head and took off." *It's not a lie, really*, he told himself, *it's just not the whole truth*.

The women stared at him for a moment, stunned at the bald statement.

"And where are you going with all these men?" Megan asked.

Vickersham moved to her side of the wagon and gazed up at her. "To find them."

"Do you know where they went?"

"No, but Del can track them."

"Did they steal horses?" Reena asked with obvious trepidation.

Vickersham looked away. He was a horrible liar and knew it. They were asking questions that he knew would be forthcoming if they confronted him, and he suddenly wished the troop had left one hour earlier. This only made him feel more guilty.

"What's wrong, Vic?" Megan asked. "Is there something you're not telling us?"

Megan's beautiful brown eyes locked with his, and he knew he couldn't carry off the sham. "Listen to me. There are things happening . . . that . . ."

"What is it?" Megan asked with impatience.

Reena glanced around at the passing troop. "Where's Hunter?"

"He already left. Late last night."

"To go where?"

"Reena . . . Megan . . . I really can't discuss this, it's—"

"Liam is our brother. I think you *can* discuss it." Megan said, her eyes flashing.

"No, it's not like that." Vickersham shook his head in frustration. "I've got a troop of men to lead. I really need to go—"

"Vic!" Megan cried, hastily stepping down from the wagon seat. "Please come over here."

Vickersham followed her to stand beside a lodgepole pine. When she faced him, he didn't see anger as he expected, only concern.

"My brother is in serious trouble, and you're speaking in riddles. We're very worried, Vic. Please be straight with me. I won't tell them if you don't want me to, but you've got to give me the truth." She placed a hand on his arm. "I deserve that, don't I?"

Vic smiled and nodded. "Yes, my dear, you do. This is going to be a shock, but here goes. We arranged Liam's escape so he could lead Meecham to us. We weren't having any luck finding him, so—"

"You *arranged* his escape?"

"Yes."

"And in the process put him in more danger by having him go back to that killer?"

"Well . . ."

"Vic, how could you?"

"He agreed to it, Megan. If he and Pod pull it off, they'll go free."

"And if they don't, they're dead."

Vickersham shifted his feet uncomfortably. Reena and Jenny were watching them from the wagon, and from Reena's look he could tell she knew that her sister didn't like what he was telling her. Vic sure didn't want *both* of them angry at him. "The boys are in some danger, yes. But this is an opportunity for them to make right what they did wrong. Liam's smart, Megan. He'll get them through it."

"Liam's smart, but Pod could get them both killed with a careless remark." Megan shook her head. "Did you come up with this brilliant plan?"

"No."

"It was Hunter, wasn't it?"

"It doesn't matter, Megan—it's done."

"I should have known it was him. Reena's never going to speak to him again."

"Then she doesn't have to know. Let him tell her after it's over."

"When will it be over?"

"In a matter of a few days, hopefully. Pod and Liam have to find Meecham first." He reached out and brought her chin up with one finger. "He's going to be fine, Megan. I promise."

"I'm scared, Vic."

Taking her in his arms, he whispered, "I know. Just pray for all of us."

"I will."

Stone, Becker, and Del Dekko worked at greasing the axles of the wagon they had brought to Pakowki Lake, one hundred miles east of Fort Macleod. The lake flowed into the Milk River valley, and the area was crisscrossed with various drainage channels, some of them dry. Here and there stood large formations of hard sandstone sculpted into strange shapes by wind and rain erosion. To Stone, they seemed to be sentinels of the prairie.

The day was overcast and cold with the promise of snow hovering in the crisp air. Del blew on his hands to warm them, looking enviously at the Mounties' wool gloves. Del's had holes in them from time and use. Hawking and spitting, he complained, "This just don't make no sense to me, Hunter. Here we are, just waitin' around, with a perfectly good opportunity to take naps, and you have us workin' on this wagon. What's the idea behind that?"

Stone was applying grease to the right rear axle with a stick. Grinning, he looked up at Del and said, "Working keeps you warm, Del. You should try it sometime."

"I been workin'! I's just takin' a break, that's all."

"For twenty minutes? Hand me that wheel hub."

Del dutifully handed him the hub, then blew on his hands again. "That thing's cold! Everything's cold. Sure be glad when spring gets here." Remembering the subject he'd broached, he said, "Seems to me that bein' wrapped up in a blanket inside a tent is a dandy way to keep warm, too. Didn't you ever think of that?"

"Sure."

"Then why—?"

"Give me a hand with this, Del."

Sighing deeply, Del squatted down and hammered the wheel hub onto the axle. With each stroke, his cold hands ached unmercifully. "Waste of good nap time, if you ask me," he grumbled.

"How are you doing over there, Becker?" Stone called to the other side of the wagon.

"Just about got it," came the answer.

"You need Del to come over there to help?"

A snicker. "No, thanks."

"What was that?" Del asked indignantly. When he didn't receive an answer, he called, "I'm talkin' to you, Bear Cub!"

"What was what?" Becker returned.

"That noise you made—I heard it. Didn't you hear it, Hunter?"

"What noise?"

Del gave the hub one more blow with the hammer, then threw it down to rub his hands vigorously. Fixing Stone with a glare, he said, "You two are havin' me on just like you and Vic do. I won't have it."

Becker stood up on the other side of the wagon, bending backward and groaning. "What are you going on about, Del?"

Del transferred his squint to the young Mountie. "You know exactly what I'm talkin' about, and I hope that axle falls off that stump and pins one o' your feet. Then you'd be in more trouble than a man with a wooden leg in a forest fire, 'cause I wouldn't spend the energy walkin' around this here wagon to free you."

"You're just a charmer, Del."

"I'm gonna charm you all right—with the butt end of a pistol."

They finished putting the wheels back on, then began to work on the front axles. Del chattered on but helped both men without complaining too much more. Stone kept looking around for signs of riders, even though he knew it was too early for Pod and Liam to have done their job. It could be a week before they met up with Meecham. The prospect of spending a week by the lake in the cold wasn't too appealing, and he mentioned it to Becker.

Del was horrified. "What? A week? Are you crazy?"

Stone shrugged. "It's in the hands of those boys, Del. There's nothing we can do but wait."

"Why, Liam's just a baby! And that other one, offer him a penny for his thoughts and you'd be more than liberal. He'd stick his head in an oven to get a baked bean!"

"They'll do their best."

Del stuck his hands in his coat pockets and looked depressed. "Well, I'm just a scout. Seems to me that since I've got you boys to this here lake, I'd just as well head back to the—"

"You're staying here, Del," Stone told him. "With us."

"Why? You don't need my gun, that's fer sure. Hunter, you can outshoot any man I ever saw, and the Bear Cub here can throw knives faster than I could empty a six-shooter. What do you need me here for?"

Becker slapped him on the back. "Because we enjoy your cheerful company."

Stone and Becker laughed, while Del sulked and mumbled something unintelligible.

They fed the horses, then set up the tent for the night. A herd of white-tailed deer wandered by, and Stone took one of them down with his Henry rifle. They feasted on venison and beans for supper.

After they had cleaned up and settled by the fire, Becker produced his Bible and began reading. Del sharpened a small knife, and Stone chewed on a piece of wheatgrass and stared into the flames. He missed Reena more than he could have imagined, and the strength of his longing disturbed him. He was almost sorry he hadn't let Liam go free back on that fateful day. Was his love for justice really more important to him than his love for Reena? Wasn't there something wrong with that? Yet he had to uphold the law.

He shook his head and shifted his position on the ground. Betsy crossed his mind, and with a stab of guilt he found himself comparing her with Reena. Betsy would have understood and supported him. Quickly he pushed the thought from his mind.

Somewhere on the other side of the lake, a coyote howled mournfully and was answered by another much closer.

"I hope he had his dinner already," Del commented. "Sure

would hate to be et by a coyote."

"What *would* you like to be eaten by, Del?" Becker asked, winking at Stone.

"A bear, I guess, if I had to choose."

"Why a bear?"

Del suddenly snapped his fingers at Becker. "'Cause you'd be dead like that. Take a coyote or mountain lion. He might wanna toy with you, kinda take a bite here and there, not carin' if you were dead or not."

Becker shuddered. "How do you think of these things?"

"A bear, now, he wouldn't want you rollin' or writhin' around and hollerin'. I think bears like their meals dead."

"And just how would you know that?"

"I don't know. They just seem like the type. When you're that big and strong, you can have things pretty much as you want them. I admire that." Del paused, dug around in his teeth with a fingernail, then sucked them noisily. "Yep, I wouldn't mind bein' a bear. Nobody's gonna argue with what you do. You're just free and easy to have things your way, you know?"

Becker stared at him a moment, then asked, "And if you could have things your way as a human, what would you do? What would you change?"

Del shrugged. "I don't know."

"Would you get married?"

"Good heavens, no! Whatever gave you that idea?"

"Just asking."

"Naw, I'd just end up with several little mouths to feed and one big one to listen to. No, sir, that ain't me."

The fire popped suddenly, and they all twitched. The coyotes called to each other again in their howling exchange.

"I'd want children," Becker said softly, absently thumbing the well-worn pages of the Bible in his lap. "As many as she'd allow, anyway."

"What would you do with a bunch of kids?"

Becker chuckled deep in his throat. "Love them, Del. Love them and teach them how to be good adults."

Del considered him a moment, then shook his head and turned to Stone. "How 'bout you, Hunter?"

"What?"

"Weren't you listenin'?"

"Would I want children?"

"Yeah."

Stone took the blade of grass from his mouth and threw it in the fire, watching it catch the heat and wither away to nothing. "I've never been around children, but I think I'd like them."

"Is that a yes?"

"Yes. I'd like to have children someday."

"Well, if you two don't beat all," Del drawled. "I'm sittin' here with would-be family men. Shooee!"

" 'Be fruitful and multiply,' Del," Becker teased.

"That's ridiculous. I'm too old and set in my ways. I know that'll break a lot of hearts, considerin' how handsome I am."

The three men laughed, and for a while Hunter Stone forgot about the ominous reason they were there.

And about Reena.

———

Liam and Pod didn't have to wait long before Meecham found them. The gang showed up in the late afternoon the day after the boys arrived.

Pod spotted them first. He was sitting on the edge of the canyon, tossing rocks down the grade and howling gleefully as they bounced. The higher one ricocheted into the air, the more he enjoyed it. Liam was getting tired of Pod's simpleton ways, but thoughts of that vanished when he saw the boy suddenly twist his head around, drop the rocks, and leap to his feet to face south.

"Here they come, Liam!"

Now that the moment had arrived, Liam felt a twist in his belly and wished that he'd lectured Pod more about their deception. Watching him on the lip of the canyon, Liam had the uncomfortable feeling that Pod was actually *glad* Meecham was coming. Doubts swirled through Liam's brain like a swarm of angry bees. What if Pod wanted to join Meecham again and betrayed Liam? Could he have fooled Liam and the Mounties that way? Was he that smart?

Liam licked his cold lips and began making his way up to Pod. He hoped he worried for nothing. Pod, in his simple way, really liked some of the men in the gang and was just glad to see them. If Liam was wrong about that and his doubts proved true, he wouldn't live long enough to worry about it, anyway.

Liam had forgotten how cold Fitz Meecham's gaze could be. He looked more tired than Liam remembered, but the force of his presence hadn't diminished. Almost every man held his gun on Liam and Pod as they rode up to them.

"Hi, Mr. Meecham!" Pod waved excitedly. "We escaped! How 'bout that?"

Meecham and Coffin exchanged glances, then Meecham fixed his black eyes on Liam. "What are you doing here?"

"Waiting for you," Liam replied. He forced himself not to look away from Meecham.

"Ain't you glad to see us, Mr. Meecham?" Pod wanted to know. Dejection was heavy in his tone, and Liam knew he wasn't acting.

Neither Meecham nor Coffin said anything. Meecham wouldn't take his eyes from Liam. Coffin held his pistol easily in his hand, arm draped over the saddle horn. Liam noticed that it was aimed in his direction, not in Pod's.

"La Belle?" Pod asked beseechingly. "Ain't *you* glad to see me?"

The dark-featured Shadow La Belle glanced at Meecham before drawling, "Sure, Pod."

The boy beamed. "That's good, that's good. How 'bout you, Trace? Surely *you're* glad to see me. I saved your bacon one time, remember?"

"I remember, Pod," the man named Trace answered. He had an unfortunate deformity on his upper lip that caused him to look as though he was constantly sneering. "It's good to see you."

"Thanks."

Meecham asked a question that made Liam realize that, as far as Meecham was concerned, no one had spoken since he had: "My question was aimed at you, O'Donnell. I asked what you were doing here."

"I told you, Mr. Meecham—waiting for you."

"I thought you didn't have the stomach for this kind of work."

"With all due respect, you were wrong. Besides, what do I have to lose? If they catch us, they'll hang us. I might as well make some money before I head back to the States."

"That's what you thought, huh?" Coffin asked in his gravelly voice. "You thought we'd take you on again?"

"Well, sure. Why not?"

"Because you're both about as hot as a two dollar pistol. Those Mounties are probably combing the countryside right now for the two of you."

Liam didn't know what to say to that. It had never crossed his mind that Meecham wouldn't take them back. If he didn't, then what would he and Pod do?

"They hung Newby, Mr. Meecham," Pod announced solemnly.

"I heard."

"Did you hear if he had any last words?"

"Nope. Just heard they hung him."

"Too bad, huh?"

Meecham shrugged. "Every man who rides with me knows the consequences." He was still studying Liam intently, as if gauging his motives.

Coffin said to Meecham, "We can't take them on, Fitz."

"I know."

Liam's heart skipped a beat, and his mind was frozen with doubt. He knew he should say something, but he couldn't think straight. To his surprise, Pod could.

"We got a surprise for you if you take us back, Coffin."

"What kind of surprise?"

Pod was obviously bursting to please them, but he managed to look sly and whet their appetites. "You'll like it a lot. A *whole* lot."

"What is it, Pod?" Meecham asked irritably.

Liam was glad the man's attention was finally focused elsewhere.

Chest swelling up with pride, Pod told them grandly, "Them Mounties got a pay shipment comin' in two days from now."

Meecham and Coffin only stared back at him in silence, but most of the other men exchanged glances.

"How do you know this?" Meecham finally asked.

"We heard 'em talking, didn't we, Liam? In the jail they were talking about it. They haven't been paid in a while, and they were grumbling about having to wait till Friday."

"Where's it coming from?" Meecham asked Liam.

"Dufferin. We figured if they're expecting it Friday, that means we could hit it on the prairie before it gets there. We even know the route they're taking."

"Where?"

"Why, we can't tell you that, Mr. Meecham," Pod said. "Then you could just kill us and take the shipment yourself."

Liam was glad Pod hadn't betrayed him and was going along with the plan. At that moment Pod looked over at him and actually winked. Liam cringed inside.

"What are you winking at?" Coffin asked.

"I'm . . . I was . . ."

"He winks at me all the time," Liam smoothly broke in, surprising even himself at how calm he sounded. "Pod likes to get approval, as you already know. Ever since we escaped, he's been excited with wanting to tell you about this opportunity."

"Yeah, that's it!" Pod agreed. "That's why I winked at him. Liam's my best friend. I like to wink at him."

Liam prayed for Pod to shut up.

Meecham glanced at Coffin, who shrugged. "It's your call, Fitz."

With seeming reluctance, Meecham finally nodded at Pod. "Go get your horses, Pod."

"Yes, sir!" Pod crowed and raced down the canyon.

Meecham dismounted and walked over to Liam. Eyes again boring into him, he said, "If this is some sort of trick—and I'm not convinced it's not—you'll be the first to die. You know that, don't you?"

"It's not a trick."

Meecham turned to the side and spat. "You heard me. You'll be the first to die. Don't forget that."

Liam nodded, wishing he could take a step back from the man. "I understand."

CHAPTER NINETEEN

A Deep Sadness

The trek to Lake Pakowki was a nightmare for Liam. Meecham, ever suspicious, never let Liam out of his sight. He even insisted on sleeping near him.

Then there was the constant fear that Pod would say too much or let something slip. The first night, Liam managed to get him alone and whisper, "Pod, hold down your chatter, will you? You can talk all you want after this is over, but for now just try to keep it down."

"Why, Liam?" He was chewing on a prairie chicken leg, and his voice was garbled around a mouthful of the meat.

"Because I don't want you to give anything away by mistake."

"I ain't gonna do that!"

"I know you won't intentionally, but I think it would be better if you didn't talk so much right now. Okay?"

"Okay, Liam."

The next day Pod was so quiet that Liam spotted a few men glancing at him strangely. One of them asked if he felt all right, and Pod just nodded and grunted, "Yup."

Liam was sorry he'd said anything, but he didn't have a

chance during the day to tell Pod to act naturally. Even if he could have, it probably would have just confused the boy more.

Toward the end of the day, Meecham startled Liam by speaking to him. He'd been his usual silent self, talking only to Coffin a few times during the ride. It started to snow at dusk, and Meecham suddenly asked, "What was the most interesting thing you learned at West Point, O'Donnell?"

It took Liam a moment to register the fact that he'd been spoken to. Then his mind raced to find the meaning behind the question, but he couldn't come up with the answer. Finally, he just answered truthfully. "Stonewall Jackson's valley campaign in the war, I guess. It was incredible."

Meecham nodded and pursed his lips. "Wasn't he the one who said, 'It's good that war's so terrible, else I'd like it too much,' or something like that?"

"That was General Lee."

"What did he mean by that?"

"His army had just won a fantastically one-sided victory at Fredericksburg. I suppose he was just feeling confident and exhilarated."

"Do you think it's true, what he said?" Meecham's eyes swung around and pierced Liam with their intensity.

Liam shrugged. "I've never been in a war."

Meecham was silent for a while, then murmured, "I think it's true."

"You were in The War between the States?"

"Nope. I just think it's true."

Liam didn't pursue it, and Meecham seemed content to return to his normal silence. The man was strange and obviously unbalanced, which only made Liam's stomach turn more flips.

The closer they drew to Lake Pakowki, the more nervous Liam grew. He wanted to ask Meecham what he had planned but didn't want to risk making him more suspicious.

They continued riding after nightfall, and Meecham sent two men ahead to scout the area and look for signs of the pay wagon.

At one point Coffin turned and asked, "How are you so sure they'll be around here?"

"Because I looked at a map. If they're due at the fort on Friday, that would put them right around here at this point, unless they're late."

But Liam knew they wouldn't be late, and he knew that the showdown could be as soon as the next morning.

The group of men moved as silently as shadows through the snowy night, with only the occasional squeak of saddle leather as evidence of their passing. When the scouts returned, they appeared as ghosts in front of them, and Coffin almost fired on them.

"You boys better let out a yell next time," he growled.

One of the scouts was Rodriguez, and after giving Coffin a sour look, he told Meecham, "They're about a mile back that way, camped."

"How many?"

"Well, it seems strange, but there's only three."

"Three!" Meecham cried, showing more emotion than Liam had ever seen from him. He looked at Liam pointedly. "Three?"

Coffin remarked, "Those Mounties are even dumber than we thought."

Liam shrugged and tried to look innocent. "I only know what we heard, and they didn't say anything about how many were in the guard. I guess they've never been robbed and don't think they will be."

Meecham's hat brim was pulled down low and, combined with the darkness, his eyes were hidden. But Liam could feel the weight of them on him. "You remember what I told you when I took you on. If this is a trick . . ." He turned to Coffin. "We camp here, then take them at first light."

———

Reena stayed with Megan and Jenny at the boardinghouse rather than going back to the Blackfoot village and worry alone. She and Megan felt totally helpless and useless concerning their brother's fate, and that fact had made them both tense and sleepless. Megan couldn't keep the secret about Liam's escape from her sister, and when she told her, Reena's reaction wasn't what she expected.

"It's for the best, I guess," Reena said after a hesitation.

"You're not surprised?"

"Of course I'm surprised! I'm just saying that it's probably better for Liam to take this risk in order to get his life back."

"Reena, he could get killed! I can't believe you're not upset."

Reena sighed and her shoulders slumped a bit. "I'm tired of being upset—with Hunter and Vic, with Liam—I just want things back the way they were. I'm not going to be mad at Hunter anymore. You were right. He's just doing what he thinks is best." She gave a small shrug. "I love him, even though I don't agree with him sometimes."

On the night that Meecham's men reached Lake Pakowki, Reena was more restless than ever. The lack of sleep was making her irritable, and the more she tried to drift off, the more frustrated she became when she failed. Finally, she slipped on a robe and tiptoed downstairs for a glass of milk. When she reached the bottom of the stairs, she was surprised to find a lamp burning in the kitchen.

Megan was standing at a window, gazing out at the falling snow.

"Megan? What are you doing up?"

"What are *you* doing up?" she returned without moving.

Reena sighed and walked over to the icebox. "The same thing you are, I guess. Worrying."

"A lot of good it's doing us."

Reena poured some milk into a coffee cup and took a huge sip. "Are you finding any answers out in that snow?"

"I was just thinking about the men sleeping out there. You know they're cold, even with fires burning."

"I try *not* to think about that. I'd suggest you do the same."

"It's a wonder they're not battling pneumonia all the time."

Megan moved away from the window and sat down at the small preparation table in the middle of the room.

Reena joined her, slumping down in the chair with a groan. "I feel as if every muscle in my body's been overworked, yet I haven't done anything."

"It's exhaustion. I feel the same way."

Reena noticed dark smudges beneath her sister's eyes, made deeper by the unforgiving lamplight. She wondered if she looked the same and decided that there was no reason why she wouldn't. The thought depressed her. Taking another sip of the milk, Reena suddenly giggled and nearly choked.

"Don't go crazy on me, Reena," Megan told her without smiling.

"I was just thinking about our situation."

"And you laugh?"

"Think about it. Here we are, two genteel Chicago girls in the wilds of Canada with our fugitive brother out there somewhere who might get shot by one of the men we love."

"Why would they shoot him?" Megan asked, horrified.

"I didn't mean intentionally. I meant by accident."

"And you thought that was funny?"

"That was an ironic chuckle, filled with fear and dread. It was either laugh or scream."

"I would have screamed."

They didn't speak for a while, and Reena restlessly spun the coffee cup round and round on its bottom rim.

"Do you have to do that?" Megan asked with irritation.

Jenny appeared in the doorway, startling them both.

"Not you, too?" Reena asked.

Jenny silently moved to the table and sat down with a heavy sigh.

"What is it, Jenny? Are you worried about Dirk?"

Still Jenny didn't speak, and when she finally looked at them, her eyes were hollow with fear. "I don't know how to pray. I think that even if I did, it wouldn't carry as much weight as yours. Would one of you pray for them?"

Megan and Reena exchanged glances. Reena knew that her sister was thinking the same thing as she: *Why didn't we think of that?*

The three women joined hands, and Reena and Megan prayed for the men out in the cold, the snow, and the dark.

———

Del was snoring loudly while Stone carefully sharpened his saber. Becker, as usual, read his Bible by the lamplight. All men wore every article of clothing they'd brought with them to counter the cold. The singing of the sharpening stone against the saber was sharp in the spacious tent. The saber didn't need sharpening, but Stone was beyond boredom and yet couldn't sleep. The slow, easy motion of sharpening relaxed him somewhat and kept his hands busy.

"Did you know," Becker suddenly related, "that what I'm holding in my hands is more powerful than what you're holding in yours?"

"Becker, don't you get tired of preaching to me?"

"No. But see, I don't think of it as preaching. I think of it as sharing."

"So why don't you share with someone besides me?"

"I do. I just haven't been around anyone but you lately. You seem kind of defensive, Hunter. Am I getting to you?"

Stone smiled lightly. "You're too much sometimes, kid. And stop calling me Hunter."

Becker looked over at the snoring Del, then back. "But it's just you and me here."

"Doesn't matter. I've told you a hundred times that if you get in the habit, you might do it in front of the men."

"So what! Now, you tell me . . . what would be so bad about that happening? Would the earth open up and swallow me whole? Would lightning strike me dead?"

Stone stopped his sharpening and looked at his friend. "No."

Laughing, Becker pointed his finger at Stone and said, "You need to lighten up . . . if I may be so bold as to say so, sir."

"All right, that's enough. Point taken. I don't really care for my friends calling me sir, anyway."

"You see? That wasn't so hard, was it? How'd you get to be that way in the first place?"

Stone began honing the blade again. With guilt, he realized that he was relieved the conversation had been turned from whatever point Becker was going to make from the Bible. It made him uneasy to talk about it. "What way?"

Becker searched for words, his mouth working. "So . . . well, you know. Strict, I guess is the word. You act like the world would end if someone broke a rule or something."

"Maybe it would."

"See? Even when you're joking, you're serious."

"I don't know, Dirk. I've always been this way, as far back as I can remember. Growing up, I wouldn't let any of the boys break the rules in our games. I was always the one to call someone down on that point. Didn't make me very popular, but I couldn't stop doing it. I got it from my mother, I think."

"Was she strict?"

"Not strict so much as unbending. Once something got in her head, it was there forever. If a job needed doing, she wouldn't rest until it was completed."

"That sure sounds familiar. What about your father?"

"He was a quiet man. With my mother's strong personality, I barely noticed he was around." He stopped and ran his thumb very lightly along the gleaming blade, then whistled in a low tone. "You could chop a tree down with that edge."

"Oh, that reminds me," Becker stated, going back to his Bible.

"Becker—"

"Just listen, Hunter, it'll be interesting to a mind like yours."

"I don't quite know how to take that—"

"Listen to this: 'Above all, taking the shield of faith, wherewith you shall be able to quench all the fiery darts of the wicked. And take the helmet of salvation, and the sword of the Spirit, which is the word of God. . . . ' " Becker looked up at him,

231

grinned, then held up the Bible on his open palm. "Behold, the sword."

"And who are you supposed to slice with it?"

"Evil. Satan," Becker returned, as if the answer were obvious. "It's the only weapon a Christian has, but what a weapon."

"Does it work?"

"Of course it works! I wouldn't believe in Christ if it didn't work."

"Get some sleep, Dirk."

Soon after Stone blew out the lantern, he heard deep and even breathing coming from the younger man's direction, even over Del's snoring.

Stone stared at the dim glow of the tent's white roof for a long time, thinking about the weapon God had given to His people.

———

Liam didn't sleep all night. A few times he actually thought of making a run for it, despite the fact that he would be a fugitive forever and never be able to see his family again if he did so. He knew it was fear of what would happen in the next few hours that caused the crazy thoughts, yet it didn't change the truth—he was scared to death of the unstable Meecham and the equally frightening Coffin. Both men slept near him, and all through the night Liam imagined Meecham's dark gaze on him, though he couldn't see the man's face. He knew he would have nightmares about Meecham for the rest of his life—if he lived, that is.

Even though Liam tossed and turned through the night, he was surprised when he saw Meecham stir from his blankets. Unlike other nights when Liam was plagued with insomnia, this night had flown past. He briefly wondered how Meecham seemed to know that it was just before dawn. It was another eerie thing about the man that confounded Liam.

The men were mostly silent as they prepared to leave. Through the gloom Liam saw Pod throw him a glance while they were saddling their horses, and Liam saw the same fear and uneasiness that he was feeling. Liam nodded at him, hoping to instill confidence he himself didn't feel, but he didn't think Pod was fooled.

"Get mounted, O'Donnell," Liam heard from above and behind him. He turned to find Meecham already on his horse, glaring down at him. Liam finished tightening the saddle cinch and climbed up on the bay mare he'd been given by the Mounties.

"Just one thing," Meecham said, then he reached out and withdrew the pistol from Liam's belt.

"Oh, come on now, Mr. Meecham—"

"If those Mounties try anything, they're plenty outnumbered. I'd just feel better if I held on to this until after the job is done." The dark eyes glittered in the growing light of dawn. "If this goes smooth, you'll be well rewarded—with both money and my goodwill. So you don't have anything to worry about."

Liam could think of nothing to say, but he noticed that no one took Pod's pistol from him. *Oh, God, please just get me through this*, he prayed silently. *I'm so tired of being scared.*

Meecham sent a man ahead again to make sure the situation hadn't changed. Liam shivered as they started off; the morning was dawning with no sign of clouds in the sky, but during the night the temperature had dropped severely after the snow stopped. As they rode along at a walk to give the scout time to get back to them, Liam tried to ease his horse back from Meecham and Coffin, but the two men sagely kept step with him until Coffin said menacingly, "What's the matter, O'Donnell? Hopin' we don't get there?"

"No," Liam returned innocently, pretending he didn't know what Coffin was talking about.

"Maybe you're giving them Mounties a chance to get away?"

"What's the problem, Coffin?"

"If your horse slows down any more, we'll be standin' still."

Liam let the slack out of the reins, and the mare returned to her normal gait.

The scout appeared an hour later. "They're still there—just

the three of them. Looks like they're breaking camp, getting ready to move."

"At the gallop, Fitz?" Coffin asked, anxious to prevent their money from escaping.

"No, we'll just come up on them normally and hope they don't get alarmed."

"Twelve men appearing out of the blue? Of course they'll get alarmed."

"I said no, James."

"All right. It's your show."

When Liam spotted the Mounties—one of which wasn't even in uniform—he wondered how they were going to prevent Meecham from robbing them. Did they plan to let him take the money, then catch them later? That wouldn't make any sense, since they'd be right back where they'd started with Meecham roaming the countryside. Liam scanned the whole area in front of him for signs of extra men but saw none. It still wasn't fully light, but he thought he'd be able to see the scarlet jackets if there were more around. Then the Mounties spotted them moving toward them, and he saw Hunter Stone stiffen. The other fellow with him was the one who liked to play with knives, but Liam couldn't recall his name. Becker, that was it. Neither Stone nor Becker seemed alarmed that a gang of men was almost upon them. They stopped striking their tent and watched them approach.

"Mornin'," Meecham drawled as they pulled up around the wagon. Liam managed to maneuver his horse so that Coffin was between himself and Meecham.

"Morning," Stone nodded.

"You boys having some trouble out here?"

"No. What makes you say that?"

"I thought maybe your wagon had broken down. Thought we'd see if you needed some help."

Del Dekko stepped forward, his Remington rifle in hand, pointed casually to the side. "That so?" His eyes were on his counterpart, the scout Shadow La Belle, who had guided them into the trap at the mesa.

"What are your intentions wiz dat rifle, monsieur?" La Belle asked.

"Intentions? To shoot me a varmint, I expect."

La Belle looked around at the snow-laden ground. "I believe all ze prairie dogs and muskrats are safe and warm in their dens dis morning."

"I'd say not all the varmints," Del maintained, with obvious meaning.

Liam saw Stone's eyes pass over him but didn't see any sign that Stone wanted him to do something. Liam wasn't armed, anyway, but with the heavy coat on he was sure Stone didn't know that. What was he supposed to do right now?

"We appreciate you stopping by," Becker told Meecham, "but we're fine. We'll just finish packing up now."

"I don't think so," Meecham shot back.

"I beg your pardon?"

"You can beg all you wanna, but your plans and mine differ slightly. What's in that strongbox in the wagon?"

"Supplies. Documents," Stone answered.

"Must be pretty important supplies and documents."

"That's why they're in a strongbox."

Meecham gazed down at Stone for a moment, then asked, "Haven't I seen you before, friend?"

Stone shook his head, once. "I don't think so." He wore the Adams pistol holstered around his coat, with the saber sheathed on the other side. Liam wondered if he was actually going to try to take all these men with only those weapons. Becker was similarly armed.

"Mmmm. You sure look familiar." Meecham nodded at the wagon. "Let's us have a look inside that box."

"Nope."

Meecham considered him calmly. "Look, mister, it ain't no skin off my nose. You can either lose that lock by this man here"—he nodded at Coffin—"shooting it off, or you can reuse it later by unlocking it."

"I don't have the key."

"Well, that's mighty unfortunate." Meecham glanced around, then pointed at Liam. "You recognize that boy?"

"No. Should I?"

"You've never seen him before?"

"I've never seen any of you before," Stone said, becoming irritated. "Are you going to point out each man here and ask if I've seen him before?"

Del snickered, then spat.

Meecham's eyes narrowed. Without taking his eyes from Stone he called, "Pod, open up that strongbox."

"Me? Why me, Mr. Meecham?"

"Just do it, boy!"

"Yes, sir. I just thought you said Coffin would—"

"Shut up, Pod." Meecham nodded at the three men on the ground as Pod pulled his horse up to the wagon and jumped down into the bed. "You fellas ease those pistols out and drop 'em down. And you," he said to Del, "hand over that Remington real careful like—butt first."

Del reluctantly did so, scowling fiercely at Meecham. Apparently he wasn't as affected by Meecham's relentless glare as Liam was.

In the wagon, Pod drew the pistol at his side, looking back at Meecham uncertainly.

"Fire away, Pod."

"What about those swords they got?" Coffin asked. He'd drawn his own pistol without Liam noticing, and he pointed at Stone's belt with it.

"What about them?"

"Shouldn't they—?"

"They're fifteen feet away, James. What can they do?"

Coffin still looked uneasy.

Liam glanced at Stone and Becker, but they only watched

Meecham calmly. Stone remarked, "You're making a big mistake, mister."

Meecham was losing his temper, something Liam had seen before. "You keep your mouth shut. I don't like you, and your life is hangin' by a thin thread right now. After this is over, I may just decide to end it for the fun of it."

Stone shrugged slightly. "To tell the truth, I'd expect nothing less from a dog like you."

Meecham began to shake, and every muscle in his body seemed to tense. Slowly and deliberately, he drew his pistol. "*Nobody* talks to me—"

Stone turned his head to the side and shouted, "Vic!"

As if rising from the ground itself, Jaye Eliot Vickersham and forty-three Mounties appeared behind Stone about fifty yards away, all aiming rifles at them.

Liam just had time to comprehend that they'd been in one of the dry creek beds, hiding, before things happened very fast.

Pod, finding himself between the Mounties and most of Meecham's men, threw himself down flat on the wagon bed with a thump.

Meecham turned to Liam, his face twisted into the ugliest mask of fury Liam had ever seen, and pointed the pistol at his face. Liam could not move, so he closed his eyes

A strange whistling sound was followed by a solid *thunk!* and Meecham grunted.

When Liam opened his eyes, the handle of a sword was protruding from Meecham's torso, and his gun had fallen to the ground. The wrath on Meecham's face had turned to pain and disbelief. Liam looked over to see who'd thrown the sword, certain it was Becker. Hunter Stone, with a slightly sick look on his face and an empty saber scabbard on his belt, walked over to Coffin and took his pistol from him. The rest of the Mounties were upon them, and Meecham's men, stunned by the sight of so much firepower directed at them, gave up without a shot.

Meecham gazed weakly at Stone before gasping in a choked voice, "How did you do that?" Then he pitched forward over the saddle horn, and Stone caught him before he hit the ground and placed him on his back.

"You left me no choice, Meecham," Stone said softly.

Meecham's eyes were having trouble focusing on the man above him, and Liam saw that they were now filled with fear. He looked vulnerable and pitiful as he clutched at the blade in his midsection and moaned. *He's just a man after all.* Liam thought. *Just a scared man.*

The realization didn't raise any sympathy in Liam for the ruthless man. He didn't know what the first part of Meecham's life had been like, but the last of it had been full of violence, brutal callousness, and disrespect for human life, which induced no pity for the man—only revulsion.

Meecham took one last heaving gasp, then the eyes that had instilled so much fear in Liam closed forever.

Stone remained squatted over Meecham, his back to Liam. Liam whispered, "He deserved it. Don't feel bad, sir."

Slowly straightening up and turning, Stone gave Liam a look he didn't understand.

It was a look of deep sadness.

CHAPTER TWENTY

The Test of Time

Megan and Reena had heard the result of the encounter with Meecham from Colonel Macleod, who had called on them personally. The ladies had been relieved beyond measure that everyone was all right. Megan, unable to control her soaring good humor, gave Macleod a note to pass along to Vic.

"Do you want to invite Hunter to dinner?" she'd asked Reena.

Reena thought a moment, then nodded. "Yes."

"Are you sure?"

"Yes."

"Well, try to control your excitement."

When the men returned to Fort Macleod at noon two days after the confrontation with Meecham, Vickersham and Stone turned over the prisoners to Macleod, who beamed with satisfaction. After congratulating Pod and Liam on a job well done, he allowed Liam to go to the boardinghouse, free at last. Exhausted, Liam managed to stay awake long enough to be fussed over by his sisters; after fixing him a meal, they found him in the parlor sprawled on the sofa, snoring. They threw a blanket over him, and he slept the rest of the afternoon.

Reena was nervous about seeing Hunter, and when the two men arrived at dusk, she knew it had been a mistake to invite them over. They were obviously as tired as Liam had been.

After giving Vickersham a tender hug, Megan pulled away and said, "Maybe this wasn't such a good idea after all. You both look like you're going to drop any second."

"A hot meal, my dear," Vic said cheerfully. "The prospect of a hot meal right now will keep me upright."

"It's almost ready. Come into the kitchen with me while I finish the preparations."

When they left the parlor, Reena and Hunter were left facing each other awkwardly. They hadn't taken their eyes from each other since his arrival, but neither spoke. Finally Reena offered, "Let's sit down."

"All right."

They sat on the sofa, Reena with her hands clasped in her lap, and Stone leaning back into the plush cushion with a deep sigh.

Smiling, Reena said, "Don't go to sleep on me like Liam did earlier today."

"How is he?"

"He's been asleep since he got here."

"I'm not surprised. He's had a tough month."

Reena could hold herself back no longer. Slowly she leaned over and lightly kissed him on the cheek.

"What was that for?" he asked with a pleased smile.

"Liam told us how you saved his life. Thank you."

Stone said nothing but inclined his head gratefully.

"But that's not all it was for. It's part apology, part relief, and mostly love."

He turned to her, his face serious. "I've been thinking about our situation a lot, and . . ."

"Hunter, you don't have to expl—"

"Yes, I do." He took a deep breath and let it out slowly.

Reena could tell he was weary to the bone and not thinking too clearly. She saw lines on his face that she hadn't seen since the time he'd been recovering from near mortal wounds. The temptation to shush him and send him back to the fort to get some rest was strong in her, but at the same time she wanted to clear the air between them and hear what he had to say.

"Actually I've been thinking about a lot of things—things that would surprise you, but I don't want to go into that right now. What I'm trying to say is . . . I'm stubborn. I know that's not exactly news to you, but I've learned through all this that what's number one on my list of importance isn't necessarily number one on anyone else's. I should have listened to you and taken time to consider your feelings after I arrested Liam. I'm sorry I didn't do that."

Reena's eyes burned. Through all the time she'd known him, she had never heard him admit he was wrong about something. Seeing the pain in his face while he apologized compelled her to say, "It's all right to be human, Hunter. You don't have to be strong all the time."

He nodded slowly, then took another deep breath that hitched in his chest. Reena was astounded to see the look of vulnerability on his face. Squeezing his eyes shut, Hunter leaned over and laid his head on her shoulder. Reena placed her arm around his shoulders and gently stroked his face.

"I'm so tired, Reena," he whispered, his voice hollow. "All the years of . . . I'm just tired."

"It's all right, my darling. It's all right." She could feel him trembling and could feel hot tears rolling down his cheeks and her own.

––––––

In the kitchen, Vickersham sat at the preparation table and watched Megan work. Seeing her skilled and compact movements brought a question to his mind. "Where did you learn to cook like this? I thought you were the pampered woman from high society Chicago."

Megan gave him a crooked smile. "You haven't tasted it yet."

"I meant—"

"I know what you meant, Vic. It began as a case of survival

on my part, but I've found that I *like* cooking." She turned and placed a dish of butter on the table and kissed him on the forehead. "Especially for a hungry man."

Vickersham felt such a surge of love that he reached out for her and pulled her to him.

"Vic, I've got flour on me, and—"

"I don't care." He kissed her, enjoying her warm lips and the mixed aroma of dough and perfume. Into her ear he whispered, "I miss you every minute I'm away from you, Megan. It's . . . it's painful."

"Mmmm. Tell me more."

He drew back and took her face in his hands, watching intently as her grin faded into a look of wonder. "I'd love to tell you more. When I look at you, everything else fades away, just *vanishes*, and you alone are in my sight." He kissed her again. "I go to sleep with your face etched on my mind and wake up with it still there." He put his fingers to her lips and murmured, "No, don't say anything." Gently, he eased her down onto a chair.

Megan watched him in surprise and pleasure as he knelt down on one knee in front of her and took her hands in his.

Vickersham looked deeply into her eyes and declared, "I love you, Megan. I want you in my life forever. I want to share my life with you, take care of you, protect you, and bring you joy. I love you so much, Megan. Would you do me the honor of marrying me?"

Megan ducked her head, and Vic couldn't see her expression. Her shoulders began to shake, and he saw a tear fall to the apron on her lap, then another. Slowly it began to dawn on him that he might have scared her, which was the last thing in the world he'd wanted. When he heard a small moan escape her, he said, "I'm sorry, darling, if I—"

"Don't you dare apologize, Vic!" Megan cried, bringing her head up to face him. "Those were the most beautiful words anyone has ever spoken to me, so don't you apologize!"

Vickersham swallowed back another apology. Breathless, he controlled his tongue and waited for her answer.

Megan withdrew her hands from his, lifted the hem of the apron to her eyes, and dabbed the moisture from them. In a choked voice she said, "There's nothing I want more in this world than to be your wife, Vic."

Grinning broadly, Vickersham stood and raised Megan to her feet, crushing her to him. She placed her cheek on his shoulder, breathing unevenly, and he held her for a long time, silently thanking God for the woman He had given him.

———————

The day after the Mounties returned, Becker took Jenny to the Meecham farm to tell the family the news of Meecham's death. Macleod had ordered another man to carry out the task, but Becker had persuaded Macleod to let him to do it. The children would be upset, and no one was closer to Lydia and Timmy than Jenny.

Becker tried to make conversation with Jenny in the wagon on the way, but she was quiet and preoccupied. Becker finally gave up and left her alone with her thoughts until she asked him a strange question.

"How did Lydia's father die?"

Becker hesitated. "You don't want to know."

"Was it bad?"

"Yes. Why?"

"I was hoping to be able to tell Lydia that he died quickly and didn't feel any pain, but I don't want to lie to her."

"He died quicker than some other men I've seen. I think it would be all right to tell her that."

Jenny didn't answer, but Becker could see she was worried sick about the duty she had to perform.

When they reached the farm, Catherine Meecham met them at the door with a resigned expression. Jenny saw Timmy and Lydia behind their mother, staring at Jenny curiously.

"I know what this is about," Catherine said calmly. To Jenny, she looked as if she'd aged ten years since their last visit.

243

"Mrs. Meecham," Jenny said tentatively, nodding toward the children, "could I—?"

"You want to tell them?"

"Yes."

"You think you could do it better than me?"

"Oh, of course not, ma'am! I just wanted to save you the pain of it."

Catherine stared at her for a moment through sad, tired eyes. "All right."

Jenny motioned the children to her, and together they walked to the stables. Lydia took her hand on the way, while Timmy merely walked beside her with his head down, leaving Jenny with the impression that he already knew what was coming.

"What are you doing here, Jenny?" Lydia asked.

"I've got to talk to you."

" 'Bout what? Is something wrong?"

Jenny led them out of the biting wind and inside the barn. Timmy climbed up on one of the horse stall doors and avoided her eyes. "Climb up there beside your brother, Lydia." Jenny helped the little girl scale the door, then took a deep breath. Her mouth opened, but she couldn't think of the words to say.

"It's bad, isn't it?" Lydia whispered.

"Yes. I'm not gonna lie to you. It's . . ."

"Just say it!" Timmy suddenly cried.

"Timmy, what's wrong?" Lydia asked.

"Pa's dead. That's why she's here!"

Lydia swung around to face Jenny. "Is that true, Jenny?"

"Yes, it is. I'm sorry, Lydia—"

"Why? What happened?"

Jenny placed a hand on Timmy's thigh, the other on Lydia's. "Your father was . . . doing some things that weren't right. The Mounties found out about it, and when they tried to arrest him, he didn't give up easy, like he should have."

"The Mounties killed him," Timmy murmured in a choked voice.

"They didn't have any choice, Timmy!" Jenny declared sharply. "Don't you go blaming the Mounties for what your pa did. It wasn't their fault!" Both children began to cry, and Jenny took them in her arms. "The same thing happened to my pa, only I knew my pa was bad. I'm sorry you didn't know yours was."

"We knew," Lydia whispered.

"What?"

"Everybody knew. They tried to keep it from us, but . . ."

"We just don't know *why*," Timmy said.

"And you may never know," Jenny told them. "That's why you've got to start doing something right now." They both drew back from her, wiping tears from their faces with their coat sleeves. "Are you listening to me?"

"Yes," Timmy replied, and Lydia nodded.

"You've got to keep from blaming your pa and try to forgive him. If you don't, it'll eat you up inside to stay mad at him."

"I'm not mad at him," Lydia said.

"I am," Timmy said, looking at her defiantly.

"Why? He didn't get killed on purpose!" Lydia said.

Jenny nodded. "That's right—he didn't. So you stop that being angry, Timmy. Your pa loved you in his way. It's just not the normal way. Just like my pa. You've got to forgive him and go on taking care of your ma. Do you understand?"

"Yes." Lydia nodded, beginning to cry again. "I understand."

"Timmy?"

No answer.

"Timmy? Tell me you understand."

"I understand. It just ain't easy, Jenny."

Taking them both in her arms again and feeling her own eyes fill with tears, Jenny wrapped up the children and held them to her. Their small bodies shook, and the sounds of sniffling and crying filled the small stable.

"It's gonna be all right," Jenny said reassuringly. "You just wait and see. We're all gonna help each other."

Relieved, Jenny felt two small heads nod against her shoulders and the comforting feel of little arms squeezing her as tightly as she squeezed them.

———

Donald Davis, who owned the I.G. Baker Store in Fort Macleod, graciously donated the use of his brand-new warehouse for Jack Sheffield's revival meetings. The North-West Mounted Police provided the folding wooden chairs. However, on the first day of the revival more people showed up than had been anticipated, so many of them were left standing against the walls of the building.

Reena looked around at the mix of people: settlers, Mounties, and Indians from all the local tribes. No one seemed to mind having to stand—the building was warm from the heat of four stoves and the presence of so many people. Outside, the temperature was below zero and it was snowing, which made it seem even more remarkable to Reena that this many people had turned out for the service.

Sheffield himself seemed surprised and slightly taken aback by the size of the crowd. Reena sat between Stone and Megan seven rows back from the front, with Vickersham on the other side of her sister on the aisle, and Liam beside Hunter. Sheffield looked down at her from the makeshift podium and pulled a face that said, "This is more than I'd bargained for!"

Reena smiled at him, trying to give encouragement across the distance. It had been his idea to schedule the revival—of course, with God telling him to do so, what choice did he have?—and Reena had seen him become increasingly worried as the day approached.

"I'm used to dealing one on one with people, Reena," he'd told her the night before. "How can I speak to a whole group?"

"You've spoken to groups of Indians, Jack. Just pray before you get up there and let God take care of everything else."

Reena had seen him praying from his chair behind the podium, but apparently God hadn't taken hold of his nerves yet.

Glancing over at Megan, Reena saw that her arm was laced

through Vic's, with his hand over it. They were speaking in low voices, smiling, their noses almost touching. Reena couldn't help grinning. Over the past two days, her sister appeared happier than Reena had ever seen her, and Reena felt she deserved it.

"Sickening, isn't it?" Stone whispered beside her.

"What?"

"Those two. They act like schoolchildren, whispering and giggling together."

"Oh, you're just being an old bear! You admire them, and you know it."

"Admire them! They're making a spectacle of themselves." Stone shifted in his chair uncomfortably and looked up at Sheffield expectantly.

"Why are you so nervous?" Reena asked him. "You haven't sat still since we got here."

"I'm not nervous," he answered quickly. The areas around his eyes were still etched with fatigue, and his face was pale.

"Hunter, were you telling the truth about sleeping all right?"

He looked at her. "Yes. Why?"

"You're *not* telling the truth. What are you trying to hide from me?"

Sheffield cleared his throat loudly, and the room hushed. Stone looked relieved that their conversation had been terminated.

"I'm not forgetting where we left off," she warned him.

After giving a short welcome, Sheffield asked them to stand for the singing of a few hymns. There weren't enough hymnals to go around, but Reena found that she knew the songs by heart, anyway. Stone stood silently beside her, shifting his feet almost continually. Out of the corner of her eye, Reena noticed Vic and Megan glancing over at Stone occasionally, then giving her questioning looks. Reena could only shrug at them.

When the hymns were sung, the crowd sat down, and Sheffield wasted no time beginning his sermon.

"I've studied and prayed for a theme for tonight, and one thing kept going around in my head—it literally would not go away. So if you have your Bibles, would you please turn to Mark, chapter twelve.''

Reena turned to the passage, noting that Hunter had his hands clasped together in his lap, but they weren't still. He was running a thumb across the other palm over and over. Sometimes his leg would begin bouncing, but he seemed to be aware of that and stopped it at once. When she held out the Bible between them so he could follow along, he barely glanced at it, keeping his gaze straight ahead at Sheffield.

"In this passage, Jesus was answering the religious leaders' questions in Jerusalem," Sheffield continued. "They were trying to trap Jesus into saying something for which He could be arrested. But Jesus knew it wasn't time for Him to be apprehended yet, so He answered every question wisely and thoughtfully, as was His way. One scribe, who was standing nearby and had heard the truth in Jesus' answers, asked, 'Which is the first commandment of all?'

"This scribe wasn't asking the order of the commandments as Moses gave them to the Jews. He was asking what was the most important charge that had been given to the followers of Christ. Jesus answered him, 'The first of all the commandments is, Hear, O Israel; The Lord our God is one Lord: And thou shalt love the Lord thy God with all thy heart, and with all thy soul, and with all thy mind, and with all thy strength: this is the first commandment.' "

Sheffield paused and looked around the room.

Reena admired the way he had regained his composure. Once he'd started speaking, the nervousness had vanished. Beside her, Hunter was still fidgeting, and Reena wasn't even sure if he was listening. His gaze seemed to be fixed somewhere behind Sheffield.

"Four things," Sheffield said, counting them off with his fingers as he spoke, "heart, soul, mind, and strength. In other words, with every part of our being we are to love God the Father. It's a perfect love, many times beyond our puny human abilities, but Jesus said we are to strive for that kind of love every day.

"You say to me, 'Preacher, that's impossible! I can't even love my wife or my husband that way.' And you know what? I say to you that yes, it is impossible. Without the help of the Great Comforter, the Holy Spirit, in your heart, it *is* impossible. But that's why Jesus sent the Holy Spirit—the very Spirit of Jesus himself—because He knew we were only human and needed His help in times of weakness."

Reena found herself so drawn into Sheffield's powerful message that she forgot about Hunter beside her. Sheffield went on to teach about the love of God, of Christ, and the love men should have for one another. When she sensed he was drawing to a close, she was disappointed, for she wanted to hear more, even though the simple message was one that she'd heard before. Jack Sheffield had a way of speaking that made the room shrink, and she was sure that every person in the warehouse thought he was speaking to him or her personally.

"I'm going to ask some of you to do a very courageous thing," Sheffield told them. "This room is filled with brave men who perform feats that the rest of us can't. But the courage I'm talking about now is of a different kind. It involves publicly showing your love for your Creator. While we all sing 'Every Hour I Need Thee,' I want you to come forward to receive the greatest and purest love you'll ever know." Sheffield scanned the crowd with his deep blue eyes, seeming to light on every person. Then he began singing the hymn.

Before three bars were sung, Stone turned to Reena and asked, "Would you excuse me?"

"What?" Reena didn't know at first what he meant, then she realized with a joyous shock that he wanted to go by her to get to the aisle.

"I'm ready, Reena. I've been ready for some time."

"You're—? Oh my." Reena spun to her sister and whispered intensely, "Megan, Vic. Move out of the way!"

"What is it?" Vickersham asked, alarmed. His eyes went to

Hunter behind her and rounded in surprise. "Oh my!" Then he hastily scooted into the aisle out of the way with Megan following.

As Hunter moved by her, Reena whispered, "Hunter?"

"Yes?"

"May I go down with you?" When he smiled weakly, Reena realized that he was scared—an emotion she'd never before seen in him.

"Yes, come with me."

Reena followed him to the front, barely feeling her feet on the wooden floor. This was what she'd prayed for and wanted for years. Other people were moving toward the front to accept Christ, but Hunter reached Sheffield first.

Sheffield, unable to keep the elation from his face at the response that was taking place, took Hunter's hand in both of his. "Sub-Inspector, I'm so glad—"

"Call me Hunter, Jack."

"Hunter, we've prayed for this moment for a long time—especially Reena here has."

Reena stood next to Stone, looking up at him, and saw tears welling in his eyes.

"I just can't take the burden of it anymore," he whispered. "The death, the guilt, the anger . . . I can't handle it alone."

"I understand," Sheffield nodded.

Then Hunter broke down completely and began to weep. "I'm so weak . . . I *need* God's strength in my life!"

Reena couldn't control her emotions either and placed her hands over theirs, crying openly. She listened to the man she loved—the man who had carried bitter despair to the point of breaking after his wife's death, the man who had stolen her heart with his kindness and gallant ways, the strong-minded, strong-willed man who had never before broken—she listened as he cried out in repentance to God and acknowledged his need for Jesus. Then she watched, still in elated disbelief, as he knelt down before God, asked for His forgiveness, and received the miracle of salvation.

She was there for it all, and she was the happiest she'd ever been in her life.

———

Following the service, Stone received congratulations and words of encouragement from countless people. He was still slightly dazed from the experience, but inside of him welled a peace he had never known. He felt a softening in his spirit, a fulfilling and yet an emptying. He tried to put into words what he was experiencing but soon gave up. The fulfilling peace was enough.

When most of the people had left, Stone found himself surrounded by his closest friends—Reena, Vic, Megan, Becker, Jenny, and even Del, who was watching him strangely, as if he didn't know him. Liam stood beside Reena uncertainly, obviously feeling the camaraderie that he wasn't quite a part of.

"It's all right, Del. I'm not going to sprout angel wings or anything, I don't think."

Del cackled and shook his head. "I'm sorry, Hunter."

"Don't worry, Hunter," Vic told him with a grin, "he stared at me like that for days after my conversion."

"Now, see, that's just it," Del pronounced. "That word 'conversion.' It's like you're all gonna turn into somethin'."

"We *have* turned into something, Del," Vic told him. "Inside of us. And you're next."

Del said nothing, but it was clear he was pleased.

"Unless someone else beats you to it," Becker said, glancing at Jenny beside him.

Jenny's face colored, but she smiled shyly.

Becker said seriously, "Congratulations, Hunter. I thought all my preaching around the campfire was bothering you."

"It *did* bother me. Why do you think what happened tonight happened?" Stone looked around at all of them. "Everyone bothered me, and I thank you for it." He noticed Liam standing slightly to the side and asked, "What are your plans, Liam?"

"West Point, sir. I'm going to do my best to get back in."

"Good luck, then."

"Thank you."

Reena put her arm through her brother's. "I think a lot of people have learned valuable lessons over the past month and a half." Her eyes came around to Stone. "A lot of people, including me."

Stone smiled at her, still unable to comprehend the magnitude of what had happened to him that day. Into a small silence he asked, "So what do brand-new Christians do after the church service?"

"A feast!" Vic announced. "I believe it should be a tradition to eat afterward, don't you think so, Del?"

"I'm always ready for a feast, you know that."

Vickersham turned to Megan. "Does Mrs. Howe at the boardinghouse have enough to feed this lot, my dear?"

"Mrs. Howe always has enough. I don't know how she does it."

"That's it, then! Onward!" Vic slapped Stone on the back as he passed him.

By silent agreement, Reena and Hunter lagged behind the group on their way to the boardinghouse. The bitter cold couldn't dampen Stone's elation, so he placed his arm around Reena and said, "Guess I surprised you, didn't I?"

"Surprise isn't a strong enough word. Astounded, maybe?"

"I didn't mention my intention to you, because I wasn't sure I could go through with it. Now you know why I was so agitated and why I haven't been sleeping."

Reena suddenly stopped and spun him around to her. With incredible gentleness and love, she reached up, took his face into her mittened hands, and kissed him. After she broke the kiss, Stone could still feel her warm lips against his, despite the biting cold.

"What was that for?" he asked.

"That," Reena answered softly, "was purely for love."

252